BURI

Set both in the presen
Angola in 1976, *Burie*
about men and women and ...

To the strains of the music of Bob Dylan and in long periods of boredom and inactivity, South Africa's soldiers tried to make sense of a war they could not see.

RICK ANDREW, himself a conscript at that time, allows his comrades to tell their stories. We get to know Manie Dippenaar, whose hunting trip threatened to turn into an international incident; Private Smith, the boy from the Bluff who had Love and Hate tattooed on his knuckles and chose a novel way to roast a chicken as his means of revenge on a bad tempered major; Morphine Sister, who 'handled a gun like a mamba'; and Spek, the surfer-boy who dreamed only of catching the next big wave.

Poignant, funny and dramatic, *Buried in the Sky* will strike a chord with anyone whose life has been tarnished by war and espcially those who found themselves on 'the border'.

BURIED IN THE SKY

Rick Andrew

PENGUIN BOOKS

PENGUIN BOOKS

Published by the Penguin Group
80 Strand, London WC2R 0RL, England
Penguin Putnam Inc, 375 Hudson Street, New York,
New York 10014, USA
Penguin Books Australia Ltd, 250 Camberwell Road, Camberwell,
Victoria 3124, Australia
Penguin Books Canada Ltd, 10 Alcorn Avenue, Toronto, Ontario,
Canada M4V 3B2
Penguin Books (NZ) Ltd, Cnr Airborne and Rosedale Roads, Albany,
Auckland 1310, New Zealand
Penguin Books India (P) Ltd, 11 Community Centre, Panchsheel Park,
New Delhi – 110 017, India
Penguin Books (South Africa) (Pty) Ltd, 24 Sturdee Avenue, Rosebank,
Johannesburg 2196, South Africa

Penguin Books (South Africa) (Pty) Ltd, Registered Offices:
24 Sturdee Avenue, Rosebank, Johannesburg 2196, South Africa

First published by Penguin Books (South Africa) (Pty) Ltd, 2001
Reprinted 2002, 2004

Copyright © Rick Andrew 2001
All rights reserved
The moral right of the author has been asserted

ISBN 0 141 00304 9

Typeset by CJH Design in 10.5/12.5 point Charter
Cover photograph: Angus Peacock
Cover design: African Icons
Author photograph: Silvi Judd
Printed and bound by Interpak Books, KwaZulu-Natal

Except in the United States of America, this book is sold subject to
the condition that it shall not, by way of trade or otherwise, be lent,
resold, hired out, or otherwise circulated without the publisher's
prior consent in any form of binding or cover other than that in which
it is published and without a similar condition including this condition
being imposed on the subsequent purchaser.

This book is dedicated to Gill and Fran and to my buddy Butch

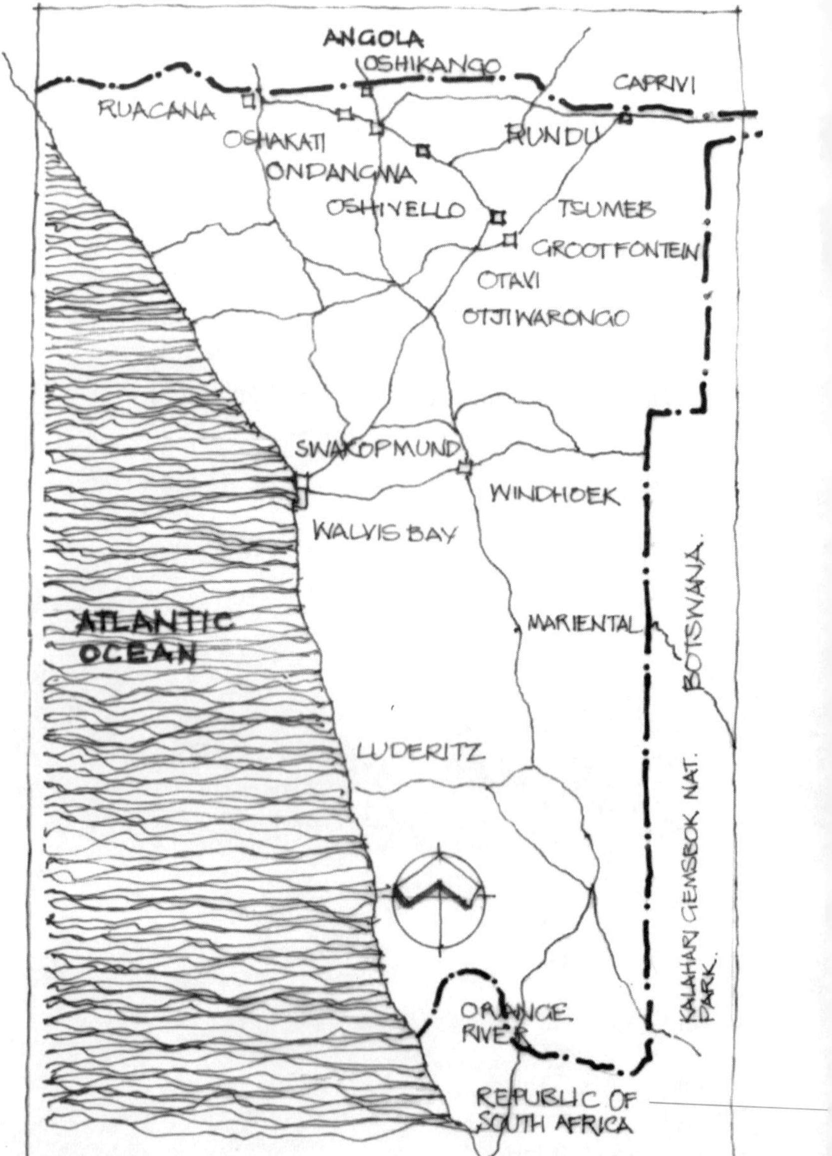
ANGOLA
OSHIKANGO
CAPRIVI
RUACANA
OSHAKATI
ONDANGWA
RUNDU
OSHIVELLO
TSUMEB
GROOTFONTEIN
OTAVI
OTJIWARONGO
SWAKOPMUND
WINDHOEK
WALVIS BAY
ATLANTIC
OCEAN
MARIENTAL
BOTSWANA
LUDERITZ
KALAHARI GEMSBOK NAT. PARK.
ORANGE
RIVER
REPUBLIC OF
SOUTH AFRICA

Ashes

Near the reservoir there is a dump in the no man's land between the mud-walled shacks and the suburban order. It smokes sourly as flames come through the ash to devour the new piles of rubbish. Raking through the refuse, the silhouettes of women stand shrouded in the haze. Hessian, paper, glass, plastic and steel. Meditating on the waste. Looking for treasure.

Approaching the fire, I acknowledge and greet the women. *Ja, mama, I know you. Close as my lips.* Then I withdraw, selecting for myself a section of waste, enjoying the warmth of the flames in the late afternoon.

The year is 1988.

I see a magazine half burned and stained. A glossy bikini-clad body, no head. Beer bottles and broken glass sweat inside a black plastic bag. A broken electric fan. A ribbed plastic pipe from a swimming pool cleaner. A miniature wire picket fence. A container explodes with a muffled pop somewhere deep inside the mound of hot ash and junk.

Sifting carefully for fear of broken glass, chemical poisons and sharp steel, I lift the weight of settled ash and damp paper. The faint smell of mildew and urine. More magazines. Pictures of Hollywood stars. Impossible America. Sentimental murderers. Impossible Europe. A grainy black and white picture of cadavers piled high. The refuse of another Hades. A crossword puzzle. An old broken cuckoo clock. A used condom. A lurid cardboard schoolhouse with cartoon bears holding hands in front of wooden walls and gothic windows . . . for kids . . . some big cartoon butterflies rising into the sky. Imported from Ontario. Made in China.

And then, strangely, a large piece of curved grey plastic. I recognise it immediately. I pull it out. It's the plastic inner of an army helmet – a 'mosdop' – but too damaged for any child to rejoice over. It has been crushed, scratched, burned and split down one side. The canvas and leather inners are mildewed and rotten.

Here is a vein of my own history. A battered part of the rind.

I take this broken relic to my car and drive once more into the order and quiet of the suburbs, where television screens flicker in evening lounges.

My mind begins to fill with images . . . of convoys and men moving in the bright sunlight, of boots and dust and rifles . . . and candle-light, and the faces of friends remembered . . . of Butch . . . and Keith . . . and I can feel the weight of the past returning.

Back to Before

Leaving Pietermaritzburg in December of 1975 I was pursuing a dream. I saw myself as a minstrel in a green jacket. My hair was long, touching my shoulders, and I was standing under the night sky of the Wild Coast, my guitar in my hand.

It was time to break free.

As art teacher at Maritzburg College, a wide gap had been forming between the restrictions of the job and the needs of my soul. I was tired of working to the background music of cadet bugles and the cane flapping the backsides of boys in grey flannels. I had had three major disagreements with the headmaster, who was a mathematician. After our short, formal, and rather strained encounters, each time I was left feeling that he did not believe the study of art to be a worthy academic pursuit. I believed that art was life itself. However, he was the headmaster, confident and composed, though I noticed a momentary tremor in his eyes when he saw the small ruby earring in my left earlobe. I was turning into an alien right there – in the corridors of those sacred rugby precincts.

I resigned, fitted out a Combi, and hit the road with my wife and small daughter.

We left in the rain about a week before Christmas, and headed south, performing at various hotels along the coast. I have memories of thick, muddy flood waters powering to the sea beneath the bridge at Port St Johns, moonlight on the waves at Coffee Bay, and halls packed with Christmas dancers at Kei Mouth and Morgan's Bay.

In the ablution blocks of campsites along the way I would invariably catch the news on someone's portable radio. It was not good. The South African army had penetrated deep into Angola. In some of the newspapers there were pictures of armoured convoys in an empty landscape. Something serious was going on, but press restrictions limited our knowledge and made it difficult to build up a picture of the situation. However, it seemed like war – the real thing – on the international chess board of power.

Like a dark rolling cloud, this news pursued us on our journey.

For the month of February we worked in East London at the Sportsman's Bar in the Queen's Hotel. Food and accommodation were supplied. We used to play the cocktail hour and the evening slot from eight to twelve, with a fifteen minute break in each hour. Gill and I both played guitar and sang, some cover versions and some of our own compositions.

On slow nights a few travelling salesmen sat watching us, sipping their drinks. At the end of a set we might receive a note with a request, or the offer of a drink. We'd look across the room and our latest patron would wave us over to his table. Usually he would feast his eyes on the singer – my wife – hardly pretending any interest in me.

By April of 1976 we were living in Cape Town – Claremont – and playing two nights a week at the Hard Rock Café in Rondebosch. We met James Davidson who, like so many of us at the time, was into music. He joined us on bass and harmonica and we named the group Orion, after the constellation which dominated the evening sky when we arrived at the Café.

We lived in a house in June Street with Annie, a friend whose husband was in Johannesburg working as a musician. In the backyard, where the walls were streaked grey from the winter rains, Gill and Annie would do the washing in a cast iron tub. They would chat, and cook, and we'd entertain all kinds of visitors. Our daughter would suck sesame salt and toddle about in the kitchen and the yard.

I walked around Claremont making drawings, writing and thinking about South Africa – something I'd always wanted to do, but never had the time. I would sit on the pavement somewhere . . . anywhere . . . in the middle of the week, and watch the people, and say to myself, *So . . . this is my country*.

I was reading a paperback of the letters of Vincent van Gogh, and there was a passage in one of his letters to his brother Theo that I pored over continually. I wrote it out in my sketch book. It put into words the kind of vision that I found inspiring, but was unable to articulate at the time. Van Gogh was quoting from *Philosophe sous les Toits* by Souvestre.

. . . Your own country . . . is everything that surrounds you, everything that has brought you up and nourished you, everything you have loved – those fields that you see, those houses, those trees, those young girls that laugh as they pass, that is your country! The laws that protect you, the bread with which your labour is repaid, the words you speak, the joy and the sorrow that come to you from the people and the things among which you live, that is your country! The little room where you used to see your mother, the memories which she has left you, the earth in which she reposes, that is your country! You see it, you breathe it everywhere! Figure to yourself the rights and the duties, the affections and the needs,

the memories and the gratitude, gather all that under one name, and that name will be your country.

I was always disturbed by the phrase 'The laws that protect you'. Apartheid put a fence between me and the others – those excluded by the Whites Only signs. It kept me in a kind of exile. *This was my country? Was this my country?*

Our rent in Claremont was low because, in the language of the time, the suburb had been 'expropriated' from the 'coloured' people and declared a 'white' area under the Group Areas Act. So, when we were living there, it was a kind of no man's land. Many coloured people were still living there, but they knew that they had to leave, most likely for Mitchell's Plain, a new township on the Cape Flats, thirty-five kilometres from the humane familiarity of their old neighbourhood. This was the law.

The kind of white people who were prepared to live in Claremont at the time were not particularly concerned about the colour of a neighbour's skin. They were there because the rent was low. And, as is well known, low rent attracts students, artists, and weirdos. One couple was so into alternative lifestyles that they dressed only in hessian robes or clothing made of flour bags. And in their attempt to escape the cage of the corporate world they were trying to return to nature, by living on grass – the kind that makes up the front lawn.

It was a good time and a bad time. There was a sense of excitement in the air. We were young. We met many like-minded people who came to hear our music at the Hard Rock. The big round table in front of the band would fill up with interesting looking people, sipping wine and smoking. Many were varsity students or people who were working but who needed to connect with others – to live out some kind of culture . . . find some kind of community. Music was at the core of it somehow.

As a group, we couldn't get a grip on any kind of national or political identity. We couldn't associate ourselves with the politics of the 'white' government but, as 'whites,' felt ourselves to be in an involuntary collusion. We always felt like we were waiting. Marginalised. Disqualified. On hold.

The dogs of the regime were vicious. The politicians ranted like angry fathers. Their ugly words and unlovely visions violated the spirit. Like abused children watching a drunk and brutal father attacking the garden, we watched the buds of community being daily hacked to pieces. Something was seriously wrong.

Then, as if we didn't have problems enough, the politicians assured us that the 'Communist Powers' were preparing to roll into South Africa. There were communist Cuban troops in Angola. The 'final onslaught' had begun.

There was much discussion about the war in Angola. South African troops had penetrated north to Luanda, but had apparently been called back by the Americans. The government line was that South Africa was sharing America's burden of keeping the communists at bay. *Here you are, white man. Here's another burden for you. Take this gun and help us get the commies out of Africa.*

Every now and again news filtered down that more South African soldiers had been killed in the operational area. The operational area. Was that Angola or the border? No one really knew. The press was restricted so no one could tell us.

Discussions raged on after our performances at the Hard Rock. White guilt and white collusion were often the topics of the day.

The manager threw out one of our fans because he had only purchased a single cup of coffee all night. Dressed in jeans, a blue-striped apron and a white T-shirt, he had the non-spender by the scruff of the neck and held him over the bonnet of a parked car. He was determined to make money.

So, while the country continued on its path of madness, we were between a rock and a hard place, playing music at the Hard Rock.

It was at this time that I received a brown government envelope. My call-up papers. I was instructed to present myself at the headquarters of the Durban Light Infantry on May the

22nd, 1976, at 08h00. Three days after my twenty-ninth birthday.

That's it. Time up.

I had completed nine months of military training in 1965 when there was still a ballot system of call-up for all white, school-leaving males in South Africa. After training we were required to complete three, three-week camps, within a period of ten years. I had completed two camps, one in the Kalahari desert, and one at Oudtshoorn, but when called up for the third and final camp, my employer would not spare me. By contacting the army, he managed to postpone the call-up. At the time I thought little of it, but the result was that I now had to do a three-month camp on the border, in order to make up for it.

The SADF had become more and more demanding. The global threat of communism had intensified and the ANC – believed to have strong communist links – was becoming increasingly militant. By the '70s the conscription system was well established – all white males in South Africa were compelled by law to undergo military training. The duration of this training had steadily lengthened, and by 1978 it was a full two years. After training, soldiers still had to complete a number of camps of various durations, and because of the situation in Angola, most men did their camps on or near the Angolan border.

The small print on my call-up papers stated quite matter-of-factly that failure to report for duty would render the addressee liable for six years' imprisonment.

My situation became an interesting case study at the Hard Rock late night discussions. A young hippie couple whose father (on the girl's side) was paying for their passage to England said that I had no choice but to leave South Africa. To stay would mean prison. To go to the border with the SADF would be to side with the racist regime and to go against all that was moral and right.

However, it wasn't easy for me to leave the country. I had a wife and child to support and very little ready cash. Besides, I didn't want to leave my country. I wanted to live in it. Learn about it first hand. I wanted to play music. Find the stories and tunes to express the truth of our experiences. Despite the evil in the land, people were living here, and neither hope nor acts of human kindness ever ceased. I wanted to see change and beauty. I wanted to see my country bloom.

I didn't know then that the seed of the future was germinating in silent determination on Robben Island – some three kilometres away. *Staring beyond the bars of his little cell. Staring through the mountain . . . A deadly and unflinching vision for justice . . . Nelson.*

However, as I didn't want to go to jail for six years, we packed the Combi, said goodbye to our friends, and headed back over the mountains to Natal. On the drive I was thinking.

What shall I do?

Shall I stay and go . . . or leave?

I couldn't leave.

I knew that I would stay . . . and go.

A part of me was curious to see what the border looked like. A part of me wanted to experience war.

Will I be able to handle war?

Maybe I'll be able to do something positive with my guitar . . . some subversion . . .

Ah, what the hell . . . it'll be an experience.

Maybe one day I can even write about it.

The bottom line, though, was that I didn't have any real options that would not mean abandoning my family and my country.

Farewell

The sun was shining as I kissed my wife and daughter goodbye. I closed the Combi door, picked up my kit, and walked through the gate of the DLI headquarters.

We formed up in our companies with the commander leading

the parade. Emerging from the bridge under the racecourse, we turned towards the station. Traffic was held up as we marched by. What remained of Greyville Indian quarter could be seen on our left. Once a bustling residential area, with flags on bamboo poles, dogs, children, mothers and marigolds, it had gone the way of District Six in Cape Town. Expropriated. It was now a forlorn grid of streets and empty plots, covered with garbage and rubble. The people's houses had been expropriated and demolished because the area had been rezoned for 'white' business by the Department of Community Development.

We must have looked a motley crew as we marched along. Many of us still had the old khaki uniforms, some were wearing shorts, and some full battledress. All of us were laden with kit and carried our rifles in the shoulder arms position. Apart from the anomalies in our dress, I was aware of the looks on some of the spectators' faces. Some young Zulu men watched in resentful silence, others in apparent amusement. A coloured woman with two children looked on with questioning eyes. *Whose side would she be on?* An Indian man stood with his arms folded. He appeared angry. A group of white housewives, perhaps mothers of some of the men, jumped about together and waved and cheered us on. Some old indunas raised their hands in un-enthusiastic salute. They still wore the iziqhaza – large decorated wooden plugs – in their earlobes.

Such was our farewell. What were we defending? Who were our allies? Who were we fighting for? Who was the enemy?

Once the march was over and the streets of civilian life left behind, we formed up along the platform of the old Durban station to await the arrival of our train. Suddenly a group of girls appeared. They had come to give some last-minute provisions to one of the soldiers. The lucky soldier turned out to be the fair-haired private, Hollard, the youngest man in the regiment.

When the train arrived we boarded it.

Next stop . . . Bloem.

Bloem

Bloem is short for Bloemfontein which, literally translated into English, means 'flower fountain'. In the legends of Afrikaner history, when wagons groaned across the heat and dust of an empty unknown, it was a find, a spring, a water source where flowers grew.

It was also the place where I was first introduced to the army – the South African Infantry.

Basic training. 1965.

A rifleman with a new ungypo'd cap and shiny springbok badges, standing to attention with thousands of others.

Bloem was where I first learned to wait, and to kill time outside smouldering hangars in the heat. Bloem was where I was issued with a trommel of kit, a steel helmet, an FN rifle, some blankets, and a fuck suit. This latter exotically named garment consisted of a khaki jacket with brass buttons and a mandarin collar, which was worn over a pair of khaki trousers that were tucked into puttees at the ankles. This outfit, with boots and 'mosdop', was worn for daily work and exercise.

There we starched and ironed the edges of our beds with our dixies, Brasso'd the taps in the toilets, and stood to attention for inspection on Friday mornings, while instructors stalked the bungalow. I saw trommels full of carefully ironed shirts overturned onto the dusty floorboards. The greasy dust from the light bulbs wiped across our white towels by the corporal's finger.

There I learned that men were mad, and that things were twisted.

And now I was back.

Saturday Afternoon Blues

Five days in uniform. Somewhere in the veld outside Bloem. It's a Saturday afternoon. We're being kitted out for the border. *Taking the weight.* I take a bog-roll and make my way to the the toilets, a line of brown plastic long-drops on a strip of concrete. A corrugated iron roof. Creosote poles. No walls. No privacy, except that today there is no one about. I look into the first bowl to see a huge mound of human excrement. Varied ochres and browns, with wads and coils of toilet paper moistened by urine, and well visited by flies. I wince at the biting, ammoniacal stench. I look across the veld and into the sweltering distance.

In the silence, time becomes oppressive. Huge. I look at my watch. The thin shadow of the second hand marches in tiny steps . . . I look down at my legs. My trousers are below my knees, covering my boots.

No magic here. No festival. A time line without music. Only these piles of human waste, the excretions of a thousand bowels on army diet. Stews, canned food, dried apricots, and coffee with condensed milk. The empty solitude of this lost Saturday. Flies buzzing lazy . . . and the stench.

Dung man with wristwatch.

Leaving

The whole battalion was waiting in the veld near De Brug for the train to take us away. It was dark and cold. We were sitting, fully kitted and in company formation, alongside the railway track. Rifles propped against rifles in upright clusters. A few small fires made from bits of dry wood found in the vicinity, and the brief flares of matches as men lit cigarettes, gave a sense of drama to the scene, capturing here and there illuminated faces and the sharp silhouettes of soldiers in full battle gear.

Eventually we heard the shrill whistle of a train and saw the bright headlight of the engine in the distance. We couldn't tell how far off it was or at what speed it was moving. We watched in animated suspense as this bright, white light moved down the track toward us. Then we could hear the panting, hissing pressure of the boiler and see the stoker moving by the light of the furnace in the driver's cab. With a squeal of brakes, the engine with its coaches stopped before us, a huge smouldering machine, linked and clanking, hot, hissing and heavy. The beam of its headlight stabbed the darkness.

Orders were given and the regiment entrained for South West Africa.

Further On

The troop train pulled into a small empty station somewhere on the way to South West Africa. It was late afternoon. Men lay on their bunks looking out of the windows. In my compartment we were playing guitar and singing the songs of Rodriguez. *Cold Fact*. We became aware of some disturbance outside on the platform. Practically every member of the regiment looked to see what was happening. There on the platform stood a single black man wearing a jacket. He was gesticulating and cursing us.

'Fuck you! Fuck you all! You white rubbish. I hope you die by a bullet!'

It was difficult to believe that a single black man would have the gall to insult a troop train full of white soldiers. *Looking for trouble. For sure.*

The first response came from a fair-haired medic wearing glasses. He swung down off the train and made a lunge at the offender, but withdrew quickly when the African produced a knife. Suddenly one of the men in my compartment climbed through the window and jumped down onto the platform. He ran straight at the African and kicked his feet out from under him. The knife went flying as did his pack of thirty cigarettes.

The African now looked beaten and frail as this strapping soldier stood over him. There were cigarettes lying all over the platform.

'Have you had enough, kaffir?'

There was no response.

Perhaps this soldier, whom I later found out was a provincial soccer player, had saved the face of the regiment. I suppose someone had to reply to the challenge. At least his response had been fast, physical and unsadistic. When he came back into the compartment he sat down heavily. His powerful thighs were apparent.

'Come on. Let's play guitar,' he said.

Despite the admiration in the eyes of many of the men, I sensed in him a feeling of guilt. I don't think he was proud of his action. What had appeared to be a menacing opponent turned out to be only an older man, weakened by liquor.

As the train left the station, I watched him quietly picking up his cigarettes from the platform. One or two men jeered as the train went by.

Chickens and Bats

We are freshly arrived, and on our way from Grootfontein to Oshivelo, where we are to be initiated into bush warfare, when the driver of our Magirus pulls up in the shade of a large tree. As he cuts the engine we become aware of another truck, a Unimog, parked in the shade on the other side of the tree. We peer at it in the dappled light, and see that the inhabitants of that vehicle are peering across at us. It takes a few moments before the situation becomes clear to all. The inhabitants of the Unimog are all paratroopers – bats – border veterans, soiled and unshaven, recently returned from a follow-up action, and they see clearly that we are all novices, untried. They look on us with a mixture of contempt and amusement.

Eerily, and softly at first, one of their number begins to make

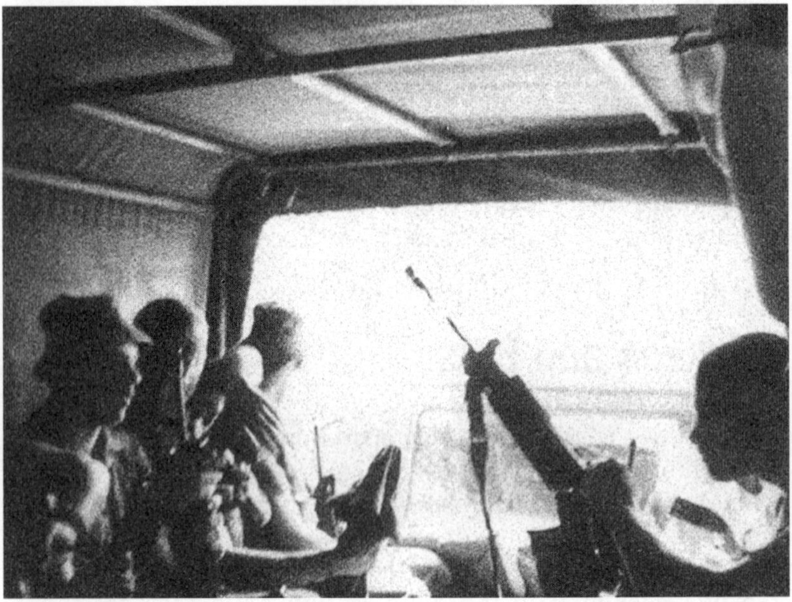

a noise like a chicken.

'Pok pok pok pok pok pok pokurk. Pok pok pok pok pokurk.'

Gently a few more join in until they are emitting the quiet, but collective sound of a chicken run. No words are exchanged, but we get the message. I catch the eye of one or two of our guys and can see that they feel as put down as I do. Our officer stares ahead. We are very relieved when the driver starts the truck and we drive out of there. Not one of the bats laughs or says a word.

Welcome to the border.

Cool Facts

We were on the border during the lull after Operation Savannah – that major push into Angola and back which ended in April of 1976. Most of our time was spent in the operational area of Ovamboland, waiting around in a defensive posture. Action was sporadic and contacts were few.

However, the nature and level of conflict in the region while we were there is recorded in Brigadier W J Matthews' breakdown of various contacts in the first two weeks of July of 1976.*

1) On July 1 five security force members were wounded when they drove into an ambush and insurgents raked their three vehicles with fire.

2) On July 2 security forces killed two insurgents in a contact just south of Ovamboland.

3) Also on July 2, insurgents killed a tribal policeman, a woman and child, evaded pursuing security forces and escaped over the border into Angola.

4) On July 4 security forces made contact with an insurgent group near the border and killed six of them.

---

*Steenkamp 1989:63

5) On July 7 security forces killed one insurgent on a 'skirmish' (type unspecified).

6) On July 8 security forces killed one insurgent in a firefight at the border.

7) On July 10 insurgents sprang an ambush from the Angolan side of the border, but inflicted no casualties and suffered none.

8) On July 10 eight insurgents died in two separate contacts along the border.

9) On July 11 a police vehicle – presumably a mine-protected one – detonated a landmine near the border but its occupants were unscathed. A follow-up action resulted in the deaths of two insurgents who were believed to have been responsible for the mine.

10) On July 13, in an action of unspecified type, one insurgent was wounded and taken prisoner and a large number of Russian weapons were captured.

11) On July 14 six insurgents were shot dead in a contact along the border.

Butch

When I first saw Butch he reminded me of a gum-chewing American GI. He had no moustache, and wore a beret and a pair of mirror-lensed wrap-arounds. He looked neat in his uniform, and had a clean trio of sergeant's stripes on both upper arms. He smoked Chesterfield, and occasionally Lucky Strike. He kept the packet neatly available in his top left-hand shirt pocket. To light a cigarette he produced a Zippo lighter with a wind guard. He would click the flint and, cupping his hands about the flame, would take his first draw – a draw so serious and focused that Humphrey Bogart would have been envious.

We were in the same compartment on the train from Bloemfontein to Grootfontein. *Flower Fountain to Big Fountain.* His dog tags hung glamorously on his chest, and he wore his army shirt with the ease and comfort of a beach shirt. The journey took two days and three nights so we had plenty of time to talk.

We chatted about music, drank beers and smoked. His musical taste was radically different to mine. He liked Neil Diamond and I could never play any of his requests, like *Cracklin' Rosie*, *I am I said*, or *Sweet Caroline*. He hadn't listened to much Dylan, but he'd been a fan of Elvis, Cliff, the Beatles and the Stones. Back home he was training to be a manager at Payne Brothers' department store, and was, for reasons I could never fathom, a member of the police reservists. In fact, his girlfriend was a cop.

We became friends.

So, by the time we got to the training camp at Oshivelo, where we were ordered to find a 'buddy', Butch and I didn't have far to look.

A buddy in the SADF is your soldier partner. The guy who guards your back while you take a leak, reminds you to check your ammunition, and walks patrol with you. Another set of eyes, and the first to notice should you go missing or get injured.

Butch and I were buddies. He liked being the official buddy of a guy who was a bit of a weirdo, a musician and an artist. I liked being the buddy of a guy who was a sergeant, a reasonable person, and a bit of a romantic. This I could see in the touches of glamour expressed in his appearance. We shared our food, cigarettes and confidential anecdotes, and Butch kind of saw himself as my protector even though I was four years older than he was. I saw him as a younger brother, less knowledgeable than me, but far more adept at handling the military.

It was Butch who helped me to catch some of the butterflies near the water-trailer because I wanted to draw them. I did these drawings especially for my daughter (who was still too young to read), and enclosed them in one of my letters home.

In the evening I would play guitar and sing, and guys would come over to listen, smoke, drum away on thighs or fire cups, and chat about music. Butch really enjoyed these impromptu gatherings. I mean, 'culture' is attractive, especially in a place as aridly unpoetic as the army. I remember on one occasion, when I was feeling a bit emotionally wasted, Butch protected my privacy and, like a stage manager, postponed the concert.

Butch and I never made demands on each other or invaded each other's space. We slept within talking distance of each other, and once the duty rosters were under way, we often went for days without seeing each other.

One night soon after we had arrived at Oshivelo, Butch approached me hurriedly and said, 'Grab your ammo and gat, we've got an errand to run.' To this day I cannot recall what that errand was, except that we ended up driving a Hippo through the bush, lost, and far from the road, with Butch talking at great length about his old school buddy, Keith.

Apparently Keith had flipped out while training – before he had even reached the border. This seemed to be of constant concern to Butch. It worried at his mind day and night and he would share this concern with me at different times and in unguarded moments.

The Hippo that we were travelling in was not in good repair because the lights kept flickering off each time we hit a bump. Bushes and trees loomed up at us out of the darkness and we flattened a few of them. Then it started to rain – unusual for Ovamboland in June.

When we finally managed to find our way back to the camp, all our bedding and possessions were wet through.

As we sat looking at all our drenched belongings, I suggested to Butch that he write to Keith's family. How could he possibly know the full story otherwise? He agreed to do it, and I heard no more about Keith for a good while.

The following day we found a very unusual frog. It must have come out of the earth in response to the rain. It was about five inches long with a deep green back and a yellow underbelly. What really shook us was that the inside of the frog's mouth was blood red. It looked as though it had been drinking blood.

Butch's comment: 'It must be a vampire frog. Probably sucks blood from all the dead okes under the ground.'

Butterflies

       I saw my first butterfly on the steps of the regimental headquarters in Durban. It was dead, and lay in a stairwell under the arches and columns of the colonial building. Predominantly red-orange in colour, it was an African Monarch, with a thick black outline around its wings and white spots on the wing tips. I stopped to look at it, noticing the contrast between its fragile, colourful beauty and my heavy, brown, rubber-soled boots.

I had just said goodbye to my wife, and this was my first morning in uniform. I held this image in my mind. It seemed symbolic.

The next butterflies I saw were in Oshivelo. They were white, with touches of orange ochre on their wing tips. Swarms of them would gather to sip the water on the ground left in the vicinity of our water-trailer. They would disperse when anyone approached to fill a water bottle or to wash a dixie, only to return once the trailer stood alone. Hundreds of delicate white wings alive on the breeze. Butterflies as camp followers, sipping the moisture of our mechanical passage.

Oshivelo

       At Oshivelo the regiment was deposited in the veld for eleven days of fire and movement training before going on to the border proper. We pitched the Ops tent and set up field kitchens. Pits had to be dug for garbage disposal and latrines. We worked hard in the sun, still eager, and in anticipation of getting to that place called 'the border'.

We slept out in the open. The weather was dry and sunny, but cold at night. Most mornings I would wake to find my sleeping bag, greatcoat and guitar case covered in frost. Looking across at Butch I'd see his sleeping form dusted with white frost.

Before breakfast we all had to participate in half an hour of rifle PT.

We'd climb out of our sleeping bags, dress in fatigue pants, boots, and a brown PT vest. Grab the R1 rifle and jog down to the PT point, which was a dust road.

Each morning on my way to PT I noticed a large human form motionless in a sleeping bag. The sleeper made no effort to rise and join in the morning's activities. *Lazy bastard*.

At the PT point a Bedford truck without a canopy was parked with its tailgate open. Standing high and proud on the back of the truck was our sturdy instructor, sergeant-major Piston du Toit. A bull of a man with a large moustache. We all formed up on the road, standing about and chatting until his stentorian voice called us to order. He was a true believer in the cause. The complete soldier. Polite, macho and massively confident.

He would demonstrate each exercise and then give the command for us to repeat it. With our hundreds of heavy boots running on the spot we drummed up a cloud of dust, holding our rifles high above our heads.

'Halt!'

The squad came to an uneven standstill.

Although he was Afrikaans speaking, Du Toit used English to drill us. He acknowledged that we were an English regiment. In fact, when the training period was over he gave us a serious talk about how very lucky we were to be members of a regiment that had a long and fine tradition in action.

The Durban Light Infantry began its life in 1854 as the D'Urban volunteer guard, a militia to protect the small outpost of buildings, thatched cottages and dust roads near the mangroves on the north side of the bay, and which is now the city of Durban. In 1935 the regiment became the Royal Durban Light Infantry, with the Queen as the colonel-in-chief. The 'royal' bit got lost when South Africa declared itself a republic in 1961.

The regiment has a long list of battle honours: the South African War (1899-1902), the Great War (1914-1918), and the

Second World War (1939-1945) where the regiment was active in the Western Desert, El Alamein, and in Italy. The regiment even has its own song, 'The Evening Stars Are Shining On The DLI'. Our regimental badge contained the Latin motto 'Primus In Africa'. It appeared we had connections and a good pedigree.

'Now we is going to use the rifle as weights to strengthen the muscle of the shoulders.'

Du Toit demonstrated by grasping his rifle barrel just behind the flash-hider, and slowly lifting it up, supporting the full weight of the weapon with his deltoid muscle. He kept his powerful arm as straight as the rifle. This was to be done ten times with each arm.

'Reg is julle. Now the left arm. One, two, three, four . . .'

Our difficulty on the ground was to find space to manoeuvre without injuring one another. It was a jostling, dusty, crowded way to start the day, but it had the effect of building unity and cheer. By the time we were released to go off and shave and dress for breakfast, most of us felt wide awake. Many whistled as they shaved in the sun.

On our return from PT for the first few mornings I watched the large form in the sleeping bag emerge and shuffle off to the toilets. His shoelaces were undone. He had made no effort to wash himself since we had been there. He was still wearing an old, outdated uniform. Somehow during the week we had been kitted out in Bloem he had managed to avoid receiving the latest uniform 'browns'. He seemed to be in his own world. He'd be at breakfast in a crumpled uniform. The odd man out, in shorts and a beret, his corpulent belly straining at his shirt buttons, which were seldom symmetrically fastened. When questioned about his intentions, whether by officer or private, he said that he was on light duty and had to go to sick report each day.

Once, ordered to go and shave, he moved off and proceeded to do as requested, but at a snail's pace. It took him an hour to shave. First the slow walk to the water-trailer. The journey back to his kitbag, carefully carrying his dixie so as not to spill the water. Then the lighting of an Esbit to heat the water. While the

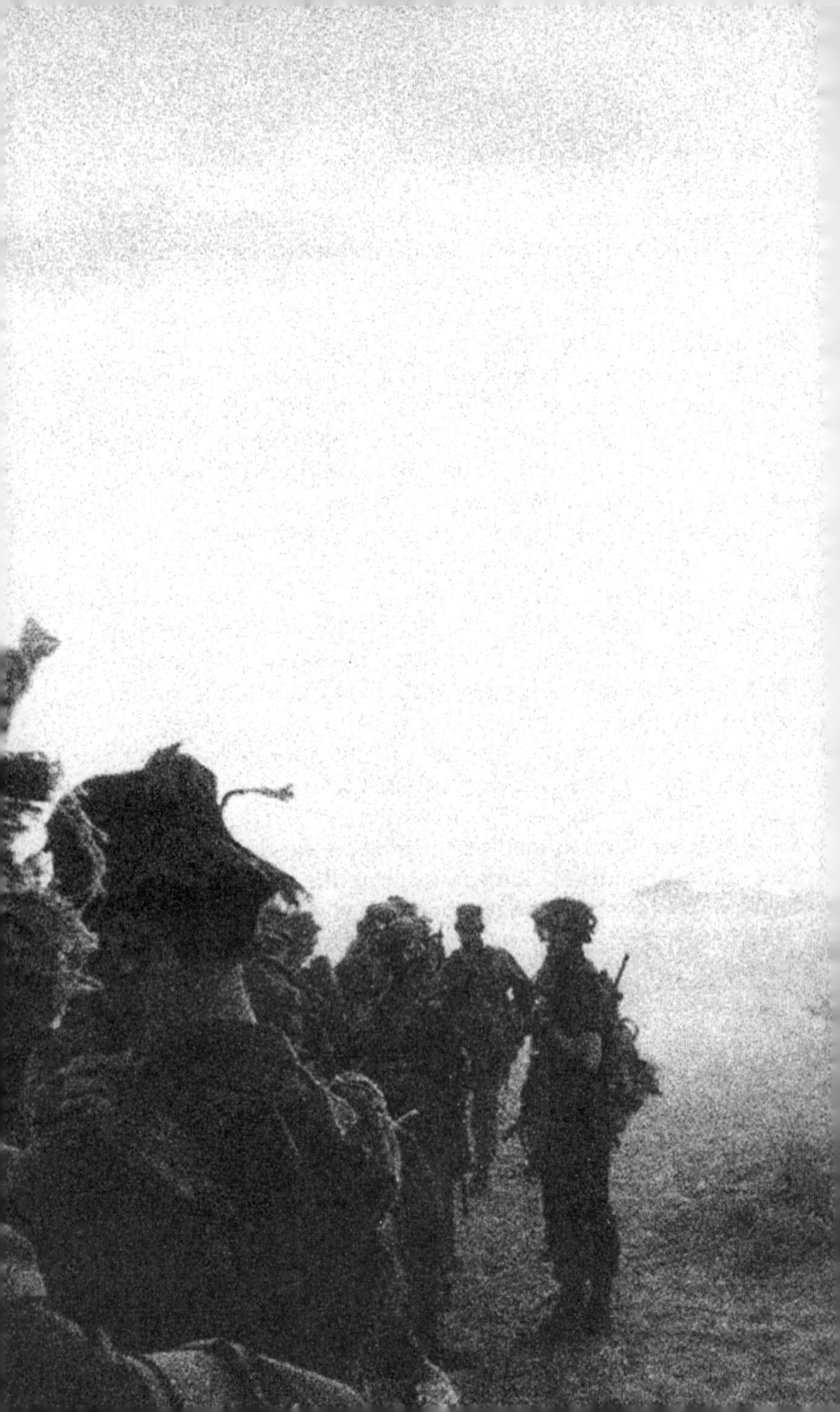

water was heating, he unpacked his kitbag, item by crumpled item, looking for a razor. He had one, but it was blunt judging by the uneven shave he managed after all this effort.

Most people lost patience with him and left him to his own devices. After breakfast each day, he'd sit down heavily outside the medical tent to wait for the doctor, doing nothing, reading nothing, just staring dully into the distance. I don't think the doctor knew how to deal with him. His appetite was normal. He never missed a food queue.

Corporal Mac confessed to me that this character was his uncle and that he ran a tyre retreading business in Sea View. Apparently he was married and had children. Mac winked at me and said, 'There's method in his madness. He's just going to pull this act until everyone gets sick of him and he gets sent home – unfit for duty. You watch.'

I found this difficult to believe, but there was a perverse kind of determination in his disregard of everything going on around him. *Married with kids? Hard to believe.*

A few days later I saw him waiting with all his kit up at the medics' tent. A truck arrived and he embarked. We watched his solitary figure diminish into the distance. He didn't wave goodbye.

Later Mac said to me, 'Ja, that oke's not lazy. He's going home. He used his brains to get out of all the shit that we're in.'

Maybe.

Blind

Although there were no signs of previous military habitation when we arrived at Oshivelo, there was a story that came with the place . . . almost as though it were a part of the vegetation. We called it the blind story.

A platoon of light infantry, not our own, was setting up camp in the vicinity. They were digging holes, holding poles, pulling at ropes, and hammering away at tent pegs. In an attempt to speed up the process, there being only one hammer available per tent, one of the men started looking around in the sandy terrain for something to use as a hammer. He could find no stones anywhere, and was just about to give up when he saw a piece of metal sticking out of the sand. He pulled it up out of the earth. It was an old unexploded mortar shell – a blind – weathered to whiteness. In the lulling memories of suburbs and Guy Fawkes parties, he considered it a dud. Figuring that it would make a great hammer, he carried it over and took a whack at a tent peg. It worked like a charm. Satisfying.

One of the men saw what he was doing and yelled out.

'Don't use that! For Christ's sake don't use that!'

But the soldier, already enjoying the feel of knocking in the peg, said, 'Ah fuck off, man.' He took another two whacks at the tent peg and then the blind exploded. Miraculously none of the other soldiers was badly hurt by the shrapnel. They were still standing, conscious but stunned. The man who was using the blind had disappeared. Only his legs remained behind. They lay some distance from each other . . . boots still neatly laced.

The bloody tailfin of the mortar ripped through a mess tent one kilometre away.

Blind.

The Major's Basin

Standing around and waiting. As usual. Word comes down that major Mills requires a designer, or someone skilled with their hands. I volunteer. I am that person. *Perhaps the job will take me away from here. Meet new people. Visit exotic places.*

I present myself to major Mills.

'Corporal Andrew, sir. I believe you need someone who can use his hands.'

The major explains that he needs someone to make a stand for his basin. He wants it raised to about waist height so that it will be easier for him to shave. The basin is a round, brown hemisphere, made of metal, and about one and a half feet in diameter. I ask him if he has access to any tools. No, he doesn't. Neither does he have any material that I might use to make his basin stand. I will have to improvise. *OK.*

I wander about looking for some timber that I can work to make a tripod that will be able to be folded flat for easy portage. As nylon rope is available from the store, my design will be made with rope and timber. I feel quite free wandering about on my mission. Nobody below the rank of major can hustle me into some new task or undertaking. For the moment I am my own man. *No, sorry, lieutenant, I can't help to dig that garbage pit. I am working for major Mills.*

Outside the Ops tent I find an empty ammunition box. The wood is certainly not the best. It's like that cheap, dry South African pine they use for tomato boxes, only this is harder, and slightly thicker. The planks are long enough to lift the major's basin to the required height. Now the problem is to find a way of cutting the wood. No one has a saw, not even the storeman. Eventually I manage to borrow a Swiss army knife with a small, blunt saw blade. I set to work.

I cut the strips of timber along the grain. It takes a while to do the cutting with such a blunt instrument, and to make it easier, I let the blade follow the flow of the grain. I quite like the organic quality of my construction. Three timber legs to support major Mills's basin. Certainly not your usual, right-angled item of furniture. My timber uprights look quite African, by which I mean unobsessed with the rectangle, the right angle, and the straight line. They waver and flow like snakes.

Hey, I'm feeling good. I'm getting somewhere.

Now I need to remove the splinters from the edges of the three timber supports. Of course there's no sandpaper to be found, so I use stones, sand and lumps of shale to round off the edges. I place these carefully worked pieces of timber on the back of a small truck parked outside the store and pop in to ask for four metres of rope for major Mills's basin stand. While the storeman is unwinding and measuring my rope I go back outside to check that my timber is still there. It isn't.

I stride up and stare in disbelief at the empty bakkie. I look around and see a plump corporal loitering in the vicinity. I suspect that he has seen the thief, if he isn't the thief himself. I am very angry and my language conveys it.

'Jesus Christ! Who the fuck has stolen my timber?! I've just spent two hours working it! This place is full of thieves and fucken arseholes!'

And to instil a bit of fear, 'Oh well, I'll just have to inform major Mills that someone in HQ company has stolen his basin stand!'

The plump corporal comes over to me. I can tell that he knows where my timber is. However, he takes it upon himself to give me a lecture on blasphemy.

'You took the Lord's name in vain. Don't do that.'

'Look, I'm sorry about that. It's not my usual way. But shit, I've just had two hours of hard work stolen here!'

He tells me to wait and he'll see if he can find out something about it. He returns some minutes later, carrying my timber.

'I found it around the corner. Someone must have tried to hide it. You're lucky I found it.'

I know he is lying but I can't prove it. I take the timber back and enquire of him whether it is not as bad to steal as it is to blaspheme. He assures me that the crime of blasphemy is committed against the Holy Spirit, whereas stealing is a lot less serious. *Ja, you poephol. Dream on.*

I get the rope and go back to work near my sleeping bag. With a bayonet I make a small hole near the mid point of each support. Rope is used to unite the legs. To hold the basin at the top of the three-legged x-shaped tripod, I use a loop of rope to unite the uprights and to contain the basin snugly. In order to get the size of the loop right, I need to work with the actual basin, so I go to the major's tent which he shares with the commander.

Inside, the tent has the usual smell of canvas under the sun. Water drips from a canvas cooler bag. It is quiet inside. So this is where our great commander sleeps. Jackets with brass-laden shoulders hang from hangers attached to the central tent pole. Both officers have stretchers to sleep on. I notice a book on the commander's stretcher. The title, *Her Majesty's Royal Armies in India*.

So this is his fantasy. Leading a royal regiment into the great unknown of Africa. Shit, he doesn't seem to realise just how fragmented this whole regiment is, or the SADF, or South Africa, for that matter. How the hell is anyone supposed to keep the faith when the world has condemned the system of politics under which the Nationalist government is ruling South Africa? The same government that is blowing taxpayers' money on this present military display. Communists? They are the ones to blame? Does the commander think that we are blind, or retarded?

Oh well, he enjoys playing soldiers. However, many of us have been forced to participate in this production by guarantee of a jail sentence. We have to be on stage, in uniform, at the required time. *There you go. Life in the SADF – a prison farm for young white males.* A theatre of war? A play? *A farce, more like it.*

I fit the major's basin into its new tripod and it stands there soundly, even when filled to the brim with water. I get my koki pen and write on one of the legs, *Made in Ovamboland on a scenic tour with the SADF*.

Mac

'I walk into the works, and the fucken arsehole dobs me out. I check that the big boss is there.

' "You've fucked up the whole run," the oke tunes me, checking me out with his ugly red fucken eyes.

'Look, the oke never liked me – not from day fucken one. I was his appy, but he treated me like a piece of shit. Whatever I did was fucken wrong. My haircut was wrong . . . my clobber was wrong . . . *I* was fucken wrong. The fucken prick . . . he was a miserable old cunt from Scotland or Wales or some rainy place where all the appies are super obedient and tidy and have no fucken lives of their own. Some of the okes tuned that he had a really sexy daughter . . . but they reckoned he would shoot any bastard that went around his house to try to put the moves on her.

'Anyway, this time I fucken know that I am not to blame . . . so I tune him straight, in front of the boss, "Look, Mr Williams, I wasn't here when you started the machinery . . ."

'So the old cunt checks me out, like, "How dare you contradict me?" . . . like I'm a fucken liar . . . and he still tries to put the fucken blame on me. But there was no fucken way . . . I wasn't going to take it . . . I mean the job was just fucken . . . fucked! . . . like thousands of rands lost! So I tune him straight, "Look, fuck off, you old cunt!" . . . and that's how I lost my job.'

This was Corporal MacIver, a printer's apprentice from Durban.

Dead Weight

Private Collins, nicknamed Bibleman, was young, withdrawn, and had a bad skin. Wherever we went and whatever we did, he was to be seen reading his Bible. He emanated an accusatory anger about the sinful state of the world, the army, and our company. He was not a friendly person. He believed himself to be one of the chosen – the saved – but his behaviour so drearily lacked the imagination of compassion.

We were striking camp at Oshivelo when the Bible-reader and I were required to carry a heavy metal trunk full of ammunition for loading onto the trucks. When I say heavy, I mean nasty, dead weight, industrial heavy . . . and so awkward in size that you want to drop it, walk away and join another civilisation – one which builds lightly and organically . . . has a better relationship with nature.

If you've ever carried an old-fashioned stove, enamelled, with solid metal cooking plates, up a narrow flight of steps in a block of flats that has no lift, then you'll know what I'm talking about.

Anyway, it is my destiny to be a member of the civilisation that built the mills that manufacture engine blocks, refineries, air-conditioners, cranes, bulldozers, guns, penicillin, and which, at that specific moment in time, needed me, with Bibleman, to carry this heavy load. A metal trunk filled with seven point six-two millimetre bullets.

As we were staggering along between the trucks with this weight between us, we saw that the gap ahead was too narrow to pass through as we were. We'd have to change formation to get ourselves and the burden through. I assumed that we'd find some way of collaboration. Instead, without warning, Bibleman just dropped his side of the trunk and let it hit the ground. Besides the sudden unexpected strain on my back and the skin grazed from my knuckles, I felt angry that he had made no effort to communicate. I expected more from him.

I'm not talking about doctrine, dogmatic arguments and definitions, just what happened, and what feels real.

Moonlight Visitation

Travelling north from Oshivelo to Ondangwa on the back of large Magirus trucks, we saw the sun sinking into the orange dust, and behind us a full moon rose into the sky above the thorn trees. Alone. Orange, and silent. We all peered back to take in this sight. Our convoy stretched to the horizon.

As we travelled on into the night, the air became cold. The moon climbed higher and became small, silver, white.

At about eleven o'clock our convoy pulled off the road. Instructions were issued that all were to bed down and get some sleep. Guards needed to be posted as we were in unknown territory. I was tired and keen to get some sleep, but on this occasion luck appeared to go against me. I was given the first shift of sentry duty for our section. I had to put aside my disappointment and walk a careful patrol of the area.

Most of the men were tired, and within half an hour a deep silence reigned. The only sounds to be heard, besides my quiet footsteps in the sand, were the occasional cough or movement from the men as they changed position in their sleeping bags.

Distances drew nearer. What was close seemed far. Shadows had a blue lunar clarity about their edges and a darkness within. The mind stopped its probing, and the soul unfolded in fear and cool joy. I watched my shadow walk ahead of me, touching the base of a truck a while before I would get there. Trees became horsemen and moved and breathed in the silence . . . dark trudging pumps. The voice of fear, twentieth century South African fear, to die-in-an-ambush-by-moonlight-on-the-border fear, insinuated itself into my mind.

I was walking beat, like that, when I sensed movement out of the corner of my eye. The movement moved with mood. I stopped immediately. Fascination overwhelmed fear. In the silence I watched a form emerge. A presence. A being. A figure. He stood before me in the moonlight. Silent and still. A Bushman . . . San . . . with limbs, naked and nimble under animal skins. He wore anklets, thongs and beads. His hands and fingers moved with precision and refinement. He had a small bow and a quiver of fine arrows slung over his right shoulder. He was a hunter; an artist; a storyteller; a man.

My lizard being slid for comfort . . . and joy.

He spoke to me in a silent language of signs and transmitted energies . . . of love and of humour. He had seen so much more than I had – this I knew, as did he – of my sorrows. Our forms are worn with memory and they breathe deeply by moonlight.

He signalled with his hand down, across his wrinkled face,

and closed his eyes . . . and I saw his lips . . . and I thought how Bushmen are considered to be on the way to extinction.

And then we expanded to a bigger but closer space, and he let me know that all would be well . . . but my mind was too uncomfortable to believe . . . to accept this. I was terribly aware of the machinery that had brought me into his presence. My 'civilisation', this convoy, this life-threatening, mechanical nightmare of which I assumed he had little knowledge.

But he knew the danger and geometry of tyre prints. His sorrow and wisdom were deep. I had much learning to do. Many were waiting.

Song Trading

At Ondangwa the regiment was required to take on, and sign for, its full quota of weapons, ammunition and transport. This involved some waiting, so we found an ablution block and had showers with warm water for the first time in three weeks. It was a good feeling to be sitting about, clean, and without any pressing duties. Of course this was an ideal time to pick the guitar, and it wasn't too long before our group was joined by another soldier carrying a guitar.

'Howzit,' he said, and squatted down. Men moved aside to make space for him in our circle. His name was Gary. Then began the usual ritual of musicians in deference to one another. Since I had already been playing for a while, I invited him to contribute a song.

'No, you carry on. I'll just jam along with you,' he said.

I was relieved to see that, like me, he had given a fair portion of his life to the guitar. He had a good sense of rhythm, played with a sensitive hand, and knew all the necessary chords.

'Let's see your guit,' I said.

A solemn exchange of guitars followed. We both fiddled about, showing off various flourishes and licks. The new guy and I were

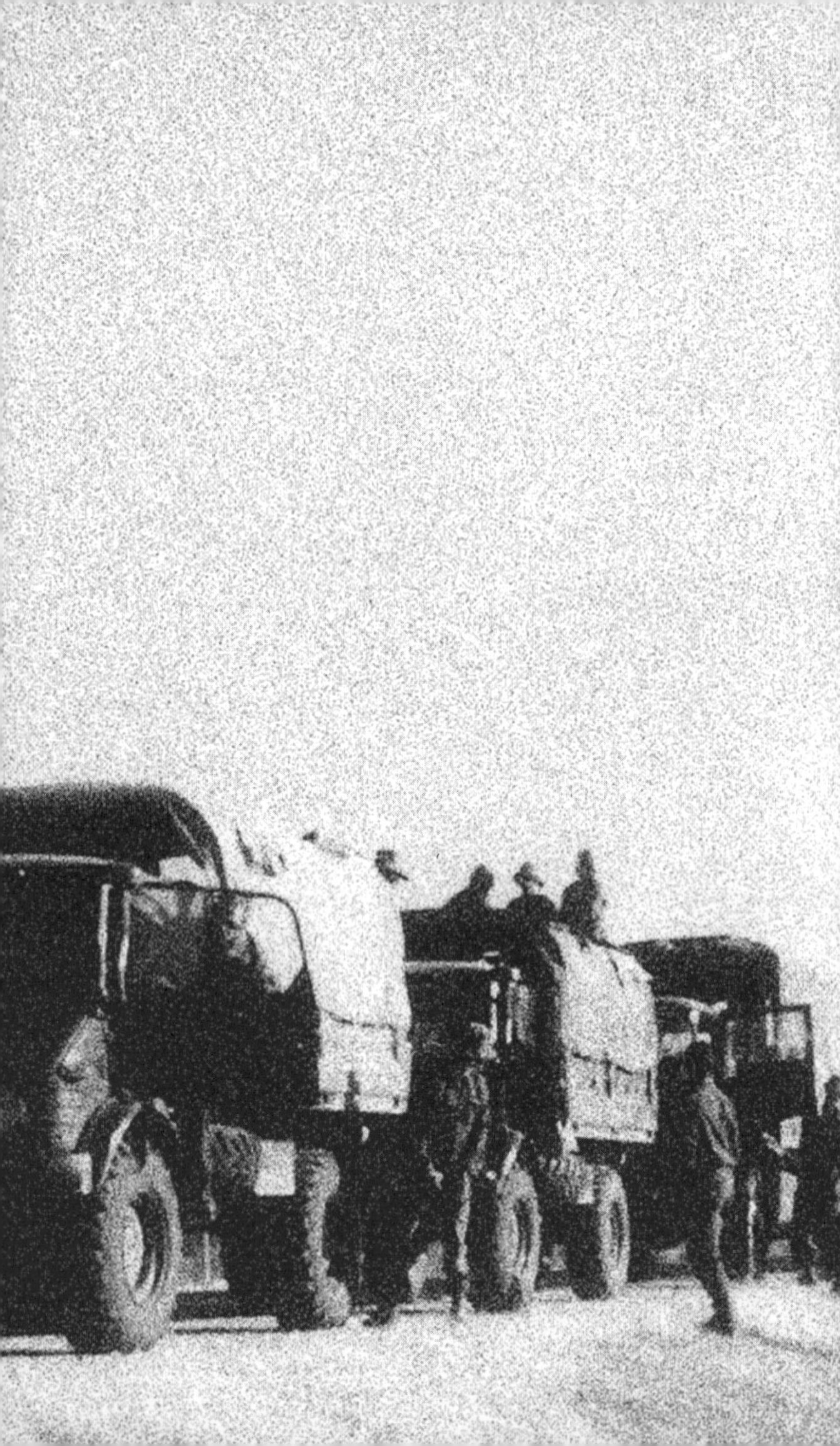

pretty much on a par when it came to technique. He played some bits with a Flamenco flavour, while I tended to be more bluesy in approach, using twangy bass notes to make the rhythm hop. His guitar had steel strings and a hand-painted ban-the-bomb sign on the headstock.

'Nice action. What sort of stuff do you play?' I asked, handing back the guitar.

He laughed.

'No, man, this guitar's my travelling guitar. You want to see the one I keep at home. That's got an action you won't believe. Perfect harmonics. It's a Yamaha, modelled on a Martin . . . Ay, I play anything, but mostly I like blues, Leonard Cohen . . . the Byrds.'

He started to play Leonard Cohen's *Suzanne*.

Suzanne takes you down
to her place near the river . . .

But he and I could see that our audience found the song a little too demanding on their listening skills, so he cut to the chorus:

And you want to travel with her
you want to travel blind . . .

He then launched into a Sonny and Brownie number, working it into a beat that got everybody moving together.

I watched the new guy, Gary. He looked a bit of a skate. His brown sun hat included a display of crude ballpoint pen drawings, a yin-yang symbol, and the strangely incomplete *no fortune bro* . . . His head bobbed forward on his neck as he sought to engage you with his eyes. He'd smile a knowing smile, enhanced by the cigarette dangling from his lower lip. He was sturdily built with strong arms and a big stomach. His dog tags swung from his neck, and tapped on the guitar every now and again as he hunched over it.

I called out a Dylan song and he knew it, *Knocking on Heaven's*

Door. Easy to play and to jam to, an easy round. G, to D, to A minor, followed by G, to D, to C. Most of the men knew the song so we had harmonies and impromptu drumming on thighs and on water bottles. As guitarists we could have fun taking occasional lead breaks, since there was always one of us to carry the rhythm. Consider how our situation increased the poetic resonance of Dylan's lyrics.

Mama put my guns in the ground
I can't shoot them anymore
There's a long black cloud
and it's coming down
I feel like I'm knocking on heaven's door

Well, things got under way. The group grew, and we played and sang all the usual requests: Donovan's *Catch the Wind*, Dylan's *All Along the Watch Tower*, *Love Minus Zero*, and *Mr Tambourine Man*. Country Joe's protest song about Vietnam, which most people knew who had seen the Woodstock movie . . . as usual, our revised SWA version . . .

Now come on all of you big strong men,
Uncle John needs your help again . . .

Richie Havens' *Freedom* (also revised) . . .

Hey, lookie yonder
Who's that you see
Marching to the 'Vamboland war
It must be handsome Johnny
With his R1 in his hand
Marching to the 'Vamboland war

Rodriguez's songs were requested, particularly *I Wonder*, and I was relieved to see that Gary could play it because I had never liked it enough to learn it. Neither of us could play Led Zeppelin's

Stairway to Heaven, though Gary managed a few tantalising notes from the intro.

We had to satisfy all requests before we dared venture forward with any of our own compositions. Usually it was only a fellow musician who really took the time to actually listen to anything original. Music, as most guys knew it, was something that came through the radio, an import from England or America. Live music was seldom part of their daily lives. People wanted to hear music that sounded like the radio. I recall one guy asking me with a straight face, as I sat with a nylon-stringed acoustic guitar in my hands, 'Can you play *Dark Side of the Moon* by Pink Floyd?'

I mean, think about it.

Eventually we aired a few of our own songs. Held them up like unfashionable underwear. It was difficult to play them with the same conviction that we projected into the songs that had had air time, and that the others knew – the songs that had taught us to sing.

While Gary was playing his song, I could see the OC and some of his acolytes peering over in our direction. Like us, they were mere chattels of the military at that moment, and were forced to bed down in the dust with the rest of us.

The only difference was that they were standing outside the music.

Dust

Once on the road, we all settled back and watched the countryside roll by. Every now and again, when the road took a long curve, we could see the immense length of the convoy which included armoured vehicles, artillery and supplies. The vehicles raised a huge cloud of dust as they thundered across the open spaces of Ovamboland. We saw small settlements and villages, cattle, fields of grain and women, their breasts bare, crushing grain in their mealie stampers. These were like large wooden mortars and pestles.

Settlements close to the road presented high walls of dried branches behind which we could see small thatched huts. The eyes of semi-naked youngsters looked up through the roadside dust at the trucks carrying soldiers. I noticed that these youngsters were covered in a pale ochre-grey dust so that the whites of their eyes and teeth were strikingly noticeable. I looked at the men on the back of our truck and they, too, were covered in dust, all of one pale grey-ochre colour. Hands, uniforms, boots, rifles, faces . . . all covered in dust. Darker streaks and rivulets form around eyes and mouths which contain their own moisture. Whites of eyes . . . and teeth.

Thus we arrived at Oshikango.

Saturday

I am standing just inside the entrance of the tent. I have a cigarette in my mouth and I am counting out some money, the coins cradled in my left hand. *How much do I need for a six-pack of beers?* I become aware of a presence and look up to see the indignant face of the commander. Large ears, pursed lips and hostile eyes.

'Don't you salute in the presence of an officer, corporal?'

I put on my mask of deference and attempt to respond with prompt obedience, but I have a problem. I can't salute with a cigarette in my mouth, and I can't remove the cigarette while my hands are occupied with the money.

I become aware of how foolish the whole farce really is, so I slow down. Calmly I pocket the money, remove the cigarette from my mouth, transfer it to my left hand, and salute solemnly. He returns my salute but continues to stare at me. His attention then wanders towards the outdoors, and he strides away from the tent.

In the sun a group of soldiers are standing around the water-trailer filling their water bottles. Some are cleaning their teeth, spitting out a mixture of toothpaste, saliva and water, leaving puddles on the ground. Their shoulders are harnessed with webbing, their rifles propped against the trailer.

He walks straight past them and goes to his favourite spot. Here he proceeds with his usual morning routine. Lighting a cigarette, he paces up and down in front of his tent. The intense but faraway look in his eyes makes me wonder what he is thinking. Maybe he sees some purpose in this spectacle, this performance. This regiment of men from the city of Durban encamped in Ovamboland. Border duty, it is called.

Everywhere through the trees you can see brown tents, sandbags and trucks. Soldiers move about in the clear air. Radio masts and aerials are sticking up above the trees. This is HQ company, dug in and waiting. Somewhere out there the enemy is breathing and scheming, priming detonators and oiling rifles.

Inside the Ops tent I can hear the incantations of the radio operator.

'Ah . . . Oscar Papa, ah . . . Romeo . . . Over.'

Through crackling static comes a distant answering voice. A heavy South African accent from one of the outlying patrols.

'Ja . . . Ah . . . Oscar Papa . . . We are moving to the rendezvous point . . . ETA fourteen hundred hours . . . We need two Bedfords to transport personnel back to base . . . Over.'

Next to the brown radio, an empty Coke can, a crumpled Chesterfield pack, and an ashtray filled with cigarette butts.

I stroll back to the kraal that Butch and I have made. We've enclosed an area in the bushes by fencing it off with branches. On a vehicular patrol I found a large piece of plank near a bullet-riddled building. I loaded it on the truck. Back at the camp I raised the plank off the ground by placing it on sandbags. The first piece of furniture in our home. On it I put my shaving gear and a collection of stones and feathers I found about the place, bits of wire, and my guitar in a plastic case.

Butch is there, sitting on his groundsheet, eating a biscuit dipped in creamed cheese. As usual he is wearing his GI sunglasses. He's seen all the movies. On his upper sleeves are his sergeant's stripes.

'I've been asked to accompany the body of private Hollard back to Oshakati this afternoon,' he says.

'Shit. Not very lekker,' I respond and proceed to lie back on my sleeping bag.

'Ja, the guy that shot him – his buddy – has had to go for treatment. He's really cut up.'

Who would be surprised? Within two weeks of our arrival, private Hollard has been shot in the back by his best friend. It was an accident. Apparently the rifle went off as they were disembarking from a truck. All looked around to see Hollard crouched and holding his stomach, dark blood spreading quickly across his shirt. He died almost instantly. A fair-haired youngster, and girls on a station platform.

Off at the waterpoint I can hear men showering. Someone's tapedeck is playing the flutings of Jethro Tull.

Saturday. Oshikango. 1976.

Saturday Night

Emptiness and boredom. Feeling the pain of separation from home. Hating the schizophrenia. *'Defending' South Africa against 'communism'* – while back home the country took flame.

The Soweto riots took place while we were on the border. We heard about it the day after it happened. It had to happen. We saw no newspapers or pictures, heard only brief reports over the radio. Corporal MacIver wrote a poem. I just wanted to get out of there and go home.

Butch got back late from Oshakati that evening. He looked tired and was unusually quiet. He'd accompanied the body-bag to the airport. A plastic sarcophagus for a soldier. The youngest man in the regiment. He'd witnessed its loading onto the

Hercules with all the other supplies and paraphernalia. He'd watched the lights winking into the sky. A parcel for the Hollard family, delivered to 'the states' – the term we then used for South Africa – care of the SADF. *Another nightmare.*

And there too, at Oshakati, by the strangest act of coincidence, Butch had bumped into his friend Keith, newly discharged from hospital and on his way to rejoin his unit on the border. Butch had managed to talk only briefly with Keith, and he still seemed very concerned about him.

They had been close at school – *Keith was a guy you would really have liked, Rick. We were like brothers, man* – and he still couldn't understand how Keith could have ended up in a psychiatric ward.

I'd become almost as interested in Keith as Butch was. We'd discussed his situation on many occasions. *Some kind of a breakdown.* I asked Butch to tell me more about his meeting with Keith, but he didn't want to talk.

'Let's go get a drink,' he said.

So we went to the cooks' tent and drank a few beers.

The cooks projected their usual cheerful cynicism, commiserated with Butch about his experiences, and chatted gaily about the absurdities of army life. Their domestic routine of feeding the company kept them busy and away from the military activities outside. By the time we got up to leave, we were feeling a bit more cheerful.

Outside the night sky was huge. Scorpio was clear among a million stars. Tents loomed in the darkness. We were numbed by the liquor and soon fell asleep.

I find myself lying on a mechanic's trolley, pushing myself along with my boots. A heavy canvas shroud is stifling me. I keep holding it off my face as I wheel along on the trolley. Eventually I get clear of what seems to be a collapsed tent. I stand up. There is a cast-iron tub filled with ice and water, cans of cooldrink and beer. A party! All my friends are there. Annie, with her long red hair, smiles. I know I love her. Ekkie turns to greet me.

Richard! Howzit! He is carrying a guitar case.

Andy is standing with his hands in his pockets and talking quietly. Cookie is there and laughing. And Cally, a ghost-like and troubled waif. And Dick in a purple vest and jeans. Long hippie hair. Rolling a joint. Crucifix hanging from a chain around his neck. Knowing, conspiratorial smile . . . an ex-altar boy. And there my own dear family. Gill holding my daughter on her hip. Home at last. Communion.

'You're on duty . . . Wake up . . . You're on duty.'

Someone is shaking me gently. I wake to see a man's silhouette. He is already leaving.

'You've got ten minutes. It's ten to two.'

I sit up and light a candle. I'm back on the border with my face and my hands, but my being is humming with the pleasure of the party. It was only a dream, but it envelops me and comforts me like a precious garment. *Ja, it's friends who make up my real world.*

I put on my greatcoat and make my way to the Ops tent. I lift the flap and blink my way into the smoke-filled interior. Gas lamps hiss on the trestle tables. Only the radio operator is there. He greets me with a nod. The two to six shift of night duty isn't conducive to conversation. I am glad, though, because I just want to hold on to my dream. It is more real than this dismal scene. Before me on the table is the map, covered in clear plastic and filled with the plottings of flare sightings and reported gunshots. It is my task to record these things on the map with a chinagraph as the reports come through on the radio. The radio hisses along with the gas lamps. Out there is the war. Within, I bask in the love and warmth of my friends.

Marginalising Manie

Manie Dippenaar had been transferred to the DLI. He was a supremely fit streetwise parabat who hated officers

– especially officers of the DLI. He saw them as a bunch of pommie wops with obnoxious class pretensions, and made no effort to hide his arrogant disdain. He had returned from two years of active service in the operational area with a record of bravery under fire, the tracking skills of a Bushman, and a high kill rate. It was rumoured that he was completely bossies.

He wore canvas combat boots despite efforts to make him conform to the leather footwear of the regiment. He carried a pistol, and a bat's R1 with a fold-up butt. Promotion to the rank of sergeant had made no difference. He could not be forced to respect the officers, most of whom were younger than he was. None of them had anything like his combat experience, if they had any at all. Few officers felt up to challenging him when they stood before the aggressive fire of his gaze . . . or heard his laughter.

At Oshikango it was decided that one company of the regiment should be sent to Ruacana to assist the troops in that vicinity, and to monitor the activities of the Cubans on the Angolan side of the Ruacana dam. The consensus of the officers was to send C company, which coincidentally contained Manie Dippenaar.

Many officers breathed a sigh of relief as they watched C company depart for Ruacana with Manie and his special equipment: three trommels of clothing, personal gadgetry and food.

In Ruacana C company dug in, taking over the camp from the Umvoti regiment. Major Rutling was in command and he soon found himself becoming distracted by the presence of Manie. It was not only that the man was insolent, but all the men looked up to him as the most experienced soldier in this terrain. Any orders given by the major were run past Manie to test their validity. Even major Rutling found himself becoming curious to see Manie's reaction to his ideas.

Manie was slowly draining him of his credibility and authority. He was getting angry. He watched Manie regaling a group of city boys with his tales. He couldn't stand any more of that laughter. *The bastard's fucken bossies. He'll have to go.*

The following morning the company was called on to parade. A special assignment was announced. The major stressed the importance of the mission, its vital necessity to the campaign generally, and also for the protection of our own in the face of Cuban insurgents from the north. In a formal voice he said: 'We have to establish an observation post south of the Ruacana dam which, as you may know, is presently being held by Cubans on the Angolan side. This observation post will be sixty kilometres north of this camp and three kilometres from the dam. It is well within range of the enemy, and in a vulnerable position in the event of an attack. The seven men who will man this position have already been chosen in view of their experience and skills. They will need to be alert. Self-discipline will be required as the post will be isolated from the regiment for long periods of time and will not be subject to the daily routines and discipline of this camp.' He then proceeded to read out the names of the seven who had been chosen.

As their names were read, the seven chosen ones smiled to themselves. Camp discipline was something they could live without. Five of the group were close friends who had vowed to stick together – a gang known as 'the five fingers'. The other two individuals were Jeff Bacon, a surfer who lived on his own planet, and Manie Dippenaar. Seeing that Manie held the highest rank – sergeant – he was assigned to command the OP.

So it was that seven soldiers, Greg Savage, Deon Bristow, Jeff Bacon (nicknamed Spek), James Cockhead (the butt of endless jokes), Eddie White, Neil Carter, and Manie Dippenaar, were dumped in the veld sixty kilometres to the north of the camp with their rifles, a light machine gun, two eighty-one millimetre mortars, ammunition, a radio, a water-trailer, food, and a Unimog with its floor sandbagged in case of mines.

They were to dig in and spend their time watching the dam in the valley.

The major felt extremely pleased with himself as he watched the seven potential trouble-makers heading north in a cloud of dust.

Out of sight, out of mind.
For now.

Dagga

It was on the train from Bloem, as we were chugging our way to Grootfontein, that I first caught a whiff of that old familiar smell. I smiled to myself. *Someone's hitting the dope.* I could imagine a compartment of conspirators passing around a slow-boat, feet up on the table.

The following morning early we arrived at Grootfontein, that huge military depot, stretching for miles in all directions. Ammunition dumps, tents, radio aerials, paymasters, quartermasters, vehicle yards, ablution blocks, parade grounds, fuel depots with large plastic fuel bladders, barbed wire, razor wire and all the other paraphernalia of that vast military enterprise. At the station we disembarked and stood in company formation while our kitbags were offloaded from the baggage trucks. I remember thinking that it was going to be difficult to find my own bag among the hundreds of identical bags piled high in the pale morning light.

Suddenly a group of military police pushed urgently through the ranks and boarded the train. We looked at each other enquiringly. Eyebrows were raised. Shoulders shrugged.

It wasn't long before the police appeared again, but this time they had in tow the soldiers of the compartment from which had been issuing the familiar aroma. All were under arrest.

They had stayed on the train and were about to bust another pipe when the military police arrived. I could imagine the scene, a still life: the brown paper of the zoll; a box of Lion matches; pips scattered across the surface of the compartment table; a clay pipe, loaded and tamped down, awaiting the flame; the lappie wrapped about the narrow end.

The OC had made a clear statement. Dope smoking was not going to be tolerated in the DLI. It was taboo. We heard that the smokers were to be sent to DB for two weeks and then tried in a civilian court. The rumour was that they would be spending up to a year in a civilian jail. They never made it to the border.

We all made a mental note of the occurrence.

We'd been on the border proper – at Oshikango – for about a week when dope made another appearance. For days we had been digging in. The Ops tent had been pitched in a hole the size of a swimming pool, which took us two days to dig. From morning to night we shovelled sand, working bare-chested in the sun. We were looking like soldiers, fit, shorn of hair, and tanned. We enjoyed our food and the camaraderie of manual labour. One lunchtime, a friend by name of Clive drew me aside. As he took off his bush hat I saw that he'd asked the barber to cut off all of his hair. His close-cropped pate was lily-white, in contrast to his tanned face and body. He smiled and said, 'I've got some zani with me. Do you want to join us for a smoke after work this evening?'

It seemed like a good idea – a relaxing, pleasant smoke after a hard day's work. Tonic for the soul.

'Ja, sure,' I said, 'but we'd better make sure we don't get busted. You know what happened to those okes on the train.'

Clive smiled.

'No problem. I've already thought of that. There's an open spot of ground behind the toilets which is screened from the camp. It'll be cool to smoke there. We'll be able to see anyone coming well before they can get to us.'

So, after work, I joined Clive and a few other mates that he'd invited at the appointed spot. A big, fat slow-boat was being passed around. We all participated in the age-old ritual, squatting down in a circle.

Some sucked deep and held the smoke in their lungs, their eyes bulging. Others smoked more elegantly, treating the reefer like a cigarette. We all felt the effects. Increased heartbeat, a wooziness, a rise of smiling energy, a sense of conspiracy and the relaxing of conscious resolve. Then, a touch of mild paranoia. I looked out across the trees in the sunset and watched some hornbills nesting nearby. Ovamboland was an alien but beautiful place.

Suddenly a whistle blew and we had to assemble. We threw the joint to the ground and scrambled off to our various units. Once assembled we were given a lengthy lecture on the maintenance of rifles in sandy terrain. A waste of a good high. I decided then to give dope a miss. Besides the risk, this wasn't really the place to enjoy the shadows of the mind.

An interesting story about dope was doing the rounds, though. It was professed army policy to win the hearts and minds of the South West African populace, so soldiers were expected to behave civilly and to be ambassadors for the 'great power', South Africa, which was there to assist them in the battle against SWAPO, the Commies, and the Cubans. A group of soldiers out on patrol had entered a kraal where they had been royally welcomed. The chief, a generous man, had fed them tenderly grilled meat, freshly slaughtered, and each man was invited to drink from a calabash of African beer. He did the whole traditional thing – the calabash was presented by a maiden on her knees, her breasts like nesting doves, her eyes cast down in obedient humility.

All were enjoying themselves when the chief lit up a large reefer and passed it around the circle. Some of the men declined, but those who enjoyed a toke participated. The officer in charge smiled to himself. Sometimes the role of ambassador made unusual demands, and in some ways the tokers had made a sound contribution to national policy.

The Patrol

This particular morning I find myself standing ready to go on patrol with the South African Police. Last night a report was received about a disturbance some sixty kilometres north-east of our camp. I and two others from Intelligence have been drafted to accompany the police patrol. Perhaps the major felt that the regiment needed some intelligence personnel to bring back first-hand reports on the 'disturbance'. Perhaps he'd been drinking with some police officers and said something like, 'Take some of my troops with you. They could do with the experience.' *Who knows?*

I have two loaded magazines of ammunition in my web pouches and a full magazine in my rifle. More important, though, in my kidney pouches I have a pack of dog biscuits wrapped in cellophane, a can of fruit salad, some dried apricots, and a few sticks of biltong. Our water bottles are full and hang heavily at our sides.

We've been delivered by truck to the police camp and here begins the inevitable waiting while the Hyenas are fuelled. I stroll over to the canteen to buy a Coke and some cigarettes. It is heavily sandbagged and cool inside. Scope magazine centre-spreads are stuck on the wall behind the bar. A collage of voluptuous female forms. Breasts and bums and thighs and provocative faces.

Words are inadequate to describe female beauty, the curve of a thigh, or its power. It's a painful reminder of another world. Eros. And all I've seen for the last few weeks are men. Men's bums, thighs, cocks, torsos and necks, in uniform and out of it. Great if you're into men, but gnawingly painful if you need women. In fact, the sight of this feminine beauty just makes the reality of my situation worse. *Who the fuck dreamed up this nightmare?*

Eventually, after a roll-call, we embark, strapping ourselves into the bucket seats so we won't be thrown upwards against the roof if we hit a landmine. A tracker-cum-interpreter is on board with us. He too is dressed in a military uniform, a khaki sun hat and shorts. Apparently his family had been wiped out by SWAPO so he has reasons for hunting his own kind.

Opposite me sits a young policeman from Pretoria, sporting a large moustache. His adam's apple is large, and he is a pipe smoker with short and stubby fingers. He moves with a slow deliberation. Besides a nine millimetre pistol, he carries a twelve bore double-barrelled shotgun – his weapon of choice. It is lovingly maintained, glowing with a bluish patina of oil. He is musing aloud about the problem of a rocket ambush, but concludes, 'As die ding jou naam op hom het, dan is 'it jou tyd, boet.' Ja, true, if the thing's got your name on it, then it is your time. He had just returned from honeymoon with his new bride only to find that his call-up papers had arrived.

We drive for miles along the dusty roads, passing a few settlements among the trees. There are no phone poles or pavements or fences. Only an endless cover of trees and bush across a land without grass. Visibility is poor from within our metal vessel. The bullet-proof windows are misting with dust. Mostly we just sit in silence, rifle barrels pointed at the ceiling. A Beatles tune is looping repeatedly through my mind. *We all live in a yellow submarine . . . a yellow submarine . . . a yellow submarine . . .*

After about two hours of driving, the whole patrol pulls up outside a small country school. We stretch our legs while the officers confer with the headmaster. His concern is that several of his older pupils in standard seven, who are nineteen and twenty years old, have gone to join up with SWAPO. Their angry idealism has contaminated the innocence of some of his younger pupils. One of the truants, or 'freedom fighters', has left one of the girls pregnant. *There are many reasons for going to war.* He suggests that we visit a nearby kraal which seems to be the epicentre of these disruptions.

I look at this small school. A corrugated iron roof, no ceilings, and many of the windows broken. A single white butterfly drifts across the dusty playground. A few pupils dressed in various combinations of school uniform stand in the sun and watch the exchange between their headmaster and these armed strangers.

'Klim op,' comes the command, and we climb aboard and drive out of there. I watch the school grow smaller and disappear in our dust.

Our vehicles bump over ant-hills and skirt fields of mahangu, occasionally breaking branches and stripping leaves as we pass by. We stop outside a large kraal. It is surrounded by a wall of dry, vertical, but irregular sticks, forming a palisade fence about

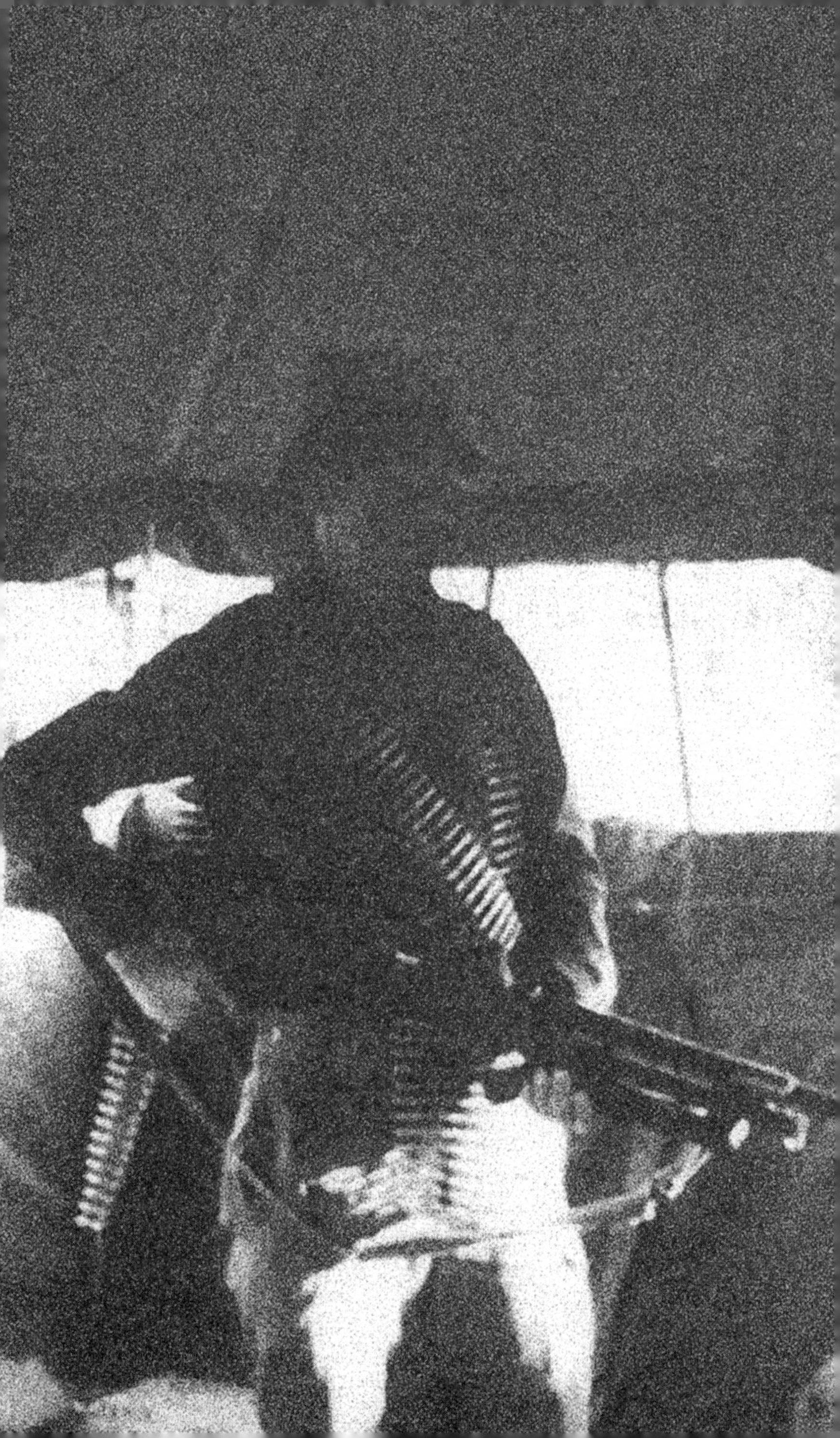

eight feet tall. We can only glimpse the mysterious internal spaces through the gaps between the posts. We enter through the southern gate. Twelve armed men and an interpreter.

Before us is a large enclosure. The sand has been swept clean. Three small dwellings, with walls of vertical sticks and loosely thatched roofs, are randomly placed within the palisade surround. To enter one of them you would have to go down on hands and knees. They have small wooden doors with bolts and padlocks.

Near a fireplace of smoke-blackened stones, an old crone sits motionless. She is smoking a pipe. Her skin is grey with dust. Her breasts are flat and wrinkled. They have fed many mouths. She watches our approach with silent contempt. Sitting close to her are three children, completely naked, their skins grey with dust too. Flies drink the moisture from their eyelashes. Occasionally, with a light economy of movement, they brush them away.

Our interpreter greets her in the Ovambo tongue. Her responses are short. She can read the meaning of the situation. Armed strangers on a mission. *The enemy*.

The captain speaks: 'Tell her that we are aware that certain young men from this place have recently gone missing. We suspect that they are involved with SWAPO.'

The interpreter translates the captain's words. She answers him in a high-pitched voice, speaking quickly.

He turns to the captain.

'She says that she knows nothing about this, but some young men have gone to seek work elsewhere.'

'Where?'

Again the discussion with the interpreter.

'She says she doesn't know. They are young. They make their own choices.'

'Ask her if she is aware that there have been reports about her support of the illegal SWAPO organisation, and that this kraal is being watched.'

As the interpreter conveys the captain's words some of the men start moving around the compound. The old woman's eyes reveal her awareness of our every movement. Most of us have by now squatted down on our haunches and are following the interrogation. Like her, I am aware of the sounds of our soldiers poking about and looking at her possessions. I watch her eyes, and for a moment they show a flicker of alarm as she hears a soldier forcing open the door to one of the huts. I, too, hear the sound of someone tampering with things inside the hut. I get up to investigate.

As I reach the hut one of our soldiers is emerging with a small and beautifully crafted bow and several arrows.

'What the hell are you doing?' I ask angrily.

'Nothing, man, I'm just taking something for back home.'

My anger rises, and in a clipped, determined voice I say, 'Put it back immediately. You're stealing from these people.'

He checks me out, sees my resolve, and reluctantly returns the souvenir.

As he emerges he comments, 'Cool it, man. What fucken difference will it make if I take a few things? Anyway these people are probably terrorists.'

'Just don't do it, OK.'

He walks off shaking his head. I'd pulled rank.

I return to the interrogation. Little has been achieved. The old lady hates our guts. That's clear enough. She sucks on her pipe, continues to avoid direct eye contact, yet manages to convey her contempt for all of us. We leave the kraal and bump onward in the Hyenas towards the scene of the reported disturbance.

A small settlement. It has been visited by death. Rifles are cocked in unison. As we emerge from the vehicles we see and know. The chief's hut has been burned to the ground. Possessions are scattered about. We stiffen with alertness. *Safety's off.* Adrenalin rush. I see a swollen human rump in a pair of grey shorts. Dead boy. Lying like a bag of discarded rubbish. *Oh fuck . . . this is real . . . we all live in a yellow submarine . . . a yellow submarine . . .*

'Move out! Spread out!' shouts the captain. 'This could be an ambush!'

Oh God why am I here? Keep calm . . . I don't want to die . . . I won't die.

I move off to the left, my senses radar wide. I move through the spaces, surveying the rape. Broken earthen pots. Rags. A discarded shoe. A photograph of a matriarch in church attire, posed formally in a studio. Then on to the body of the boy. He is stiff with death and covered with flies. The smell of rotting meat. I can't understand his head, and then I see that the top of his skull has been lopped off. It is a hive of flies. How? *Must have been done with a single blow. A panga? A boy of ten . . . yellow submarine . . . a yellow submarine . . . we all live . . .*

A shout goes up. 'Jusses mense. Hulle het vir ons gewag!' So they had been waiting for us. We move towards the voice. We want to see how, and where. Somehow we sense collectively that death has moved on. It waits here no longer. The captain stands at the top of a long track and beckons us forward. We move past the body of an old woman. Her corpse has been raked by bullets. Cartridge cases are scattered all over the place.

The captain points out the signs of a planned ambush. The bait lies close by – the body of a man, fully dressed, but without shoes. Automatic weapon fire has been the cause of death, although the wire around his wrists suggests a prelude of torture. A few metres from the corpse the enemy has dug a small defensive trench. A place to hide, and from which to open fire on those who come in response to the disturbance. They've left a few empty cans and plenty of beer bottles. We can smell their faeces in the vicinity. But they are gone. The tracker says that they left the previous morning so it would be pretty pointless to pursue them now. They'd be long gone. *Probably wearing civilian clothes. Watching the passing military vehicles. Standing with a hoe in a field.*

The chief who owns the kraal is a tribal policeman who stands for the old order – peace and quiet and the native in his place.

These policemen are issued with an old British three-o-three rifle and paid a small retainer to keep the faith and steady the boat.

Such men are seen as a hindrance to the revolution, especially if personal conflict comes into the game. Apparently this chief is unpopular with a certain faction of the youth. He has been trying to stem the tide . . . *stem the tide . . . King Canute . . . washed away . . . throne and all.*

With the interpreter's insight into the tribal drama we are able to piece together the events that led to this devastation.

Three nights previously a group of armed men visited the kraal with the intention of either convincing the chief to join their side or eliminating him. There was already conflict between the chief and one of the young men in the vicinity. However, the chief is not there when they arrive. He is in Oshakati attending an elders' meeting. The soldiers leave. Nearby there is a Cuca shop – a three by three metre corrugated iron shack that sells beer. The owner is asleep on the floor. Something changes in the darkness. Freedom fighters become killers. We guess that they knocked loudly on the side of the shop, demanding beer. Because of the dark mistrust of war, the shopkeeper refuses to open the door, so they begin raking the shop with their automatic weapons. The shopkeeper survives by lying low, and after pleading for mercy, opens the door. He is beaten about while the soldiers go on a drinking spree.

The chief's wife, once the firing has stopped, probably calls out into the night to establish what has happened. This may have triggered the lunacy which followed. She is shot down on the road and her body is strafed with automatic fire. She is punctured by at least fifty bullets as she lies on her back in the sand. Her son tries to run away but his life is ended by a viciously swung panga, leaving him as we have found him. They burn the kraal. Thereafter they decide to set an ambush for the police, and drag the shopkeeper up the road, leaving a deliberate trail. He is executed. Then they wait.

I am thankful that communications in Ovamboland are not swift, for surely we would have walked into a hail of bullets had we arrived a day earlier. It wasn't our time.

We decide to drive around the area before heading back to base. As we are walking towards the vehicles I begin to think of angels. I call on one to protect my wife and child back home. I can almost feel the winged presence of my guardian angel walking behind me. I make up my mind to treat my family better if I get home safely. I will build a new bed. Start again. Find my meaning. Fulfil my visions. As I look across into the bush, I see issuing from a hole in the base of a tree, silver rings, mysterious, wavery, like smoke rings. The O's of anguish. The O's of Oshakati, of Oshivelo, of Ondangwa, of Oshikango, of Owahimba, of Ovamboland, of Africa. I see the picture to be carved into the headboard of our new bed: A soldier standing near a tree which sings these O's. A bicycle leaning against another tree. Above, a huge winged angel . . . brooding. Some distance to the right stand my wife and child. Above them, another angel.

How the soul seeks other connections when dark forces cast their shadows over our lives.

The journey back is relatively uneventful. We stop at several settlements. Fan the rumours, tell the tale. The darkness closes in.

Back at the police base we disperse, each man carrying his share of the nightmare.

Words on Paper

To send messages of love and longing for home, I'd decided to use telegrams as a means of communication because the regular mail took at least two weeks to reach home. Letters had to be handed in to the adjutant to be censored. This he did with a ballpoint pen, covering over any information which was considered to be strategic. Once censored, the letters were put back into their envelopes and sealed. From there they went to the postal depot which was attached to the stores. There they would wait for the next vehicle to Oshakati. Then they were put onto a plane which touched down at Grootfontein before going on to Pretoria. The mail was then placed in the hands of the regular postal service of the Republic of South Africa.

Telegrams were quicker, even if a bit more expensive. Besides, things could go wrong along the postal route. Once a truck carrying stores and post was hastening along the dust track to Oshakati when its engine cut out. The driver and his companion opened the bonnet, but neither was that mechanically minded, so after staring at the hot engine for a while, they decided to take a break. Resting in the shade beneath the truck, they waited for assistance to come along. They drowsed off in the hot silence. When it started growing dark, their vulnerability became clear to them. They became anxious. Suddenly, one had the belated idea that the truck might be out of petrol. They had a spare can of fuel for such emergencies. They opened the vehicle's petrol cap and tried to sniff and peer into the pipe. They needed a torch. Without thinking, the driver lit a match and held it over the petrol pipe to help visibility. The fumes ignited, burning his face. The canvas of the truck caught alight and it wasn't long before the whole truck was being licked by flames, fuelled by its own petrol. All the letters were burned. Millions of words on paper . . .

Dear Rose,

We have been in ----- for ----- weeks now. I am really grateful for the food parcel you sent me. The biltong and honey are great. The weather is hot by day and cold by night. I saw quite an interesting sight the other day as we were driving through ----- near -----. A long green snake was slithering along beside the truck. He kept up with us for a while before peeling off into the bush.

I long to hold you in my arms again. Other thoughts come to mind but the ----- read our letters so I won't mention them. How's everyone at home? Try to remember when you reply, that letters take about ----- weeks to get here.

I'm well despite the boredom and routine. It's only ----- more ----- before we'll be back home, hopefully in one piece. Please keep writing, your letters really help to make things bearable.

I love you and long for you.
Yours forever,
Simon x x x x x

Phil's Pills

Another Saturday morning. We of the BBC (Better Breakfasts Club) – due to special friendship with the cooks – have had a meal of bacon and eggs in the kitchen. It's a sunny day and there are no immediate duties. Phil draws me aside. 'Hey, I've got some lank pills. Tranquillisers. Let's pop them a bit later.'

Why not? Anything to take the edge off the boredom of captivity.

I pick up a six-pack of beers from Bruce, who runs a kind of after-hours store of liquor and cigarettes – the HQ company shebeen. I go to Phil's tent. Blond Phil, with his lucky charms, his stories and his blue-eyed grin. He is waiting for me, listening to Dylan's *Desire* album on his small portable tape recorder. The romantic sound of mandolin and guitar, and Dylan's voice singing . . .

Hot chili peppers in the blistering sun
dust on my face and my cape . . .

'OK, china, let's drop them.'

He hands me two white pills. We look at each other, smile, and swallow the pills, washing them down with a sluk of cool beer.

'Get your guit, man. I'm tired of listening to recorded music.'

I stroll across to my tent in the heat and collect my Japanese nylon-string guitar.

Phil and I chat, drink beer, and every now and again I sing a song. We are feeling mellow. Tranquillised. Well insulated from military pressures.

I play some of my own stuff and Dylan's stuff, particularly *Love Minus Zero*, the words of which are comforting somehow. A green pasture of poetry. Every day there are requests that I play it. Staff-sergeant Giles comes at night and asks me to play it for him before he hits the sack. Clasping his arms around his knees, he tilts his head and listens, the candle flame reflecting in the lenses of his glasses.

My love she speaks like silence
without ideals or violence
She doesn't have to say she's faithful,
yet she's true like ice, like fire . . .

After a good session together with Phil, I go and relax in my tent. Phil decides to do some sunbathing.

I fall asleep.

I am woken by a familiar voice. Eugene's. He is usually a quiet, soft-spoken individual, but now his voice carries an unusual urgency. He is saying, 'Wake up, Phil, wake up. What the fuck is wrong with you?'

I know, so I go outside to investigate. Phil has fallen asleep in the sun and has been rather badly sunburned. He is lying on his back. He has a fair skin and his face is now a bluish pink. His eyelids are guinea-fowl purple. We can't get him to wake up properly, so we drag him along the sand by his feet. At the waterpoint we open up the hydrant and drench him with water. He leaps up swearing. 'What the fuck! What the fuck you doing?'

To our relief he comes to his senses. We explain that with another hour of sleeping in the sun he would have been a hospital case. As it is, he has suffered quite badly, and he uses Nivea cream to cool his burning flesh.

All the skin will peel from his lips. It will take him about ten days to recover.

Hot chili peppers in the blistering sun . . .

Exodus in Seven Parts

Manie Dippenaar and the manne had been manning the OP for eleven days now and they were getting bored. Their routine was to rise at eight am, before the sun started overheating their sleeping bags, catch a wash at the trailer, sometimes a shave, and to take a shit in the bush somewhere. For this, each man had his own spot. Neil, tall, with dark hair and a friendly smile, commented on how well his stomach worked since he had been squatting. 'You realise that the human body was designed to squat rather than sit on a porcelain throne with your legs at right angles to your body.'

Breakfast was an informal affair since none of the men really bothered to dress. Shorts or underpants were adequate and all were looking tanned as they sat around a fire cooking porridge or powdered egg.

'Jeez, I could do with some fresh fruit. All this canned stuff . . .' said Jeff. A good-humoured urbane face with a large nose.

'Ja. Tell you what I could handle right now . . . a loaf of fresh bread,' added Greg, his bony hands resting on his knees.

'Ay, ou Savage, I could chow a whole loaf right fucken now,' Manie agreed. 'It's still three more days before new supplies and the post arrive, so we'll have to wait . . . ah . . . seventeen days before we see any really fresh food. No, fuckit, you okes, this calls for action. I'm going to find a shop where we can get some bread and fruit. If you want to come, get dressed.'

Manie grabbed his hat, strapped on his pistol, and picking up his rifle, headed towards the truck. He was followed by 'Coptop' (James Cockhead), who seldom spoke and walked with his arms dangling at his sides. Deon got up and strolled towards the truck. He was very conscious of his well-developed upper torso, and walked with a rolling motion, his arms pushed out from his sides like a gunslinger. Then Eddie decided to go too. He was a confident joker with blond hair that might be better described as white.

The other three who didn't feel like getting into harness, placed their orders with Deon. Manie smiled widely as he started the Unimog and they drove off in a cloud of dust.

They found a shop ten kilometres to the east which doubled as a post office. The shopkeeper was sullen and unfriendly. All shopkeepers or bottle-store owners had been ordered by higher authorities to minimise contact with South African soldiers. For reasons of security, shopkeepers had been warned never to allow South African soldiers to post letters or to make phone calls. There was an official notice displayed above the counter to the effect that 'No unauthorised personnel from the SADF may post letters or use the telephone' . . . blah, blah, blah . . . 'offenders will be prosecuted.'

The shop was hot under its corrugated asbestos roof. There was no bread or fruit available, but they purchased some flour, some beer, cigarettes, sweets and cooldrinks.

Back at camp they dug a hole about two feet deep. In this they started a fire, adding bigger sticks of dried wood as it grew hotter. When there was a bed of glowing embers, they laid a piece of flat metal directly onto the coals. On this surface they placed the large ball of dough for their bread. It was a mixture of flour, beer, salt and cooking oil. Then they closed the hole with a piece of corrugated iron, and covered it with sand so that no heat could escape.

While waiting for their bread to bake, they sat about talking over the usual things – women, sex, what I'm going to do when I get back home, the nature of my civvy job, motorcycles, music, and some of the arseholes running this world.

Neil Carter pulled a book from his pack and informed everybody that he was going to read.

'What you reading, Neil?'

'*Exodus* by Leon Uris.'

'Fucken thick book, ou china. What's it about . . . Moses in the desert?'

'Nah, it's about the Jews establishing a homeland in Israel. You know, with the kibbutzes an' all.'

'Fuck it, man, I'd quite dig to read that myself,' says Jeff. 'I checked the movie back in the sixties when I was still at school . . . Paul Newman was in it . . . and some blonde chick. She had to give him an injection in the heart. 'Twas a good movie.' He smiled in fond recollection.

'Hey Neil, why don't you be a real china and divide the book into seven parts and then we'll all have something to read?' suggested Manie.

At first Neil didn't like the idea of cutting his book into seven parts. It was unheard of. Eventually, with a shrug of his shoulders, he succumbed to the general enthusiasm for the idea.

'It's just a fucken book, man. If it worries you, I'll buy you another copy when we get back home,' said Manie.

'But I want to read it in the correct order . . . seeing it's my book. I want to start at the beginning.'

'No problem, Neil. Lank. For us it'll be a gas to read any section in any order, and then put it all together in our heads at the end . . . like a new kind of puzzle . . . like that broken telephone game we used to play at school.'

Neil took the book, a thick paperback of some six hundred pages, and looked at it. Then, working carefully with his bayonet, he divided the book into seven parts. It was written in five books. So, he took book one, *Beyond Jordan*, for himself. It was a long section. Book two, *The Land Is Mine*, about one hundred and twenty pages, he divided up between Deon and Greg. Book three, *An Eye for an Eye*, he divided between Manie and James. Book four, *Awake in Glory*, only about one hundred pages long, he gave to Jeff, who mumbled some comment about the title under his breath. The last book, *With Wings as Eagles*, he gave to Ed, who responded, 'If I had wings you think I'd be here?'

Silence reigned as all of them started reading . . . waiting for the bread.

Night Cries

When stand-to was over and the sun was no longer a presence, we would watch the first stars of the evening appear. Celestial. Innocent. Distant.

Before moonrise the darkness would descend, and here, miles from settlement and city, the sky sang with stars.

One evening I had wandered off alone and was standing under some trees. The moon was rising. I heard the sounds of sobbing. Deep, anguished sobbing, issuing from the chest of a big man. He must have thought he was alone, or else he was beyond caring. Crying like an abandoned child in a lunar world, he was far from the short-sleeved bravado of sunny days.

I recall nights when we could all hear the African drums beating a furious pulse, and voices, mainly female, singing into the night. Probably a party. We, on the other hand, were not permitted any form of loud or jovial conviviality. We had to maintain a hushed, firm, sober presence. Of course the local people knew that there was a regiment of men camped nearby, but that didn't seem to dampen their enthusiasm. We all heard the singing and thought of home.

Another night I was on my way back to the tent, having just completed four hours of ops duty – mapping flare sightings and reports of gunfire – when I heard a man shouting loudly. His voice came from somewhere nearby. Obviously someone in HQ company. The voice had a hysterical pitch to it. He was talking fast, spitting out a delirium of words, but they were clear and made complete sense. He was berating our sergeant-major.

'You dumb, stupid pig! All you're good for is collecting money from phone booths! You wanking, dull post office clerk! If it wasn't for the army and this fucked up situation you'd be nobody.

You are nobody! Hide behind your badges. Hide behind the uniform. You better hide, because we'll find you when all this is over. On the streets of Durban. You! You cunt! You loud-mouthed prick! Clean your own shoes. Grow up. Fuck off. Take your money and go!'

This diatribe ended abruptly and silence resumed. I was startled by this sudden disembodied expression of unbridled hatred and also a trifle amused. Everybody knew that in civvy life the sergeant-major was employed in a minor administrative post in the telephone department.

It was so late in the night that even if the sergeant-major had woken to hear his denouncement, he would have been hard put to focus his consciousness and trace the voice before it was over.

I heard later that it was Clive who had delivered this tirade. Some of the guys who shared a tent with him had been startled awake by his shouting. He had been standing upright in his sleeping bag, as if to attention, while this stream of words poured from his mouth. They spoke to him but soon realised that he wasn't awake. He was in some somnolent condition. When his tirade was over, he lay down once more and continued sleeping. He professed to remember nothing of this outburst when morning came.

Another night found me on guard duty at the magazine. There was no moon and the darkness was thick. Any movement was challenged in the traditional manner.

'Halt! Who goes there?'

Most knew the password and answered. You could hear their minds working as they hurried to voice the password, always a little awkwardly, either barked out rapidly or with a slight quaver. Although you couldn't see anything, you knew that there were loaded guns pointing at you in the darkness.

Of course there were those who forgot the password, or hadn't been around when it had been given out. An English-speaking voice with a Durban accent calls out: 'Hey, it's me,

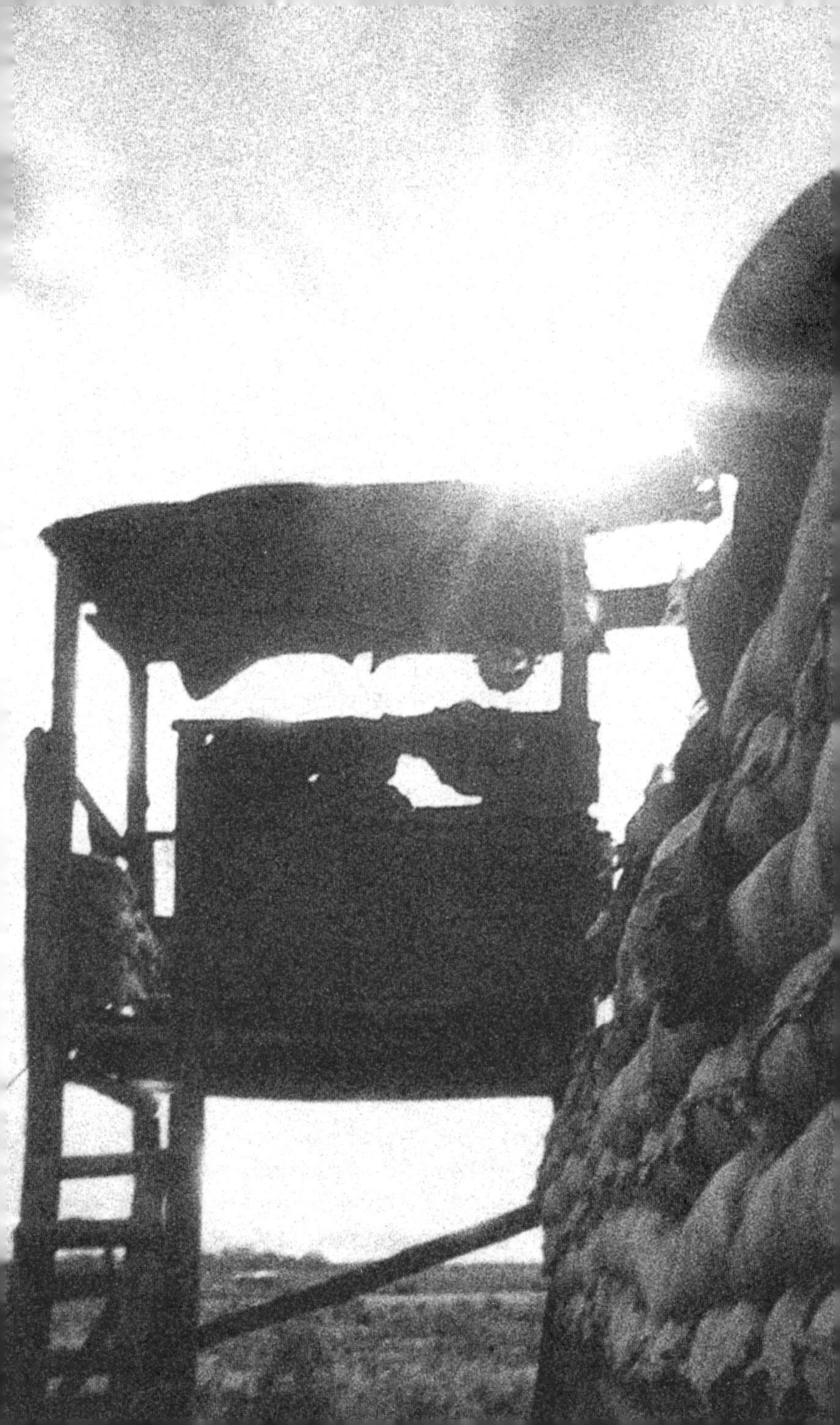

private Fraser of mortars. I was out of camp today so I wasn't given the password. Sergeant Murray is my section leader . . .'

Guarding the magazine was dull work. A complete black-out had been ordered and it was a moonless night, so there was not a light to be seen on the ground. We wandered about in the darkness, under a canopy of distant stars, tracing a path around the looming form of the sandbagged magazine as far as the Ops tent, and then back again. I was in the vicinity of the Ops tent when I saw a figure emerging. When he reached the top of the steps he stopped because he could see nothing. It had taken my eyes at least an hour to adjust to the darkness, so I was aware of how completely disorientated this person was, especially since he had just come out of a tent brightly lit by gas lamps. I drew nearer and recognised the padre.

'Good evening, padre,' I said. 'Can I help you back to your tent?'

'Please. I can't see a thing. It's incredibly dark.'

I came up close to him and suggested that he take hold of my webbing and follow me. It was like leading a blind man. He tripped once or twice, but I delivered him safely to his tent. Inside, once the flap was closed, he lit a candle, and peered at me in the dim light. I saw his greying hair and glasses. He thanked me profusely for my help. He asked me who I was and how I was enjoying the camp.

I had seen the padre only from a distance – a distance coloured by my cynicism. I'd judged him to be a little soft, a kind of voyeur, protected by the chaplain's badge, and earning a captain's salary. I was of the impression that he was having a fine time. It seemed to me that he had no specific duties other than leading the outdoor Sunday service and counselling men who had 'problems'.

Well, I had problems, so I proceeded to tell him of my difficulties. I spoke of the injustices of the apartheid government and my problem with accepting my conscription into the army. I told him of how this call-up had disrupted my life and self-employment as a musician. I asked him how I might find a way to understand the will of God in this situation.

As I expected, he didn't share my views on conscription. I should 'obey the laws of the land', he advised me, and taking up his Bible he read to me from one of Paul's letters to the Romans.

Everyone must obey the state authorities, because no
authority exists without God's permission, and the
existing authorities have been put there by God.
Whoever opposes the existing authority opposes
what God has ordered; and anyone who does so will
bring judgement on himself.

As regards the apartheid government, he conceded that the system had flaws, but that right now we were in SWA as agents of law and order – on God's side, so to speak. We were the 'good' guys. The commies were the 'bad' guys. Clearly he supported the status quo.

His parting words to me were: 'Continue to pray.'

I thought of some of the other guys whose lives had been upset by the army, like Butch's mate, Keith. There were just too many questions.

Thinking that he was being well paid to dish out a rather cold comfort, I made my way once more into the darkness.

David

We'd been on the border about a month when David arrived. He was a tall, handsome Jew, well built, neat in appearance, with raven-black hair. He had about him the air of calm that comes from a sense of belonging to an established and supportive religious culture. A tradition of wise fathers. *A history of persecution?*

He had been sent to us from B company where he had refused to carry a weapon. He'd been shouted at, given pack drill, threatened, and ordered to obey, but had stubbornly refused to take up arms. He was prepared to help and to serve the regiment, but he was not prepared to carry a gun.

Unable to get him to capitulate, the officer in charge of B company had sent him to HQ for disciplinary action. Instead of bringing him before a military court, where his trial might have raised awkward moral issues and influenced others, he was put on permanent fatigue duty. He had to heat the commander's bath water each evening, clean the latrines, run messages, and be general skivvy for anyone above the rank of sergeant.

He was given a place to sleep, and then began his long days of servanthood. He carried buckets, cleaned vehicles, delivered meals and ran messages. He dug holes and swept the Ops tent. Each day was a long routine of chores. We would see his manly figure carrying bundles of firewood across the late evening horizon.

Although he was given little time to rest, his spirit could not be broken and he remained cheerful. In conversation he deliberately spoke pidgin English like an African gardener or house boy. I'd hear him in the evenings in the tent next door regaling his mates with stories of his day's events.

'I making the fire to make it hot the water for the bath for lo big baas . . . lo kenel. Ai, she is shouting me too much this kenel. I'm going inside to that bathroom. That bathroom . . . me, I'm make it . . .' His stories were accompanied by a pantomime of exaggerated servility and manically humble gestures.

He managed to continue playing the role of menial for the duration of the camp. His method of resistance, although unorthodox, was extremely effective, and he had the stamina to keep it up. By reducing himself to this farcical role he would remind us every day of the servant/master relationship that so often corrupted civility and trust in South African society. *Passive resistance? A calm and smouldering anger expressed through humour?* Whatever it was, it was a demanding role, and David played it well and for the duration.

You prepare a table before me in the presence of my enemies.

Concert in a Mess

Word got around that I had a guitar and could sing, so some of the officers decided that it would be 'nice' to have a folk singer performing in the mess one evening. I was invited to play. Some brass from Pretoria were visiting the regiment on this occasion.

I arrived early and selected a position in the tent from which I could best project my voice. Since I had no PA system, I guessed it would be difficult to sing above the chatter once the liquor had taken hold. I lit a Texan, and waited in my corner for the signal to begin. The officers from Pretoria were ushered in. They regarded me with a vague and slightly contemptuous interest.

Perhaps the commander thought I might be able to unite all these disparate souls in some kind of sing-along camaraderie. The vibes were awkward. Although in uniform, I felt like a travelling clown – one of the acrobats or jugglers sitting outside the city, on a wall, in the company of Picasso's monkey.

Eventually Lieutenant Jansen gave me the nod, and I launched into the first song, Country Joe's *I-Feel-Like-I'm-Fixin'-To-Die Rag* – our contextualised version – which was a daily request from the men, and which was in my fingers.

Come on all of you big strong men
Uncle John needs your help again.
Got himself in a bit of a jam
Way down yonder in Ovamboland.

The chorus, usually sung in beery gung-ho voices by the men, sounded rather naked in just my own voice.

And it's one two three
What are we fighting for?
Don't ask me . . . I don't give a damn
Next stop Ovamboland

There ain't no use to wonder why
Whoopie . . . we're all bound to die

The audience was politely quiet and clapped without enthusiasm as the song ended. The next song was Graham Nash's *Military Madness*. As I sang the lyrics I remembered our digs in Greyling street a long time ago. Blankets up for curtains. No carpets. Guitars and amps everywhere . . .

It was a plaintive and melodic song, but when I got to the chorus,

Military madness is killing this country . . .

Lieutenant Jansen stood in front of me and told me to stop.

'Look, the commander wants you out. These songs are inappropriate.'

He handed me a six-pack and ushered me to the door. I knew the songs might needle those committed to the military, but I didn't expect the rejection to be so fast and so thorough. I walked off and didn't look back.

Dear John

Manie and the boys at the OP received their first mail from the main camp after three weeks. A young lieutie was in charge of the men who brought their supplies. A fresh water-trailer, food supplies, some fresh meat and vegetables, a few cans of petrol, and the mail. The men jumped at the letters and went off on their own to read them. Manie handled all of the negotiations with the officer, a freckled nineteen year old. He handed over the daily reports and laughed as he watched the intimidated officer bouncing away in his Landrover.

Later that day when they were sharing out the freshly cooked meat, they noticed that James was in a very strange mood. He wasn't wearing his hat and his hair was all awry.

'What's wrong Mr Glans?' asked Eddie.

'Nah, nothing,' said James, turning away.

'Kak, Helmet, ou china. We can check that there's something wrong.'

Everybody laughed except James. He stood up and said angrily, 'Why don't you all just fuck off and leave me alone!'

He stormed off and everyone looked at each other. *Here was trouble*. Manie was the boss so he followed James to his sleeping bag, where his things lay about in the late afternoon light. His unwashed dixie cans and utensils, his kitbag . . . half unpacked, his dusty sleeping bag and rubber mattress. And a letter.

'Ay, sorry, ou Jim. We didn't know there was a problem. Is something wrong at home?'

He noted Jim's dusty, dishevelled head, and saw that he was crying. The arrogant grensvegter became an attentive friend.

'What's wrong, Jim? What happened?'

'The fucken bitch. She's screwing my best friend. I never thought that she could do something like this.'

'Ag, women will do anything, Jim. But your best friend? That's another story.'

James was not consolable.

'She said she loved me. I never asked her to. *She* said she loved me. Check here, she gave me this ring. For what? For fucken what?' and he pulled the ring from his finger and threw it into the bush. Manie estimated its position for recovery later and continued trying to comfort James.

By now everyone had overheard the story, so, as much out of curiosity as compassion, they all gathered round. No more nicknames for now. Everybody thought about their own women back home and wondered.

Eventually James calmed down when Manie offered to take him to the shop first thing in the morning to make a phone call.

'She gets to work at eight-thirty in the morning and the best time to phone her is at nine-thirty, she usually makes coffee then. I've got to speak to her. This letter was written two weeks ago. Christ, anything could've happened by now. Fuck, this place is making me mad! I've got to get out of here. I've got to speak to her . . . see her. She could be anywhere now. I mean how could she do this to me? . . . and with fucken Terry! The oke was my friend!'

All went to bed considerably sobered by the experience of watching the effects of a dear John letter.

First thing next morning, Manie went to make sure that James was still there. He had been so hysterical the previous evening that they'd feared he might run off in the night. He was still there, though it was clear that he hadn't slept much. He seemed calmer.

Manie, James and Eddie climbed aboard the Unimog and drove to the shop.

Under the asbestos roof of the shop, the heat of the day was warming the dark interior. The proprietor was sorting through his book of stamps. He looked a little alarmed when he saw the three soldiers moving towards him. They had a sense of urgent purpose. Manie spoke: 'Lissen, chief, we need to use your phone. It's an emergency. Please.'

'No. I am sorry. Your commander has told it to me that you may not make calls from civilian phone. For security reasons.' He pointed to the official notice on the wall.

'Ja, but this is not an unsupervised call. I am the commander of this section. One of my men has an emergency and he must call home. It is under my supervision.'

'I am sorry but I have been told it. No soldiers to make calls on this phone.'

Manie unclipped the holster of his nine millimetre pistol and cocked the hammer. In silence he placed the hard, shiny barrel against the proprietor's pulsating temple.

'Lissen, fucker, we're using the phone . . . it's ah . . . it's an emergency! Now move before I fucken kill you!'

Manie, the proprietor, and Eddie listened as James tried to reach and reason with his ex.

'What do you mean that you were never sure? It was *you*

who gave me the ring . . . Oh yes? . . . Oh really? . . . So you think I'm not going to do anything?

'Ja . . . but why do you have to wait until my back is turned? . . . But you did . . .

'No, I'm not your friend . . . ever . . . and that bastard Terry . . . I'll pulp the cunt . . . you both betrayed me . . . Wait till I get out of here, then we'll see what's who!'

As James slammed the phone down he knew he had lost. His useless threats hung in the air. You can't force someone to love you. Manie uncocked his pistol and returned it to its holster. The proprietor was afraid, but held his sullen dignity. He hated these white intruders.

After paying for the call and purchasing some smokes and stuff, Manie turned to the proprietor as he was leaving the shop.

'If you report what happened here today I'll fucken kill you. And you won't be the first kaffir I've killed. Any trouble and we'll find you – you and your shop . . . and it'll be overs, china.' He used the old 'we'll cut your throat' gesture and laughed as he walked out into the sun.

Long Distance

The prefabricated offices were carpeted and airconditioned inside. Right in the heart of headquarters at Oshakati, they didn't need sandbagging. I followed the sergeant-major along a corridor lined with small offices. Desks and maps and books and files and papers and people in uniform. We entered the room at the end of the passage and there on a dark wooden desk was the phone.

I had made formal application to make a long distance call home. My wife had mentioned some problems she was having with accommodation and I was troubled about it.

I thought the sergeant-major would leave the room to give me some privacy for my call, but I was mistaken. He became quite formal and, like a policeman, warned me that he would be standing over me with a loaded Uzi hand-carbine and that if I was to divulge any strategic information during the course of my conversation, I would be arrested, if not shot on the spot. What could I say? Nothing. Just make the call.

After navigating the various clickings and exchanges, with telephone operators who seemed impatient and half deaf, I could hear the phone ringing. *I hope she's there.* I could picture the white plastic telephone as it rang in the hallway of her mother's house. The sergeant-major was standing in front of me with his hand-carbine slung over his shoulder.

Someone answers.

'Hullo.'

It's one of the African maid servants.

'Hullo. Please call Miss Gillian to the phone. This is her husband phoning from the army. Please tell her to hurry.'

Eventually the phone is picked up and my heart races to hear that familiar voice.

'Hi, babe, it's me.'

'Oh, Rick, it's good to hear your voice. How are you?'

'Fine, babe, fine.'

The presence of Mr Moustache and his hand-carbine becomes less oppressive as I talk with my wife. It appears that she has moved to her mother's farm and is living in the old store-room above the garage. She has privacy there and her own bathroom, so she is reasonably comfortable. I feel considerably cheered to hear that she is settled and secure. We talk about time. Another two months must pass before we can embrace again. Gill cries. I hurt. We send love and blessings. We say goodbye.

'Thank you, sergeant-major. At least I know that my wife and daughter have got somewhere to stay while I'm away.'

I could tell that he didn't think much of me – someone so unprepared for the military and its demands, and to be caught off guard in this way.

Outside in the sun we split up and I wandered over to the post office to send a telegram home.

As fate would have it, the sergeant-major and I arrived back at the Landrover at about the same time and we sat in the front, drinking Cokes, with the windows open. We were waiting for the four soldiers who had travelled in the back to complete their business in Oshakati. I thought that this was a good time to probe the sergeant-major on his personal feelings about the situation.

'Do you really think that there's any value in our presence here in Ovamboland?'

He looked at me in disbelief.

'When are you going to wake up to the fact that there's a war on?' he asked me impatiently.

'Whose war? This is not our country. We can't speak the language. Most of these people don't really want us here.'

'Are you fucken mad? Are you going to wait until you are standing with your back to South Beach before you realise that the communists plan to take over your country? This is the thin edge of the wedge, pally. If we lose the war up here, we'll be overrun. The blacks will take over . . . and that will be that.'

It was clear that he was not to be dissuaded from his point of view, which was definite, apocalyptic and self-righteously held, so I steered the conversation towards cultural things, but success there was equally limited.

'What kind of music do you like?' I ventured.

'Not that stuff you play on your guitar.'

'Don't you like Bob Dylan?'

'It's kak. He can't even sing.'

'So, whose music do you like?'

'Jim Reeves, and the orchestra of Henry Mancini.' He became very guarded about revealing anything that dealt with feelings. Although he was only a year or two older than I was, he, like so many South Africans, had remained immune to the spark of rock 'n roll. Rock just rolled right by.

Yep, the sergeant-major and I would never have much in common. The beat and battered reality of street life held no interest for him. The 'ol' black nigger from the delta' with his gift of the twelve bar blues could not get past the guards at his gate. He'd never listened to Eric Clapton playing with Howling Wolf, or heard Muddy Waters sing.

The problem, though, was that since he had no knowledge of culture outside of his own ghetto, he tended to see my cultural tastes as being semi-criminal and subversive, and I suppose they were a threat to the closed Calvinistic nationalism that gripped South Africa – that communist-hating, fag-baiting, apartheid-swallowing, self-righteous, arrogant patriotism that included only those whities that shared your tastes and fears. Brotherhoods of big biltong-eating men in short-sleeved khaki shirts. Their women, kept 'madams'. Such fear of diversity. Such fear of the shadows within. Such repression.

Hitching a lift from Jo'burg once, I was picked up by a farmer from the Free State. It was a Sunday and he was out driving to see if he could find any girls, although 'poes' was the term he used. He had been married, was now divorced, and he needed to feel a woman. We drove around Heidelberg in the late morning, sipping brandy. He kept the bottle under the seat of the car – a VW Beetle. He stopped alongside some schoolgirls walking from church to their boarding establishment.

'Môre, meisies. Hoe gaan dit hier?'

Adolescent girls from small town boarding schools had the reputation of being wild and willing to abandon themselves to the lusts of men, but the two who peered into our car window had a pretty good sense of the situation. An older man, an oom, who had been drinking, and a 'foreign' English-speaking passenger. Adventure they wanted, but this was not the one. Providence rather than good sense saved us all. Anyway, once we were under way again this farmer, whose name was André, began to tell me how he hungered for the black women on his farm. He'd heard that they were incredible in bed – wild, and hungry for it, and that once you'd had one, 'tasted chocolate', you'd never be able to settle for a white woman again. His eyes revealed his excitement at the rumours. Yet in each small town that we entered he was immediately able to masquerade as a helpful, self-effacing and trustworthy male member of the Afrikaans community.

'Môre, oom. Môre, tannie,' he would say as we bumped gently by on the lookout for 'boude'. And them thinking something like 'That's a nice, friendly young man, looks like a church-goer too. I haven't seen him around . . . wouldn't mind introducing him to my daughter . . .'

The back doors of the Landrover were opened noisily and the other members of the expedition clumped about in their boots and settled themselves for the return journey. There was no more need for small talk as the sergeant-major drove us out of there.

Miniskirts and Bicycles

Outside Oshakati there was a bottle-store, a miniature Fort Knox, with burglar guards, wire mesh over the windows and a crown of barbed-wire coiled around the roof. Also, there was a café, a supermarket, a bank, and several trading stores. As the sergeant-major drove carefully through the crowds of African people moving along the pavements and the street, I noticed some of the Ovambo women riding bicycles, wearing miniskirts and ankle boots. Here was a unique female expression. These Ovambo women were not like the Zulu or Tswana women that I had known for most of my life, and whom I had always seen through the eyes of a national prejudice, as robust and matronly.

Well, the Ovambo girls were slender and graceful, quite petite, and they cycled along in their miniskirts in a most elegant way. There was nothing lascivious or self-consciously calculated about their movements, only a pure enjoyment of their youth and health, and the fact that they were women.

Ovambo women on bicycles reminded me of the erotic potential of life and for a moment I forgot about the dreary military realities that bound us. I turned to the sergeant-major, knowing that it would freak him out, and said, 'Hey, some of those chicks look all right. Nice legs. Miniskirts.'

He looked at me in anger and disgust. He didn't even bother to respond. If before he had been unsure of my allegiances, he now saw me as being beyond the pale. I was definitely a weak link and would have to be watched. *Friends no more*. It was really quite a relief to let him see my true colours. He was a man whose views I didn't particularly respect, so I wasn't upset that he should have little respect for mine.

Once we had passed through the town and there were no more civilians to be seen, especially female civilians with short skirts and braided hair, he cleared his throat and turned to me.

'You may remember the commander's orders with regard to the local women. We have been given clear instructions to avoid all contact with Ovambo women.'

Obviously I had made him uncomfortable and he was re-establishing his authority – regaining his dogmatic perspective. *The order of the snor*.

Yes, I could remember the commander's orders given one evening to the regiment, about how we were to keep separate from the local inhabitants, especially the women. Apparently some of the previous regiments stationed in the vicinity had been over-familiar with the local women. Such behaviour was to be seen as a security risk and the sign of low morals. I remember the colonel also instructing us not to walk around without our shirts on. Perhaps he thought that some of the young soldiers, with their tanned surfers' bodies and well-developed pectorals, might lure some women over to the camp, Eros would run rampant, and a slur would be cast on the fine colonial reputation of the DLI.

Yes, I was aware of the taboos of the DLI, which were pretty much the taboos of white South Africa. I certainly didn't labour under the illusion that a relationship between one of our city-bred soldiers and a rustic Ovambo woman would lead to bliss. Certainly not while the world is the way it is. Who would bring up the children? How would the parents-in-law communicate?

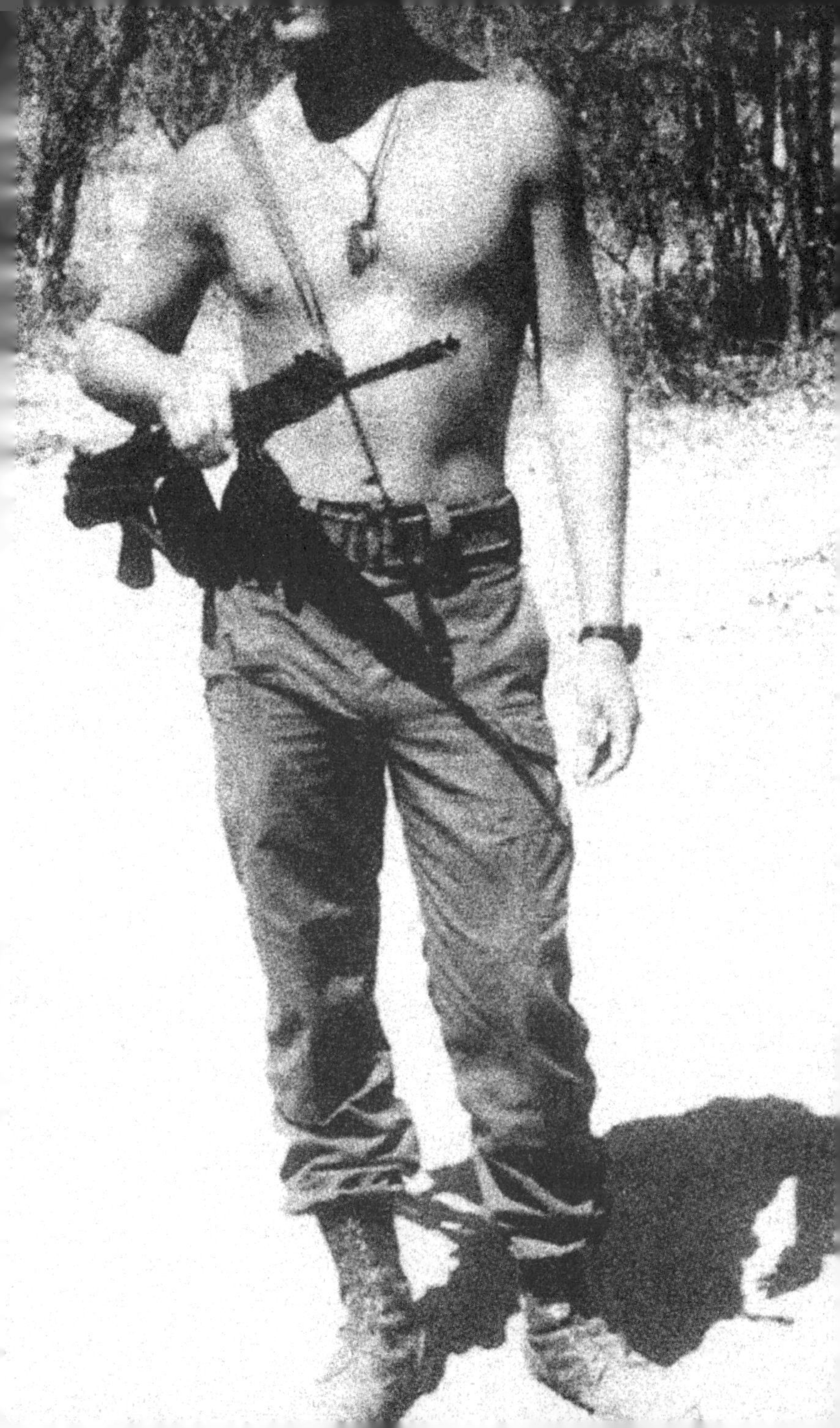

Where would the lovers live?
Ja, Eros, you must tread carefully here in Southern Africa.

The Officer's Address

We'd been on the border about a month and routine had set in. It was a Tuesday. The camp was quiet after the lunch hour when we heard that pounding, popping, beating sound of a helicopter as it curved in to make its approach. We watched it land in a wall of noise, the rotors fanning the dust and sand. Several officers emerged, held on to their caps, ducked their heads, and trotted away from the vehicle. They were in semi-formal dress, being shirt and tie, step-out trousers and shoes. They left the pilot of the chopper to tether the horses. He slowly got the rotors to stop beating the air and brought the smouldering, high-pitched engine to silence. He made his way over to the officers' mess. He was wearing khaki overalls and held the rank of lieutenant. He removed his flying helmet, ran his hand through his curly brown hair, and put on Rayban sunglasses.

A helicopter pilot is a highly admired being in the SADF. This pilot's calm walk and obviously untouchable composure confirmed this. He'd delivered the brass, and now he'd wait in the mess until they needed his skills again.

We knew that helicopter pilots were well trained, had excellent reflexes, and were cool-headed under pressure. They understood the fine tolerances of their machinery. The shafts, bearings and pistons, the nuts, bolts, blades and screws, and the axes of equilibrium which kept seven tons of steel airborne. They had rescued troops under heavy fire, in impossible situations. They could fly in sideways, the rotor blades at right angles to the bush canopy, then straighten out to land under the trees. As they rose once more, they almost sawed their way through the bush. Well, such were the rumours and they certainly made us feel a whole lot better when out walking patrol.

From the staff point of view, a chopper is the key to fast escape. Fly in. Talk to the men in the field. Witness a patrol. Get the feel. Get the information, and get out. Home for dinner. Nobody in their right mind would mess with a chopper pilot, unless you use the word to mean dine.

It wasn't long before we found out what this visit was about. Word went out that the battalion was to assemble on the road near HQ company. Attendance was compulsory. Once the men had assembled, all with their rifles, one of the officers who had arrived on the chopper stepped into the centre of the assembly and raised a megaphone to his mouth. Hundreds of white butterflies congregated undisturbed at the water-trailer.

'Good afternoon, Durban Light Infantry. I am Lieutenant-General Constand Viljoen and the purpose of my address to you all is to inform you about the situation you are in . . . To give you some idea of what has gone before . . . and why you are here.'

We found it a little unusual to be addressed with seeming civility and reason. We were suspicious at first, like a prisoner suddenly being offered a cigarette by his inquisitor. We were used to being treated like automatons . . . mindless . . . the old Crimean way . . . Ours not to reason why . . . Ours but to do and die . . .

The men relaxed before such reasoning and began to listen with interest to what this young, but high-ranking officer had to say. And what he had to say blew our minds.

'You are all aware of the fact that the Portuguese have fled Angola. Driven from the land by a communist-inspired liberation movement. That country is a complete mess of civil war. You may have seen the convoys of vehicles left lining the roads at Grootfontein.' We had, and it was Africa Addio revisited – a chaotic nightmare of bullet-riddled vehicles and homeless refugees.

'You may know about the Cuban soldiers that have been brought in on the side of MPLA. You may know that our army pushed north as far as Luanda on Operation Savannah. But . . . we were recalled by America . . . the pressures of international politics. Jonas Savimbi and his UNITA forces – our allies – are active in the south of the country – what we call Savimbiland. He is in fact the buffer between the communist forces to the north, and this part of the country that you're in – Ovamboland. However, the forces of communism have infiltrated this country too, and you are here to stem the tide. The communists' aim is to keep moving south, and to bring South Africa to its knees. Once they have achieved that, then they believe that the resources of Africa will be theirs. Their aim is nothing less than world domination.

'How can we fight a war like this – a war of insurgency? The man who mortars your camp at night, buries his weapons and uniform, and walks about in civilian clothes by day. He is African . . . probably an Ovambo himself . . . so he knows the customs, speaks the language, and is favoured by local hospitality. His intelligence network is far in advance of ours, likewise his opportunities for persuading people of his cause. SWAPO, or the South West African People's Organisation, is orchestrating this war and calling it a liberation struggle. Wittingly or unwittingly they are working for the communist cause of world domination.

'And now, how can you boys from Durban make a contribution to the defence of your own country? First you need to understand that you are here as diplomats, as ambassadors of South Africa – of civilisation. This war is not a full-scale conventional engagement. It's a war of terror and persuasion. Insurgency and counter-insurgency. It's a war of psychology. You have to win the hearts and minds of the people. This war will not be won by military action on the ground, but through influencing people towards non-communist ideas and Christian values.

'Unfortunately, the racial divide between black and white in Africa . . . and more particularly in Southern Africa . . . doesn't help our cause. The terrorists live like the people and understand the culture. Take a look at the way we live here . . .'

We all looked around at the trucks and the aerials and the tents. We were like a mechanical monster. A juggernaut. A huge growling creature that rolled over the land on thick rubber wheels. Each individual soldier was but a working part of the machine.

'And how are we doing so far, as ambassadors for South Africa? Winning the hearts and minds of the people? Well, I'll tell you.

'The previous regiment, which was stationed in this vicinity and left the area before your arrival, did quite well. They didn't mind driving their trucks over the people's mahangu fields. They didn't mind destroying the crops . . . or helping themselves to some of the poultry.

'Two geniuses from that regiment shot one of the people's cows . . . they said it was just to get some rifle practice. On Guy Fawkes night they decided to include the locals in their celebrations, so they flung a thunder flash into one of the compounds. It landed near an old man who was asleep and exploded a short distance from his head, leaving him deaf for life . . . blind in one eye . . . and badly burned. Some members of the same regiment molested one of their women.'

We were appalled at all this. How could we possibly change anything? We were the enemy. Just our presence there would be a reminder to the local people of the white man's callous disregard for a non-mechanical culture.

Our convoys of trucks stretched across the dusty landscape. We were an alien invasion. Seeing the bare-breasted women pounding corn in their mealie-stampers revealed a culture based on subsistence and tribal organisation. To me it seemed almost medieval. An African Arcadia. A paradise before the machine. Before plastic bags and television. Ovamboland seemed to live in another century, but now it was being visited by the twentieth century. Here were two worlds in parallel, side by side on the earth, yet connected through conflict and need.

As we walked back to our positions we felt devastated. There was a great deal of discussion among the men. That young officer had been most effective and articulate in his address. We felt called, even inspired, to undertake missions of help to the local people . . . to win the psychological battle. I wanted to teach English in one of the local schools. Dennis was an architect – he could help to upgrade the built environment. We were suddenly aware of how much potential there was in the regiment. Our idealism took flight. We wanted to contribute, to build community, but it was not to be. The war had come, and good intentions didn't change the situation.

On arrival at HQ company our squad of four was ordered to make a new soak-pit for a urinal. This involved digging a hole about one and a half metres deep and about one metre in diameter. This hole was filled about two thirds full with flattened cooldrink and beer cans to form a soak-pit. A plastic urinal, with an elbow like a stove pipe was then held in position while the remainder of the hole was filled in with soil. The urinal, of the required khaki/brown, military colour, stood proudly like a large trumpet or telephone, at the correct height for the standing urinator.

While we were flattening the cans by beating them with spades, Dennis began to sing the familiar refrain from the Mainstay ad, *You can stay as you are for the rest of your life . . . or you can change to Mainstay*. We could see it, the picture, with this caption below, *Singing architect flattens beer cans for urinal*. This immediately brought before our minds the contrast between the glamour and freedom of the ad – white cutter sails in the Caribbean and beautiful people drinking cane spirits – and the reality of our situation. Despite the officer's address that day, little would change. We had few options, and no choice but to stay as we were.

Seven Gentlemen

One quiet afternoon at the OP the seven could hear a vehicle approaching. It was labouring up the road from the dam. It sounded like a jeep. They quickly put on their uniforms, cocked their rifles and stood ready. Manie was wearing his shades, his fingers looped through his belt. He stood like a cowboy, his holster open. Gung-ho . . . macho.

A jeep pulled into the camp. It was driven by a bearded Portuguese soldier wearing a camouflage cap and uniform. As the dust settled, he smiled and made signs to show that his intentions were friendly. Sitting in the back of the jeep were two women, one white and one black. The driver got out of the vehicle and approached Manie. He could not speak English or Afrikaans, and none of the seven could speak Portuguese, so the conversation was conducted in a crude sign language.

What he had to say was that these two women were available for the men if they wanted them. The price was not expensive – five rand a time, and he would return a bit later to pick the girls up.

The two women climbed out of the jeep. They both looked a little jaded but they were smiling and stood to the side. Manie had no desire to touch either of them, but he had his men to consider, so he nodded in agreement. The man drove his jeep out of the camp and, by pointing at his wrist watch, indicated that he'd be back in an hour.

The women stood by quietly waiting for a response from the men.

Eddie was the first to speak.

'Hey, James, what do you say? Take one of the ladies to your hideout and insert Bert.'

'Not a fuck, china. They're both seriously ugly. Besides, I might get a disease.'

'Then fuck them between the tits.'

'Jeez, you're a crude bastard, you know, Eddie,' said James. And then with sudden realisation, 'Shit, I hope they can't understand English.'

They looked across at the women, who smiled coyly.

'I mean, Jeez, look at that one's dress, and stockings. I mean who the fuck wears stockings in the bush?'

'She does, china. Hey, man, take them off her, play a bit of doctor-doctor and then give her a protein injection.'

'Fuck off, Eddie! Why don't you do it if you're such a big deal?' Eddie just laughed.

The women, who were in their late thirties, were not beauties, but their tired emotional honesty brought the men to their senses. The truth was that the men enjoyed having a female presence in their midst . . . just watching the way they moved . . . the fit of chin to neck . . . the way they looked down while they made adjustments to their hair . . . their voices. The African lady sat down on a log and stared out at the bush, her short black hair braided beneath a doek. The other one just stood with her hands in her jacket pockets.

'Well,' said Manie, 'does no one want a fuck? All your talk about sex, and now you have a chance, you do nothing!'

'And you, Manie?' chipped in Eddie, quite pointedly.

'Nah, I want something a little more my age. Mind you, if we had a few dops I might have a go.'

By the time the pimp arrived to pick up his girls he came upon an unusual scene, a tea party, in fact, with the girls being served tea and biscuits. He was angry to discover that he had made no money, and started to ask the girls some rather aggressive questions.

Manie soon put a stop to this with his usual directness.

'Hey, you fucken Portugoose pimp, don't talk to these ladies like that. This is our camp and we'll fucken kill you if you think you can come in here and shout the odds!'

The man quieted down, and waited patiently while the company finished their tea.

The Boet's Letter

The letter that Neil received from his brother was a little disturbing. It had got through without being opened by the censors. Peter, who was older than he was, worked as a designer in the advertising department of the *Rand Daily Mail*.

> *PO Box 445*
> *Honeydew*
> *1 July 1976*

Dear Neil,

Howzit. I know that your letters are censored. It's typical of this fucked-up country. What can you expect?

Neil, I won't go into too much detail, but I have to tell you that I am leaving South Africa. You've probably heard about what happened in Soweto on June the 16th. If you haven't, then it means that the pricks are keeping you guys in the dark. For days our black reporters came in to the office in a complete state. 'Soweto's burning!' they'd say. 'The school kids are going berserk. Cops are shooting at them and arresting all and sundry.' One of my black mates managed to get a look into one of the police mortuaries and he reckoned that the place was piled high with kids' bodies! What's happening, Neil? And you're on the border.

I've been in the army, Neil, and the army and I don't get on. I'm not staying to get fucked around by them.

Anyway, to cut a long story short, I can't handle the contrast anymore between where we live in Honeydew – you know, the lawn, the rose bushes and all that – and what's going down across town in Soweto. Every time I look at my kid in bed at night I freak. And Julie just wants out. She reckons she can't stand the barbarism anymore, so we're leaving at the end of the month. I'm going to try to get a British passport through Julie. I'll write to you when I get settled.

Mom is upset, but what can I do? It's a screwed up society, Neil. Look after yourself, boet, and remember what I said to you when I came back from Europe. There's kak in this land and soon we're all going to have to wake up and choose sides. Being in the SADF is the wrong side as far as I'm concerned.

Till the next time,
*   Your boet,*
*   Pete.*

ps. Julie and Paula send their love and say they're going to miss you.
pps. This is for you, Mr Censor. Go fuck a veld-kornet.

Neil sat for a long time after reading the letter. His older brother had always been a rebel. He was always being flapped at school. He was a joller, a breker, and he never compromised. He was more willing to face up to facts and respond to his real feelings than most of the okes he knew. For the first time in his life he felt the kind of pain that would increase as the struggle in South Africa moved on into a headlong impetus of violence, polarisation and confusion.

He didn't want to discuss the contents of the letter with anyone because he knew that they'd merely say that his brother was a commie, or some kind of a moffie. The usual, 'Good riddance. If the oke doesn't like this country then he knows what he can do,' attitude.

But in his heart he loved and admired Pete. Ja, it was a sobering letter. Maybe the boet was right and he too should get out. He'd quite like to go to Israel and work on a kibbutz. Apparently the girls there were something else . . . and there was a wide range to choose from . . . Greek, Danish, French . . . even English.

The Major's Chicken

Being an English regiment, some of the class prejudices of England continued to haunt the DLI and were often a cause of hostility which could lead to pitiful acts of bitterness.

On return to HQ from a vehicle patrol one afternoon, major Mills called out for private Smith, the cook. For some or other reason the major felt hostile towards Smith. Was it because private Smith was a rebel with tattoos on his hands? *Love* and *Hate* on his fingers, and a picture of the Saint (stick man with halo) between his thumb and forefinger? Or was it perhaps because Smith did not like the major? He'd been heard to say on more than one occasion that major Mills was a cunt. Or was it because he came from the Bluff and played soccer, while major Mills was from Musgrave and favoured rugby? Whatever it was, major Mills had been heard to comment that Smith was a poor specimen of manhood and that it was because of rubbish like him that South Africa's military potential was going to the dogs.

When private Smith arrived, still fastening his web belt, he stood to attention and saluted. Mills looked at Smith, returned the salute, and made some derogatory comment about his appearance. Then from behind his back, he produced a live chicken.

'Here you are, Smith. I want it plucked, cleaned and cooked for my dinner this evening. I am having some guests tonight. Deliver the meal to my tent at seven sharp with some well-cooked vegetables.'

Smith accepted the chicken almost in disbelief. Its legs were tied together and it squawked and flapped its wings madly as he took it.

'Well, Smith, what are you waiting for?'

'Suh!' he shouted, and turned away towards his tent alongside the kitchen. 'Arsehole,' he thought, as he carried off the bird.

After cutting its throat, plucking and disembowelling it, Smith had an idea. Before taking the chicken to the oven, he jerked himself off, and with muscles stiffening, directed his spurting semen into the bird's empty ribcage. Then he placed the chicken in a bowl, and kneeling carefully in the sand behind the tent, he urinated on it thoroughly. Methodically. *Marinated in pee sauce*.

He cooked the chicken in these sauces and presented it to major Mills at seven pm with boiled potatoes, boiled onions and spinach.

The major and his guests thoroughly enjoyed their meal of

crisp free-range chicken and wine. They even sent compliments to the smiling chef.

International Incident

The seven had been manning the OP for just over seven weeks. They were tanned, seldom wore clothes, and were accustomed to the leisure of their routine. At nine o'clock one night, they were chatting quietly around the fire when a bullet whizzed overhead. Manie shouted, 'Hit the deck!'

They all flattened out near the fire, cocked their rifles and listened. Their hearts were beating fast. Fear swelled within them, choking the breath. Another bullet whipped through the air and came to rest among the trees nearby. They didn't really hear the shots, so Manie assumed that whoever was firing at them was firing from a distance. Probably from the dam below.

'Neil and Greg, get a mortar ready, we're going to return fire now!'

They set up one of the mortars. Another bullet ricocheted overhead. It had obviously hit the ground earlier because it spun whizzing through the air, its metal jacket now a tattered garment causing crazy acrobatics.

The mortar had a maximum range of just under five kilometres, so Manie's plan was to drop enough mortars to cover the full distance of the slope between the OP and the Cuban position on the Angolan side of the dam. To root out or terrify whoever was firing at them.

'OK, Neil, set the range at half a kilometre and fire.'

Greg's long, thin fingers dropped the mortar down the barrel. A muffled explosion followed. Powp. The mortar hurtled into the darkness. A fat metal bomb, avocado green. The booming explosion with its burst of metal fragments echoed in the darkness. Because the terrain sloped towards the dam, they couldn't see the light caused by the explosion.

They waited in silence for a response.

'OK. Set the range for one kilometre, and fire when ready. We'll make 'em shit.'

Powp.

Another mortar sped off into the night. The explosion took a little longer to reach their ears, and the sound carried more echo this time.

After about four minutes, Manie ordered one more mortar to be fired, this time at a range of four and a half kilometres, and aimed in the general direction of the Cuban position on the Ruacana dam.

Powp.

The mortar took a lot longer to get there, but the explosion was very loud and tinny. It sounded like they'd hit a small ammunition dump or a shed with a corrugated iron roof. Maybe even a stash of corrugated iron sheets in a storage depot. The explosion roared and echoed, but Manie figured that the impact of the explosion had travelled across the water and was echoing from the hills around the dam.

'Jesus. Imagine if we've hit the dam wall and the whole fucken thing just collapses and the water floods free!'

Spek's imagination ran wild as he remembered the movie *The Dam Busters*, and some of the great American disaster movies he'd seen. Into his mind welled up the most horrific scenes and headlines.

SOUTH AFRICAN TROOPS CAUSE NATIONAL DISASTER

THOUSANDS DROWN IN THE DESERT

SEVEN SA TROOPS TRIGGER MAJOR WAR IN AFRICA

SEVEN SOLDIERS APPEAR ON CHARGE OF MASS MURDER

They waited in silence. After twenty minutes in which there were no further sounds or bullets passing overhead, Greg spoke

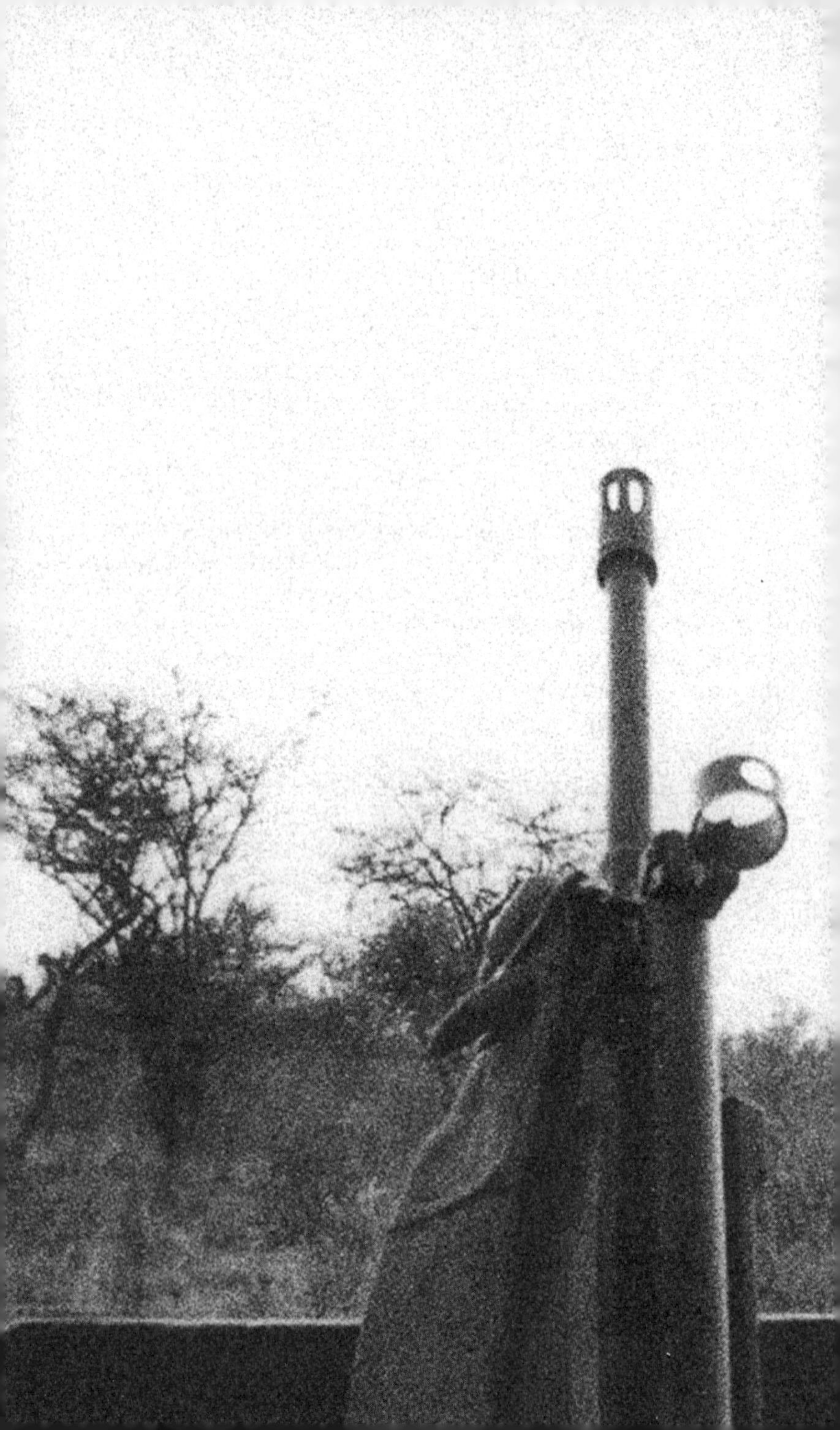

up. There was a tremor in his voice.

'What if we've hit a Cuban camp and they're finding our range with artillery or those fucken red eye rockets as we speak now?'

Fear swelled within them. Breathing was difficult. Their hearts were racing.

Manie knew that such a situation might be possible, so he rounded up the men and they moved about six kilometres to the west.

'Don't you think we should radio HQ and tell them what's happened?' asked Neil.

'And if we've started a war?' asked Deon.

'Or killed thousands?' enquired Spek.

'Ah, balls, man,' said Manie. 'You okes are fucken dreamers. When people fire at me, I return fire. End of fucken story. Anyway, one mortar can't destroy a dam! No. I reckon we just lie low for now, and see what the morrow brings.'

'Ja, but they'll ask why we didn't report the contact,' said Neil.

'True,' said Manie. 'We'd better radio a report right now. OK, this's the story – everybody listen up. We responded to being fired upon with a few mortars and we've moved, just in case they mortar our camp or turn the artillery onto us. Give them our position and tell them we'll return to the OP in the morning.'

Silence settled over the night as Neil sent in his report to the corporal on duty in an Ops tent sixty kilometres to the south. No more bullets flew above them and no more explosions tore the night. Few of them slept.

Before dawn they moved back to their original position. At six am the platoon commander arrived with a convoy of armoured vehicles. The first question of the morning was, 'What the hell happened here last night? Do you realise that you've caused an international incident? Pik Botha has had to fly to Angola to discuss what occurred here last night. You men better have some kind of an explanation!'

Apparently the Cubans had reported an unprovoked mortar attack on their base. Nobody had been hurt, but they raised the alarm, fearing that it might be the beginning of a major offensive.

Manie looked at all the officers with his usual disdain and

explained.

'We were fired upon and we responded.'

By that evening the seven were relieved of their positions and found themselves back with C company.

The Chief's Gift

At Oshikango, the local chief was a wealthy man. His compound was large and shady. He owned extensive fields of corn and many head of cattle. He decided to give a gift to our regiment for being there. No one really knew why he did this, but he must have had his reasons.

Anyway, a beast was given to each company of the regiment so that each man might have the pleasure of eating fresh meat. The beast earmarked for HQ company was a pale brown cow with long horns. It was tethered to a tree, while the sergeant-major organised its execution and butchering.

I watched the sergeant-major place the barrel of his hand-carbine on the skull of the beast, between the eyes. He pulled the trigger and the beast dropped to its knees, fell sideways and lay dead.

The butcher, who was an actual butcher in Durban, set to work gutting the animal and with the help of assistants hung the carcass from a tree where it was easier to work.

The cooks didn't let us down and, working over open fires, prepared a company braai. The smell of roasting meat was wonderful and we knew we would eat well that evening. Waiting in the queue with my mess tin at the ready, I noticed what appeared to be a slight altercation between staff-sergeant Giles and one of the cooks. As he came away from the serving table I asked him what was wrong. We shared a tent, so we were on first name terms.

'What's wrong, Mike?' I asked.

'The meat hasn't been graded or inspected. I'm not going to

risk it.'

I was amazed that he could imagine that there would be someone there to provide the rubber stamp of approval – that blue branding that government inspectors leave on the white fatty parts of the meat. Sometimes it's difficult to change ideas and assurances. Some call it civilisation.

Staff-sergeant Giles, his worried eyes peering at the flames through thick lenses, went without food on the night of the feast.

Keith's Story

After the feast Butch and I returned to our tent with some beers. Butch lit the candle near the centre pole and in the dim light we saw once again our dusty webbing and personal belongings. Then Butch lit a cigarette, and told me that he had been corresponding with Keith, and also with Keith's mother. I could see that he wanted to talk.

At last.

I was pleased, and very interested, because Butch had talked so often of Keith since the days at Oshivelo, that he had become a presence in my mind . . . a person I almost believed I knew.

I am a good listener, so I settled back and let Butch talk. We felt relaxed after the good meal. As I listened, Keith's experience began to take shape in my mind. I can't recall Butch's exact words, but the story remains powerfully vivid, and replays itself in my mind, even today . . .

Keith opened his eyes to see a ceiling . . . pale cream Rhino board nailed to pine rafters. A soft light was coming in through the window behind his bed. It was evening.

Where is this?

Then he heard a Bedford drive past the window and he remembered.

It was on the rifle range. His heart began to beat faster as he relived that moment of . . . what? . . . of breakdown? The rifle range . . . and the truck falling . . . *no, no, it was me falling . . . not the truck. But why fall?* Then he remembered the targets, and the wrenching force of confused fear.

It had started as he arrived at the range. There was something about the officers and the atmosphere, an electric quality of damnation. He could sense a huge, collective paranoia . . . the whites' fear of the black masses . . . a fear usually hidden behind a mask of arrogance and scornful derision. But no one had said anything at all. He couldn't remember any racist jokes or anything. What he sensed in his spirit started to affect his breathing. He didn't want to be there . . . he wanted to fight against this fear . . . this violation. But who or what could he fight? How? Maybe just run . . . get the hell out . . . but his mind and training told him to override his feelings.

He toughed it out and concentrated on his rifle. It was a well-crafted weapon of steel. He stared at the barrel and the flash-hider, the sights, the trigger, and the safety catch . . . *Safe, Single fire, Automatic* . . . and the wooden butt. The group ahead of them was firing away . . . getting on with it . . . each shot a clouting sound with no echo. Then he looked at his magazine, full of shiny, sharp-nosed bullets. He imagined the copper snout penetrating his chest . . . or anyone's chest . . . the breast of a beautiful girl? This thought tremored through his being. It hurt so much he nearly fainted.

He took out a bullet and pushed its hard, sharp nose into his pectoral muscle on the left hand side. It hurt, and left a deep indentation with a slight tear where it had broken the skin.

Why am I here . . . now . . . with this thing in my hands?

He toughed it out once more.

His father, who no longer lived at home, had called around before he left for the border. He was proud to see his eldest son in uniform, enthusiastic even. He made jokes about sergeant-majors and pranks; and keeping your head, and shining your boots, and being always alert. Even then Keith had felt a tremor inside him, a trickle of sand in a tunnel somewhere. His dad was going on about discipline and obeying orders, something that Keith had been doing since he could remember. *Keith, my boy, learn your times tables . . . play sport . . . make the first team . . . keep your uniform clean . . . look after your brothers . . . attend church . . . look after your mother . . .*

And when his dad had left home to live with a younger woman, his mom, feeling betrayed and devastated, joined a pentecostal church. It provided her with support and community. Keith dutifully accepted his new role as protector of the family even though, at sixteen, he was hardly more than a boy.

In the church he was promoted swiftly to youth leader. He played guitar, was in the church band, and ran two youth groups, a social one on Friday night, and a Bible study on Sunday. The pastors were his role models. They were confident and seemed to know what God wanted. His mom always praised these 'men of God', so he tried with all his heart to be like them, even though he could sense hypocrisy in the air.

When the church gave him a send-off for the border he felt another tremor . . . more sand fell in a tunnel somewhere. There was a division in the congregation. Some were all for the army. They believed that he was off to fight the demonic forces of communism and to protect South Africa from the evils of atheism and revolution. They didn't seem to have any qualms or doubts about South Africa's own human rights credentials – how the laws in South Africa might stand opposed to the things that Jesus taught.

The other group seemed to be aware of the questions that were bothering him, so their farewell was tinged with compassion and understanding. They didn't pray for victory over evil powers descending on South Africa but rather for God's will to be done in South Africa, and for God to strengthen him, body and soul, for the trial which lay before him. With this group he could identify.

Then they read to him a parting scripture from Psalms.

I sought the Lord, and he answered me;
he delivered me from all my fears.
Those who look to him are radiant;
their faces are never covered with shame.

This poor man called, and the Lord heard him;
he saved him out of all his troubles.
The angel of the Lord encamps around those
that fear him, and he delivers them.

A nurse entered his darkening room. She switched on the lamp near his bed.

'You look a lot better,' she said, as she shook a thermometer. She took his pulse. Her fingers were firm but gentle. He loved the feminine touch, like those early times in childhood when he was sick and his mom came to him, clearing his delirium with her loving radiance.

The nurse read his temperature and investigated a wound on his eyebrow. His eyes followed her as she moved about. She was quite old . . . about forty . . . Afrikaans. Obviously pro the army. She was into duty, not celebration.

She gave him some pills to swallow.

Butch looked across at me in the candlelight. 'Do you want to kip?'

'No, carry on, china. I want to hear more.'

Ward 28

Keith woke in the dark, in a different room, a ward with many beds. In the bed next to his he could hear a dog whimpering and whining. The creature was lost in pain. He stared at the bed in the gloom. It wasn't a dog. It was a man. He'd never heard a human being crying in this way . . . like an animal. It was as if the man had been wrapped around with the green and flexible branches of a thorn tree, so that every time he moved, the thorns bit deeper and tore open his flesh.

A medic came by and spoke gently to the sufferer. Drugs were given and soon all was quiet.

When next he awoke, he was in the same bed. The same ward. But he could smell the ash of veld fire, and the sweat of an African labourer. On the bed next to his, on the left, he could make out a large, dark figure . . . sitting up, with his feet on the floor. He peered at this figure in the gloom. It was an African cane cutter, preparing for a day's work, a day that started long before sunrise. Such men had been his first role models . . . well-defined muscles, skin a rich chocolate brown. Their Boxer tobacco . . .

Then he remembered the flames of the cane fires, huge and hungry, burning the leaves and grasses around the feet of the cane. The heat and flame drove out the rats and snakes, and made the shoots accessible to the cutters.

This man had a soiled red bandana around his head and two tight-fitting bracelets on his upper arms – below the deltoid, and above the bicep. He had on an old shirt with torn-off sleeves, and around his neck he wore a cheap child's necklace . . . silver plastic . . . made in Hong Kong. He was pulling on a pair of faded khaki trousers, smoke-blackened below the knees. His feet were bare, the heels cracked and thick.

When Keith next awoke, it was morning. Cheering sunlight streamed into the room as nurses wheeled in the trolleys of medicine. He was in a ward of some thirty men. There were bars on all the windows and the door. This, as he soon found out, was ward 28 – the notorious psychiatric ward of One Military Hospital.

The men were friendly to him, that is, those who could see past the pain in their eyes. In the bed opposite him was a cheerful person who introduced himself as Gerrie Papenfus, nicknamed 'Papie'. He was very gregarious and spent most of his days visiting patients in other wards: medics; nurses; the sweepers in their khaya; and even the mortuary. Papie was easy-going most of the time, but on occasion some dark shadow would eclipse his eyes and he would become restless and uneasy.

This morning, however, he was in top form, loudly greeting all the medics, nurses and fellow patients. The man in the bed next to him lit a cigarette, and lay back in a cloud of smoke, his arms behind his head. He looked across at Papie with amusement and affection. There was a scorpion tattooed on his forearm. His eyes met Keith's and he winked conspiratorially. Then, turning to Papie, he said, 'So, Mr Papie is happy today. But of course . . . yesterday he heard that his discharge papers are on their way.'

Neither Keith, nor any of his friends (especially Butch), could have imagined that anyone they knew would end up in a place like this. The psychiatric ward. The bottom of the bin. In the careless ease of their youthful chat they would have dismissed this place as a garbage dump for derelicts.

Of the patients in this ward there was a large group classified as 'drug addicts'. These were soldiers whose lives were bound by various forms of drug abuse or addiction. Some had arrived in the army fully addicted to drugs, while some had intended to use the army as a means of going cold turkey, but were unable to part with their feathers. Others found the army to be a most jarring and hostile place, and so started using drugs, usually dagga, to insulate themselves and to reduce their pain. Some of them were so desperate that they would take anything, even if it was likely to lead to further discomfort and trouble . . . like drinking whole bottles of cough mixture, or taking sleeping-pills during the day, or LSD before going on parade. Not one of their number appeared to suffer remorse.

The addict group were very comfortable in the hospital while under observation. They were in close proximity to a dispensary full of drugs and medicine. This provoked some enjoyable fantasies and discussions about how to get their hands on some of the more exotic pills, powders or liquids. Dagga, the daily staple, was readily available. It was brought in by friends and visitors, or by the medics, many of whom smoked themselves. Also, there was Simon. He was one of the African sweepers and the main merchant for the patients. He was young, about twenty-three, with an open, friendly face. Hip to partying and the reggae vibe, and keen to supplement his wage as a sweeper.

The patients were not bed-ridden, so they could go outside and smoke on the veranda, in the gardens, or in their own hiding places. This was the land of the permanent smoke-break. The sword of Damocles which hung over their heads was that all confirmed drug addicts would ultimately be sent to Greesveld . . . a harsh name for a harsh place . . . high, barbed-wire fences . . . highveld cold. Isolated, controlled detox. *Coldturkeyfontein*.

The drug addicts in ward 28 were aloof. They didn't wish to associate with the loonies – those who were disturbed or appeared to be out of touch with reality. They considered themselves to be pretty sane, merely chemists to their psychic needs . . . *'medicants'*? . . . a part of the hippie movement . . . the surfing fraternity. Even the nurses used to refer to them as hippies and they certainly made no effort to dissociate themselves from the term.

Of those who were not addicts, three in the ward had attempted suicide. A chap called Buddy and his mate Nicholas had tried to kill themselves by drinking petrol. Piet had tried to hang himself from a washing line in Bloemfontein.

There were those who took fits with a random regularity, and then there were the straightforward loonies. Those who twitched, and talked to themselves, signalled with their fingers, and dodged the knives of demons trying to stab their faces.

The day wore on. Tea and meals were brought in regularly. There were visits from nurses and medics and the doctor, who informed Keith that he had had a fit on the rifle range and that he was under observation for possible epilepsy.

Epilepsy? He went back again to that fateful morning on the range . . .

Eventually the command came down that his section was to move onto the firing line. They loaded up their magazines, cocked their weapons, and assumed the position: stomach on the ground, and the rifle supported on forearm and elbow. Safeties off. Then the command came down. 'Single fire. Twelve rounds. In your own time. Carry on.'

Keith looked at the target. It was a hundred metres away. A geometric version of an enemy soldier . . . a black shape. *Why black?* Sand fell more heavily in a tunnel . . . a chamber somewhere collapsed. Was this a racist army pursuing a race war? Killing people? *Thou shalt not kill.* I shouldn't be here! It's too late . . . I can't go back now.

He toughed it out, trying to suppress the saboteur within. He wanted to be anywhere but where he was.

He took aim at the target. His sights were squarely on the black helmeted shape. Suddenly the shape on the target became the face of his father . . . then his mother . . . then his brothers. He couldn't pull the trigger.

A sudden volley of shots along the line jarred him and he saw each one of his family's heads exploding with each shot. He jumped up, throwing his rifle to the ground and turned, staggering to escape.

He heard an officer shouting at him but he couldn't understand what the man was saying. The officer was running beside him, hitting his steel helmet in violent agitation. He was approaching a truck. He couldn't tell if it was moving or stationary. Suddenly the truck started to fall to the left. That truck is toppling! An accident? His face hit the ground and there was a snapping sound in the back of his head . . . then . . . a welcome silence.

Epilepsy? I think not. I just can't carry two contradictory views in my head. Obedient gung-ho killer for a collective white paranoia . . . or a servant of Jesus Christ. In me they can't be reconciled. They repel each other like the poles of magnets. *As much as you do these things unto the least of these my brethren you do it unto me. I think I learned my lessons too well. Help me, Lord.*

Most of the men were outside in the gardens or on the veranda. In their pyjamas and dressing gowns, they were absorbing the winter sun. Some were visiting other patients. Keith lay in bed agonising over the disgrace he had brought to his family.

A medic, who was obviously gay, approached him. He had a freshly stitched wound across his cheek where he had been cut trying to control a thrashing patient . . . a victim helping victims.

'Can I get you anything?' he asked Keith in an effeminate voice. Keith could see that he was kind and that he loved men, but . . .

Keith asked if he could have something to help him relax. Something to relieve the pressure in his mind. The maddening loop of anger, blame and guilt. Anger, blame and guilt. *Why didn't anybody tell me the truth? I'm a coward. I've shamed my friends and family.* He longed to be in another place, a place where his body wasn't. To be free of his relentless, accusing self. Free of this agonising consciousness pulsing through every nerve in his body. He saw a recurring picture of his head exploding . . . his mouth sucking death from the barrel of a revolver.

The medic gave him some pills, and he lay for the rest of the day, numb, slightly nauseous, but tranquil. Occasionally he nodded off into a sleep filled with new dreams . . .

Suddenly Butch and I heard a dog howling in pain and someone cursing and shouting. We grabbed our rifles and went to investigate. At the kitchen tent I saw the silhouette of David as he stood talking to the cook by the light of a gas lamp. The cook was holding a catapult, and his eyes were bright with excitement.

'These fucken local dogs have been trying to get to the supplies since we've been here, but tonight they've been excited by the smell of the fresh meat, so they scheme they can get pushy. I got the one bastard on the rib cage with a bullet head.'

He showed us a handful of bullet heads which he used as ammunition for his catapult.

'Usually I miss the bastards in the dark,' he said, 'but tonight I got lucky.'

Opposite Sex

'How'd you like to fuck this thing?'

I looked up to see Eugene approaching with a page torn from a magazine. He handed it to me. It contained the picture of a most beautiful, curvaceous woman, scantily clad. My eyes took in the heart-arresting curves and valleys of flesh.

I muttered something like, 'For sure,' and gave the picture back to him. I didn't enjoy being tortured this way. It was like showing a picture of food to a starving man.

Eugene took the picture from me and continued to pore over it.

'God I love women!' he said. 'It's the way they're shaped . . . so fucken beautiful . . .'

Then quite suddenly he became pensive.

'The problem is, though, that locked up in every one of them there's a personality and, man, can they cause shit.'

Later that day I noticed some graffiti written in koki pen on an ammunition box. I called Eugene over to have a look. I thought it might serve to supplement his earlier meditations.

The graffiti started off with the old cliché . . . *Poes Is Koning*, but to this was added the rider . . . *maar piel is sy baas*.

We attempted an English translation, and came up with *Pussy is king . . . but cock's her boss*, but it didn't come near to conveying the alliterative crudity or the lascivious, grinning tone of the original.

A Classic

After the 'international incident' Manie and the manne had been back in camp with the rest of C company for a few days when Eddie White and Neil Carter were ordered to drive a permanent force member of a Recce unit from Ruacana to the equestrian unit near Oshikango. They were to pick him up at 08h00 in a Landrover.

They arrived fully fuelled and ready to go at five-to-eight. The officer, a tall, beefy captain with dark curly hair and a deep, blue five o'clock shadow, ignored their presence until exactly eight o'clock. Then he ordered Eddie to get into the back and clambered aboard. His thighs and arms were huge and his hands were big and hairy, tanned and rough. He had a scar across the bridge of his nose. He wore sunglasses.

'Ry, jou fokken Engelsman!'

Neil released the clutch and they started the journey along the dust road. He tried to smile at his passenger and make some conversation but the response ended any further attempts at civility.

'Hou jou bek, Engelsman. Ek wil niks van jou hoor nie.'

Neil shut up, as ordered, and allowed his angry imagination to begin its wanderings. How he hated this fat Dutchman . . . the way his lips twisted around his guttural language. He was the kind that made you really understand why the blacks hated boere. A huge bull of a man with thighs like hams, who would and could fuck you up just as soon as look at you.

'Ry, jou donner! Jy's te stadig. Ek het nie die hele fokken weektyd nie.'

Neil put his boot on the accelerator and speeded up.

Fifteen kilometres along the road he applied the brake and slowed down when he saw some donkeys making their way across the road.

The officer shouted, 'Ry, jou fokken moer! Ry die goed dood!' and simultaneously opened fire with his hand-carbine. *Ride them over?* Neil speeded up, but he had no intention of injuring any of the animals. Both Neil and Eddie watched the officer firing over the backs of the donkeys and sending a few bullets along the ground. He didn't appear to have wounded any of the beasts who galloped away in their dust. Neil hoped that they wouldn't see any black people along the road because this maniac would be sure to cause some kind of trouble.

And that's how the journey went.

'Te stadig!' and Neil would speed up.

'Te vinnig!' and Neil would have to slow down.

The officer permitted no stops or conversation on the five hour journey. When they finally dropped him off at his destination, he climbed out of the Landrover, picked up his baggage, turned to Neil, said, 'Fok off!' and walked away.

Neil turned to look at Eddie who was covered in pale dust and nursing a full bladder. They both smiled.

A PF cunt. A classic.

Jewellery

Under a tree I find two pods which contain seeds made of a carvable, milky-coloured substance. Someone tells me that it is vegetable ivory. It is pure pleasure to carve into it with my pen knife. A blessed therapy . . . to create something small and sacred . . . something beautiful. Each ivory seed is tear-shaped so I carve away the outer skin and allow the essential shape to emerge. The forms need to be lighter, so I make a hole through the centre of each of them and work at a good formal blend of space and volume. The shapes appeal to me and ask to be pendants, but I need some copper wire and a few tools, so I pay a visit to the tiffies. The technical service depot is about one kilometre east of our position.

I wander quite a long way through unfamiliar territory until I come upon their vehicles. I approach the first person I see, a corporal, and explain to him about my jewellery-making intentions what I need and why. He listens with interest, and says, 'OK, come.'

He takes me to a trailer which is a large mobile tool kit, and begins looking into different drawers and containers. He gives me about a metre of thin copper wire, a broken hacksaw blade and some emery paper. I am jubilant. He cannot give me pliers but offers to lend me an old pair, provided I return them within the week. He asks who I am, and in which company, just in case he has to get hold of them sooner . . . like if there is an inspection or something.

I walk back feeling happy and inspired. I see movement off ahead of me, the flit and drift of butterflies, and there, moving along the sand in curving, glassy movements, is a long, pale brown snake, the colour of the sand and the dust. I stop to watch him on his journey. Of course it may be a female, but it's difficult to tell with snakes. It is about three metres long, a big, beautiful snake, and it disappears into some bushes leaving a trail in the sand. I take this to be a good omen.

Back at base I use my newly acquired tools to further work my jewellery – my small and sacred sculptures. Of the two, I choose the blemish-free one, and carefully wrap copper wire around its lower half. The wires radiate out of the centre hole like the rays of the sun. Then I attach a loop of wire to the top of the pendant so that it can be hung around the neck from a chain or thong. The silver ball-joint chain that we use for our dog-tags doesn't have the right feel for my new creation, so I use a bootlace to hang it around my neck. I keep this talisman from the eyes of those officers who might see it as suspicious – a reversion to primitivism, touching dark shamanic forces, or just being a goddamned hippie.

I wear my comforting pendant for the duration of the camp, and eventually give it into the hands of my wife when I get home and can once more hang my clothes on the back of a wooden door.

Eddie at the Inquiry

'I'd like to kick the cunt's head in,' said Eddie to Neil once they were rid of the ugly presence of the classic.

'The oke's a fucken non-human prick. A fucken burst arsehole,' was Neil's response.

They planned to rest overnight and journey back first thing in the morning, but the unforeseen happened, and Eddie was forced to remain at the camp for three days to participate in a court of inquiry.

What happened was this: Eddie, on return from the toilet, was quaffing a Coke when a shot rang out. A fat sergeant who was sitting nearby holding his rifle, cried out as a bullet hit the barrel of his rifle. It penetrated the thick, tempered steel and some of the metal fragments grazed his well-padded ribs. He was OK . . . it wasn't his time.

It all happened in a split second, but sorting it out took a lot longer. The military police subpoenaed the individuals concerned, including Eddie – as witness. The shot had come from a nearby tent. A Bren gunner, returning from patrol, and exhausted, had dropped his weapon onto its bipod, and a single bullet left in the chamber had gone off.

Neil had to drive back alone.

Eddie wasn't too happy to stay for the court of inquiry, but he had no choice. He had to wait around for three days until he was finally called up before the court to give his evidence as a witness.

'Private White, by the left, quick march!'

A sergeant-major marched Eddie into the tent and called for him to halt. He was ordered to stand at ease in front of a table at which sat four officers. He told his story. It was recorded, and he was marched out of there. He never heard what happened to the Bren gunner whose gun went off, but he listened with interest to some of the cases that were being tried during the three days that he was there.

Two riflemen from an Afrikaans regiment were being tried for attempted murder. They had shot their sergeant 'by mistake'. Their plea was that it was an accident, but it appeared that they had actually intended to shoot their sergeant-major.

The two of them were farm boys. The one had a mangled hand, the result of a childhood encounter with a mealie grinder, and the other had no teeth. Both of them seemed simple fellows, but they were sly, lawless and arrogant. Witnesses said that they were homosexuals because they slept side by side . . . in the same sleeping bag, some witnesses claimed. Apparently they were inseparable and did everything together, including pushing into the food queue.

They alleged that their sergeant-major had been insulting and intimidating them. The fact that the inquiry was at this early stage being conducted in English did not make things any easier for them.

'No, mister . . . ag jammer, ag sorry . . . major . . . the sergeant-major used to shout on us every morning. He hit on our tent wif a knobkerrie and nearly kill Jannie. The kerrie have just miss his head. One morning he pull open the door of the tent and shouts on us, "Get up, you fucken moffies, julle gatbandiete." '

He looked around in appeal as if to demonstrate his shock and indignation at this insult. The officers looked on without emotion. With a meaningful look at Jannie, who was standing dumbly beside him, he continued.

'Nou, my pa . . . my father, Bul Groenewald, he told to me that nobody must swear me like a kaffir . . . and now this sergeant-major is insulting me, and my friend. Ek is nie 'n moffie nie . . . I is not a moffie . . . ag, jammer, ag sorry, mister . . . ag, major . . . a homosexueel. Ek is nie 'n homosexueel nie. Jan is my buddy, my army buddy.

'So, after he insult us, we fink to teach him a lesson. Jannie and I dig a diep . . . ah . . . hole, there by the tent door, in the front, and we put small trees on it. And then we put sand over, soos 'n valstrik, soos . . . ah . . . how you say in Engels? . . . soos a trap, ja, a trap. Ons wou hom net waarsku . . . a warning, jy weet. We wanted to warn him . . . ah . . . to make him have a fright.

'In the morning before the sun is up, we stand-to. Our weapons is loaded. Then we hear a noise by the tent door. Dit is half donker, en ek skrik . . . I get a fright. I didn't fink . . . and I pull the trigger. Ek het vergeet . . . ag, I forget about the trap. My kop was deurmekaar . . . ah . . . I isn't awake properly. Ek hoor iemand gil. Ek ruk oop die deur . . . en daar . . . sien ek . . . ah . . . I see I have shot sersant Moolman frough his foot. Ek het gehuil. I was crying. So 'n ongeluk!

'Ek sweer jou, majoor, dit was 'n ongeluk. It was a accident!'

Bul Groenewald's son, who had done all the talking and pulled the trigger, was sent down to Pretoria to stand before a civilian court on trial for attempted murder. His buddy was sent to DB to be bullied and broken.

There were several cases of AWOL, usually older soldiers who had ducked out to take care of family matters. Eddie overheard one angry sergeant threatening to do the commander if he extended his camp or sent him to a civvy jail.

'All I did was arrive one week late because my wife was having a baby, and now I hear the cunt wants to extend my time up here by a fucken month. He'll need a month to recover when my mates and I have finished with him.' Eddie tended to believe this particular sergeant, whose gang name in Greyville was the 'Midnight Mover'.

A charge of assault was laid against a certain private Michael Kennedy. The crime had taken place in a food queue one evening. A sergeant, who was nothing more than a bully, had been picking on the scrawny private Kennedy for some time. He wanted to make him grovel, so he sidled up to Kennedy in the food queue and started commenting loudly on his appearance. 'Why do you wear such thick gogs, ou ballas? You must eat so that you can put some muscles on your bones and become a man. You've spent too much of your time pulling wire and reading, boetie.'

Kennedy had by now come to hate his tormentor, so he looked directly into his eyes and said, 'Why don't you just fuck off and leave me alone? Go pick on somebody your own size if you're such a big deal!'

The sergeant was alarmed. He blushed blood to his ears. The troops had heard him being insulted. 'I can charge you for insubordination, private Kennedy. No one tells a sergeant to fuck off. But I don't want to get you involved with court cases, so why don't you step behind the dining tent with me, and we can sort it out man to man? There you can tell me to my face what you want to say.'

Eddie could just imagine the way the private must have felt, but he went behind the tent with the sergeant . . . a lamb to the slaughter. In his nervous fear, as the sergeant squared up to him to begin the game of cat and mouse, private Kennedy kicked the sergeant as hard as he could in the balls. *Man down*.

Kennedy was tall and thin, but he swung that boot on the end of his skinny leg with all his might. It was a kick that had behind it the support and blessing of all the men. The sergeant went down screaming. He was lost in pain, moaning loudly as he was carried away on a stretcher. Michael Kennedy was suddenly one of the most popular men in the section.

Because the bully had lost face, he laid a charge, but witnesses substantiated that he had been picking on the private. Kennedy was put on orders for two weeks. He had to report to the adjutant on the hour, and undergo an hour's pack drill each evening. Then he was to be transferred to another company.

The last case Eddie overheard before his transport arrived was the case against private Godwin. He had been charged for damage to state property by the commander of his regiment. He was found using his bayonet as a stand to hold his fire cup while boiling water.

The R1 bayonet, with its blade pushed into the sand, is an ideal holder for the water bottle cup – also known as a fire cup. The open-ended cup handle, made of flat metal, fitted perfectly into the cylindrical bayonet handle. It seemed to be made for the job. The metal cup was firmly supported at the ideal height above the ground for the flames from an Esbit or a small fire.

Everybody did it.

It was just after midday when Eddie was instructed to climb aboard a Magirus truck which was returning to Ruacana. Three other soldiers were aboard. Eddie made himself a bed among the supplies on the back of the truck and fell asleep.

He woke some time later. He was covered in dust and the truck was droning on across flat country. He propped himself up on his elbow and watched with amazement as two of the men on the back were slugging it out – a full on fist fight. He couldn't hear their shouts above the noise of the truck, but he could see the anger on their dusty faces . . . sweating and bleeding. He decided to keep out of it and returned to sleep.

He was woken by someone shaking his shoulder and shouting urgently. For a moment he thought that the fight had moved across to include him, but the truck was stationary. Then he saw flames coming from the cab. He jumped up and began to assist the others to offload the cargo. The driver said that the engine had just burst into flames.

Fortunately there was a convoy a short distance behind them which took them and the supplies to Ruacana. The Magirus was stripped of all useful equipment and left to burn itself out in the darkness. There was to be another inquiry.

When Eddie arrived at camp and the manne asked him where he'd been for so long, he shook his head bemusedly and replied, 'Hey, ek sê, I dunno.'

DB – Part One

Sitting about and chatting, as usual, the manne got on to the subject of DB, Detention Barracks. Eddie's recent experience at the court of inquiry had been the cause of much discussion about DB, and prisons generally.

During his primary training with the SADF, Eddie was given the task of escorting a friend to DB, a medic who was charged not only with one month's AWOL, but also insubordination. Apparently the senior officer at the trial, a captain with one finger missing, had said to the prisoner, 'Weerman Swart, do I look like I have "fool" written across my forehead?' and Swart had replied, 'Yes, sir.'

Eddie launched into the story.

'When you get to DB, you stand in front of a huge corrugated iron gate, the colour of a Bedford truck. A peephole opens and the prisoner has to announce himself and state his crime. My mate, old Johnny, stood to attention and shouted out, "Rifleman Swart. Charged with AWOL and insubordination!" Then, with a rattling of chains and locks, the gate was opened. From that moment, Johnny reckons his life changed forever.

'I saw this heavy corporal striding across to start on him. Old Johnny was dressed formally in his uitstap uniform, standing to attention, with his black bag at his feet. The corporal shouted at him in a hoarse voice, "Optel! Jou fokken stuk snot!" I watched ol' Johnny pick up his bag and swing it onto his shoulders. "Get going! You fucken septic medic. Run! To the other side of the parade ground and then back again!"

'That's the last I saw of him as the gates were closed, but I could check the dust rising from the parade ground where the okes were running. He told me later what happened to him inside there.

'It was hot the morning we dropped him, and he reckons that he ran up and down till lunchtime without a drink of water. He reckons that the instructors had been tipped off about him. He became known as "die slegte medic" – the cheeky bastard who was always trying to gyppo the army. They really picked on him.

'During that first morning, he didn't see corporal Akals, an instuctor whose nickname was Kaffir, running up behind him. A heavy punch between the shoulder blades knocked him to the ground. He grazed his face and hands. His kit bag went flying. When he looked around in alarm he saw Kaffir grinning. He realised ... *Trust no one. Watch your back.* At lunch time he was drenched in sweat and pale from dehydration.

'He was called into the shade where four of the instructors were standing, swinging their swaggersticks and preening their moustaches. As he stood to attention, one of the corporals punched him in the face. His lip split. A blow in the guts caused him to cry out and to throw up. Another instructor kicked his feet out from under him, and for good measure, landed another kick in his ribs. Seeing that Johnny was looking a little "ongelukkig" they pulled him up and took him into the admissions centre. He was stripped down, and each item of his kit was recorded. His brand of cigarettes was carefully noted. He was issued with an overall. He was then given one cup of water and marched at double pace to the lunch queue. Lunch was eaten standing at the tables with the other inmates. Conversation was not allowed. Johnny couldn't hold down his food.

'The first two weeks in DB are aimed to break you. Everything's done at double time.

'The afternoon started with pole PT. The pole was carried on the shoulders or above the heads of a team of six men as they did various kinds of physical training. The pole, a thirty foot telephone pole, weighed just under four hundred pounds and its rough surface left splinters in the flesh of their hands. There was a special yard in which this PT took place. It adjoined the barracks that held the Jehovah's Witnesses. These conscientious objectors were in DB for two years because they refused to serve in the SADF. So pole PT was always accompanied by the singing of the Witnesses. "Halleluuja ... halleluuja ... halleluuja ... halleluu ... oo ... ja ..." which drifted over the high wall that separated them from the regular inmates.

'After pole PT, each soldier was allowed one cup of water before running to the obstacle course on a dusty field near the parade ground. They had to climb ropes and high walls, run, balancing on narrow poles, and crawl flat-out through tunnels made of forty-four gallon drums welded together. An instructor stood by, beating their backs as they emerged. Johnny reckons that they were choking in the dust and body odour. One of the ous collapsed but the others were ordered to trample him.

'After the obstacle course, there was a fifteen-minute tea-break, which was taken standing. Then they were all marched at double pace to work in the gardens. Johnny reckons the gardens were unbelievable. Filled with bright flowers, and there were ripe peaches on the trees in the orchard. Anyone caught touching or stealing the fruit was beaten and made to do chase parades at night. Johnny and three others were set to work on their haunches, weeding and picking up leaves, below the branches. This was to keep them uncomfortable, not allowing them to stand or sit while they worked.

'The instructor called one of the okes working near Johnny. Johnny kept thinking in his mind, *Keep your head. Keep your head . . . so when you get out of here you can buy a whole box of peaches and a carton of Paul Revere cigarettes*. He reckons that he kept remembering the Paul Revere ad with some oke . . . with like a highwayman's hat on . . . riding flat-out on horseback through orchards and forests. The light and shade of the leaves in the orchard reminded him of it. The soldier returned with a peach in his hand, "Here's a peach for you . . . from the corporal."

'He's thinking, *Hou kop, hou kop, keep your head*. So he says, "I don't eat peaches." The soldier looks a bit puzzled and runs back to the corporal to return the peach.

'A while later they were lined up to drink water from a tap. Two instructors were in charge of this operation. One was the tap man. He regulated the flow of water. The other oke held a stick, and beat anyone who tried to pig-out on the water. Suddenly the corporal who had tried to get Johnny to eat a peach called him to attention and accused him of eating a peach.

' "No, corporal, I don't eat peaches," he said.

' "I don't believe you! Jou fokken sak stront! Open your mouth!"

'Feeling confident that he was innocent, Johnny opened his mouth. The instuctor pushed something into it. He reckons it took his breath away and practically turned his mouth inside out. His salivary glands went berserk, and he felt as if his eye balls were rolling backwards. The instructor had put crushed aloe into his mouth. At the tap, old Johnny was so angry that they let him clean his mouth out and have a long drink. No one dared to hit him.

'After work they were all marched at double pace to the showers. Naked, they walked through the foot-baths of icy water, purple from Condy's crystals. He reckons the shower heads were set in the concrete ceiling, ten feet above them. Cold water poured down on each man for exactly one minute.

'After showers was Rookparade. All the ous who smoked were given a cigarette according to their brands. They stood in a long line, shoulder to shoulder. The instructor lit the first ou's skyf and stepped back to watch how each oke would pass on the light "donkey-style". When the first oke finished his cigarette, all cigarettes had to be put out in a special bin. The instructors made sure that filter smokers did not remove the filters from their cigarettes. Some okes had managed to use the thick filter paper to cut their wrists. The non-smokers, meanwhile, had to lean up against a wall on their foreheads, their hands behind their backs and their legs apart.

'From there they were all marched back to the cells where they were locked behind steel doors for the night. The one thing old Johnny didn't expect was the crying and wailing and muttering that he heard when the doors slammed shut. He reckons that one of the okes used to pray loudly. "O, liewe Vader God, vergewe hulle hul sondes . . ." Johhny used to wonder which okes the oke was asking God to forgive. Other okes would just cry or yell. Some okes jabbered away like madmen. Johnny was exhausted. He dropped onto the coir mattress on the cell floor and fell asleep. Gone.'

The Cut Line

The cut line was the border proper. From the air it looked like a dust highway, hundreds of kilometres long, stretching across the northernmost edge of Ovamboland from Rundu to Ruacana. It followed the border demarcation of the map through varied terrain, from the jungly swamp areas in the east, through thorn scrub and the palm belt near Oshikango, to the stony mountains in the west near Ruacana.

It was a one kilometre wide killing zone. A no-go area. It had been bulldozed clear by a fleet of large graders and dozers, each one with an armed guard riding shotgun on the back. They say the dust raised by this clearing process could be seen for miles. The only trees left standing were those which had been too big and well-established to be moved.

Many men had been injured or killed, both making and patrolling the cut line. A Unimog of parabats, tooling along the cut line, was hit full-on by a rocket launched from the Angolan side. The result ... three dead, and two young men with missing limbs left to face their changed lives at One Military Hospital. Deep muscular twitches in their stumps. Ugly stitches across skin folded inward. Inflammation and the itching of phantom limbs. The careless comments of fools, 'Don't worry, you guys'll be playing soccer again soon!' *New meditations. New worlds.*

The cut line afforded good vision for the defenders and made it difficult for insurgents to move into the area as they would be spotted crossing the open space. The DLI had the task of controlling sixty-two kilometres of the line.

At a pre-patrol briefing session with the commander, the officers were issued with binoculars and the latest instructions.

'The cut line is a killing zone which is to be kept clear at all times. The message has been put out non-stop since Tuesday over all the South West African radio stations, so all the local people should be informed about the stepping up of security in this area.'

Radio was the popular medium in Africa. Most homes had a portable. But I still felt that it was an assumption to believe that everybody would have heard the message – later to be proved right.

The commander continued. 'You are to fire upon anything that moves across that space. It doesn't matter whether it is

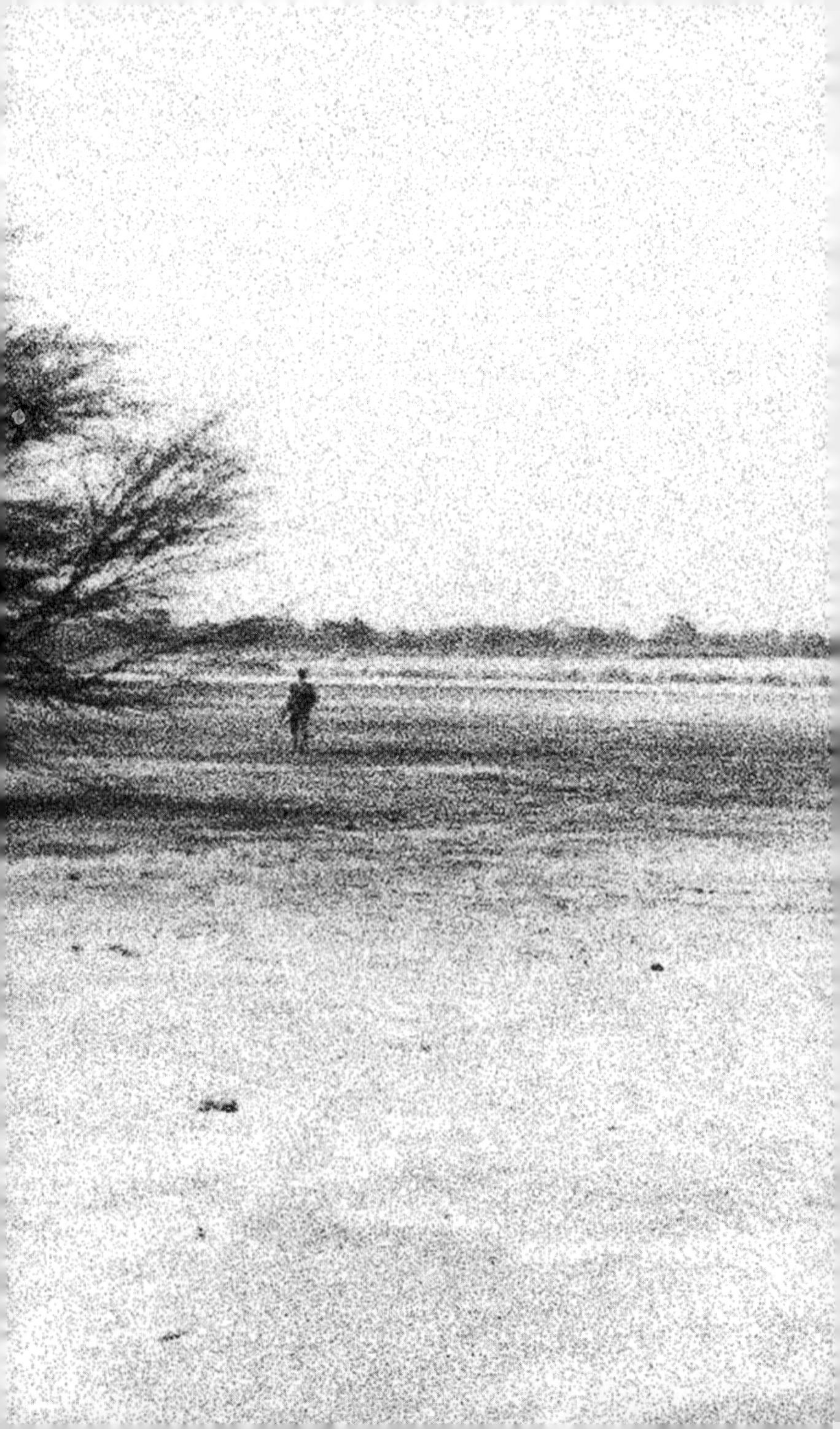

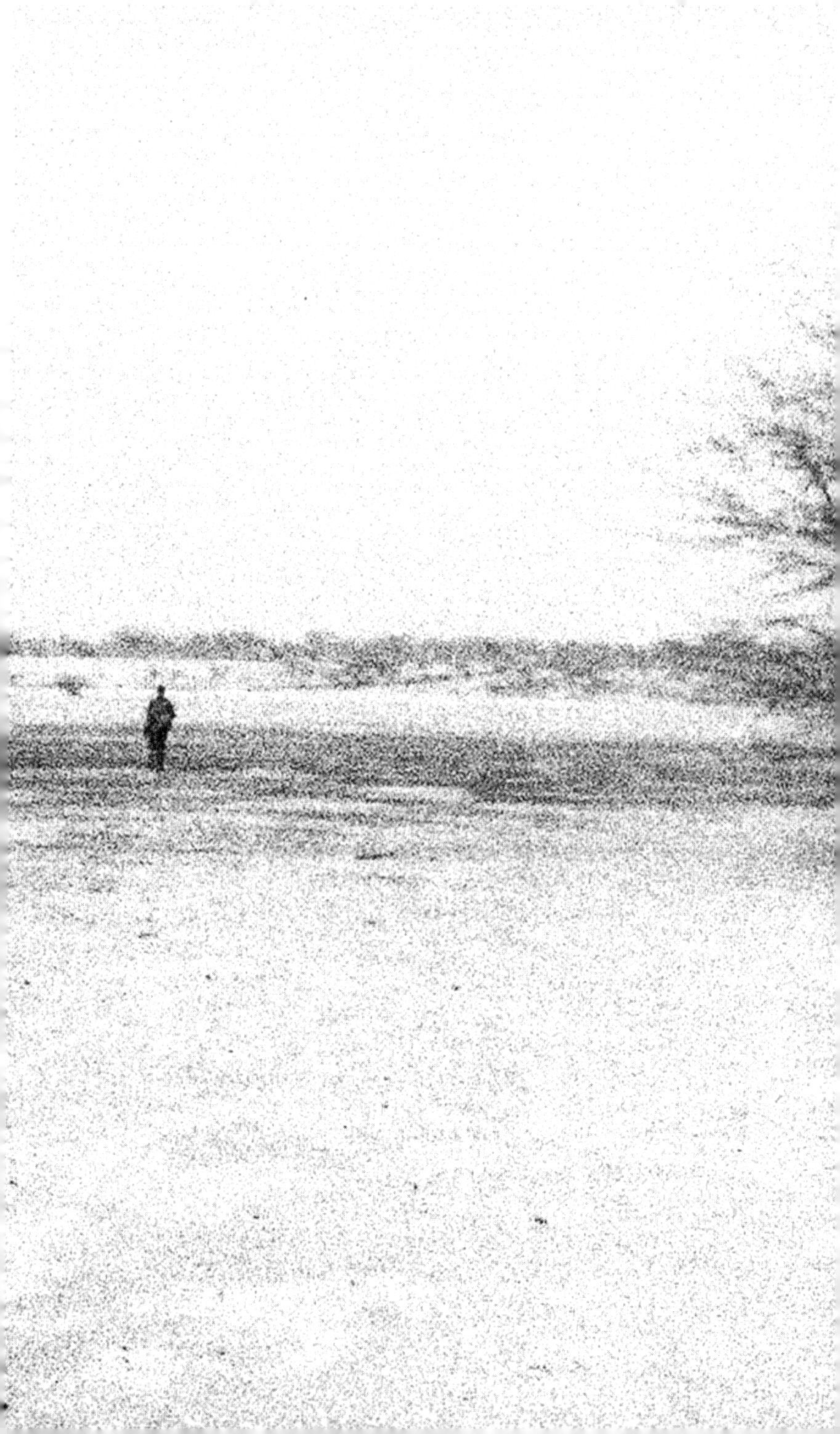

human, mechanical or animal.'

One of the officers raised his hand to ask a question.

'Does that mean that we are to shoot women and children?'

The commander thought for a moment, and then answered.

'Yes. You shoot anything that moves in that space.'

I could feel a stiffening among the officers. Almost a disbelief that they had just heard him say that. Most of these officers were professional men from the city of Durban and the idea of gunning down women and children did not sit well with them. I knew that mutinous thoughts were creeping into their minds. Once away from this authoritarian charade and on patrol with their men, they wouldn't order anyone to fire on women and children. After all, the no-go zone on the cut line had only been re-instituted two days previously. There were bound to be people who hadn't heard about it. It was far more humane to take prisoners of women or children, or better, just scare them off, and all sane men knew that.

Men? Well, according to our code of conduct, it didn't seem as bad to fire at them. Terrorists were usually imagined to be male, even though many women were active as instigators and informers . . . even fighters.

The next day the first report of action on the cut line came through. An urgent voice over the radio in the Ops tent. 'Ah, Bravo Medic Bravo . . . this is Oscar Papa . . . calling Bravo Bravo Medic . . . Please send medic to Bravo company position on cut line. We have a casualty. Over.'

Some men from B company had been lying in the shade of the trees after lunch, keeping a watchful eye on the open space ahead of them. One member of the group had climbed up a tree for better observation. Suddenly one of the men on the ground spotted movement in the trees on the other side of the line, and without warning anybody, fired off a few shots. The man in the tree took fright, and thinking that he could be seen in his elevated position, tried to get down immediately. In his panic, he slipped and fell, and broke his wrist. First casualty.

The second casualty, or casualties, happened like this. The

colonel decided to inspect the cut line, and he chose to do this in two of the Hippos. These large armoured vehicles were for the protection of personnel in case of ambush or landmine. Each one had mounted on the front of it a Browning-three machine gun. The machine gunner was positioned front centre above the driver's cab and he could spray bullets in a forward arc of some one hundred and seventy degrees.

After driving along the cut line for about an hour, the colonel ordered the driver to stop. There was nothing to be seen except some cattle grazing close to the edge of the cut line. The colonel seemed to go into a trance-like state and he shouted an order to the corporal manning the machine gun.

'Corporal, shoot those cattle.'

The corporal smiled at first, thinking that the colonel was joking. I mean, the cattle so obviously belonged to the local people on our side of the line. They were just inside the no-go area. Clearly they had been used to moving about the area to graze. There were no fences.

'Shoot those cattle, sir? Seriously, sir?'

In an impatient and angry voice the colonel reissued the order.

'You heard me, corporal. I said shoot those cattle. They're on the cut line. That's an order!'

Few envied that corporal as he swivelled the Browning around, gave one last look of appeal, took aim and pulled the trigger. The loud popping rattle of the weapon cut through the midday silence. The bullets kicked up dust as they moved swiftly to their target. An ox, two cows and a calf lay dead or dying. Ears rang from the noise of the weapon.

All surveyed the dead cattle and wondered. *Ambassadors for South Africa?* A charge of silent and mutinous anger pulsed through the men. The colonel had brought the border right through the middle of the truck. He had isolated himself from those who did not share his cause, and there were many. The rest of the trip was spent in silent anger and frustration at this display of aggressive stupidity. *Who were we to listen to? Was anyone sane here?*

Back at camp that evening I was asked to help write a protest song. Clive was so angry that he couldn't keep still. Somehow he imagined that we would be able to write a song that could express our indignation. A protest song that would give us a voice, let others know what we were going through. A song that would move out onto the airwaves of the world and . . .

Well, we didn't have much in the way of lyrics, but Clive knew for absolute sure that the title of the song was to be 'The War Boar'. It never got written.

The third bit of action on the cut line involved sergeant Christopher Cameron, a life-saver from North Beach in Durban.

I was on duty in the Ops tent when the radio operator received report of a gunshot. It was two am. We heard the section officer asking for an ambulance in the support company sector. Sergeant Cameron had been wounded. It was a dark night out there and the imagination could conjure all kinds of sightings and contacts. We listened to the reports as they came over on the radio. The ambulance arrived. Sergeant Cameron was wounded in the hand. He was OK. He could walk. He was being attended to by the medics. He was taken to a medical depot at the equestrian regiment situated a few kilometres north of our camp.

The next day when the support company returned from their nocturnal patrol, we heard the full story. While moving into position for an ambush, crawling about in the bushes at the edge of the cut line, Chris's rifle had been caught in the bushes. It was dark. He pulled at the rifle impatiently. He was holding the end of the barrel. The rifle was cocked and the safety catch was off. The trigger caught on something and the rifle fired. Fortunately, the barrel was pointing under Chris's arm . . . out, towards the cut line. The bullet passed through his palm and one of the magazine pouches on his webbing.

The small variants of fate, and what might have been, can still torment the mind to this day.

Suitcase

It was a quiet Sunday morning. I was on duty in the Ops tent when Captain Browne called me. He took me outside and showed me a large men's bicycle leaning against the sandbags. A size twenty-eight. No three-speed gear. Pedal brakes for the back wheel, and a bell. It had a carrier on the back into which was clipped a small school suitcase. The suitcase was tightly attached to the carrier with rope.

Captain Browne informed me that this bicycle had been captured on the cut line the previous night. We had set up an ambush and fired on the owner of the bicycle as he made his way towards the Angolan border. He had managed to escape by dropping his bike and running like a hare. I was ordered to search the suitcase and the bicycle in case the owner had left any incriminating evidence – presumably of his commitment to SWAPO or the liberation struggle.

There was a slight chance that the suitcase could be booby-trapped, so I set about my task very carefully. There was nothing out of the ordinary about the bicycle, except that I wasn't used to seeing such old-fashioned bikes. It reminded me of my childhood in Emmarentia. We had a servant, Sally, and I used to visit her and her friends in her small room across the yard. She told me about her husband, Isaac, and assured me that one day I would meet him. Well, one day arrived, and I came across this big black bicycle parked outside Sally's room. A size twenty-eight 'Black Gentleman's' bicycle. I went inside and was introduced to him, a tall thin man with a beard and pale-coloured hands with one long finger nail. Isaac.

This bicycle reminded me of those times . . . and the servants' quarters. Embroidered sheets and pillowcases. The bed lifted up on bricks. Straw mats on a smooth concrete floor. The smell of phutu and Sunlight soap. The loudly ticking clock beside the bed.

Carefully I removed the suitcase from the carrier. I took my time untying the knots in the rope. Placing the suitcase in front of me on the sand, I opened the hasps on either side of the handle and lifted the lid carefully. The first thing I saw was a yellow nightie with delicate, lacy shoulder straps. Beneath the silky weight of the nightie I found a fresh cake of Lux soap and a new wide-pronged comb. Then I found a child's toy and a small pair of cheap plastic sandals.

I was looking at the gifts that a father had planned to give to his wife and children.

My emotions were reeling. I left the suitcase open and stood up. I spoke in a loud and penetrating voice.

'This is wrong! What we are doing is wrong! Shooting at civilians in the middle of the night is wrong. We don't realise what we are doing anymore!'

Captain Browne emerged from the Ops tent looking alarmed. I saw him turn and talk to my buddy, Butch. I couldn't hear what he was saying because my sense of indignation and anger had taken control of me. I started asking whoever I could see in the vicinity how they felt to be part of a system that fired on innocent people. I couldn't stop my mouth. Then I heard Browne say to Butch in a loud voice, 'Sergeant Budke, if you don't take your buddy away from here immediately I shall be forced to place him under arrest. Get him out of here now!'

Butch, faithful buddy, took me back to the tent, all the while trying to calm me down. 'Cool it, Rick. There's nothing you can do. It's a shit situation. If you don't lower your voice, you'll only attract more trouble. Come on, let's just move out and cool out.'

In the tent I told Butch that I wanted to get the fuck out of there. I felt like my life had been torn in two. I wanted to steal a vehicle and start moving in the direction of home. He kept reminding me of the consequences which would follow such a course of action. He reminded me about Keith, who had flipped out and ended up in a psychiatric ward. He certainly didn't want to see another of his friends going through the same movie.

Later, on that painful Sunday afternoon, when we were

released from duty at about four in the afternoon, I made a drawing of Butch. It was an attempt to distract my mind which was tumbling in panic and pain. He refused to put on his sunglasses while he posed for me. I gave him the drawing, which I titled 'Butch without shades'.

I realised that I needed to get a grip on myself. Though I never retracted my condemnation of this particular incident, there was a war on. I decided to wake early every morning and join the PT squad. I needed to get myself a tight routine and focus on physical fitness. That way I could get through the days and nights that stretched ahead.

Prisoners

It was growing dark when we pulled up at the reservoir tower just south of the gate into Angola. We had been called to investigate another 'disturbance'. The base of the tower was surrounded by a barbed wire fence and we could see a group of soldiers standing around two handcuffed men who were squatting on their haunches.

Our officer went to investigate. The men in handcuffs, uniformed members of an Ovambo regiment, officially our allies, had been arrested for drunk and disorderly behaviour. The previous evening, they got drunk and decided, on their own initiative, to set up a road block. The first to arrive at their road block was one of the rare civilian vehicles that passed through the area. The soldiers, both fully armed, and carelessly bold on liquor, had ordered the inhabitants out of the car while they proceeded to search it. They passed lewd comments about a young lady passenger, and helped themselves to certain items of clothing while searching through the people's luggage. The occupants of the car had suffered these indignities in silence, but they lost no time, once they had been released, in reporting the crime at the first military base they came to. The two soldiers were found and arrested with the stolen possessions a short distance from the road, arguing over a fine pair of leather shoes.

I watched our officer talking to the soldiers who had arrested the men. The two prisoners remained squatting on the ground, silent and sullen, while decisions were made on what to do with them. Eventually our officer returned to the convoy with the prisoners. One of them was put into the back of the Landrover ahead of us, and the other was put into the back of our Landrover, where I was sitting with Butch and Phil.

'Corporal Andrew, you are to guard the prisoner.'

Shit, why me?

I grasped my rifle firmly and started to play the role. I indicated to the prisoner that he should sit on the seat opposite me, up close to the cab, so that he couldn't make a break for the door. I sat near the door on the opposite side and stared at him with a kind of vague and soldierly aggression. At that stage I didn't know what his crime was, or why he was a prisoner. He spoke no English, but understood the situation. It was a comfort to have Butch and Phil there with me even though they expressed amusement at my new occupation as warder.

On the way back to base we stopped at the equestrian camp, which was about five kilometres north of our camp at Oshikango. It was well established and had a lock-up facility. I had to take the prisoner along. He was still handcuffed. While the officers deliberated on his fate, he squatted down once more, rocking gently on his haunches, his handcuffed wrists projected forwards between his knees. He kept looking at me and trying to catch my eye. I looked at him and he indicated that he wanted a cigarette. I looked away, but he knew that he had reached me. By the light of the gas lamps I could feel his eyes seeking after mine. I decided to respond by taking out my cigarettes. There were only about three left in the packet so I decided to give them to him. However, I couldn't be seen to do this in front of everybody, so I waited for an opportunity.

Eventually it was decided that the prisoners would spend the night in the lock-up and that we would collect them the

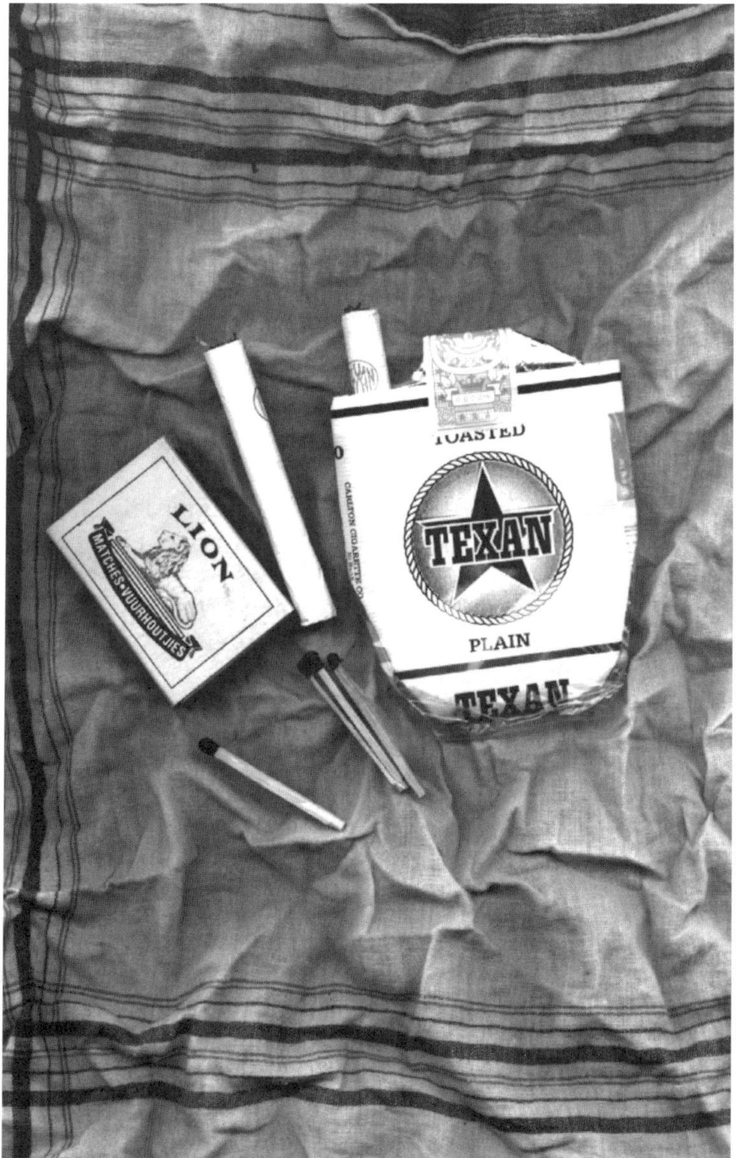
LION
MATCHES • VUURHOUTJIES
TOASTED
TEXAN
PLAIN
TEXAN

following day and escort them to Oshakati. As I left my prisoner at the lock-up, I managed to put the packet of cigarettes into his hands without being seen.

The following day at about two in the afternoon, another corporal and I were driven to the equestrian camp to collect the prisoners. We loaded them into the back of the Landrover and sat with them, holding our rifles firmly. The two prisoners were looking a little shabby at this stage. They hadn't washed or changed their clothes for two days and two nights since their drinking spree. I expected my prisoner to beg further favours from me, but he behaved in a subdued manner and seemed resigned to go along with the slow and tedious procedure of prosecution by the military.

In Oshakati we escorted the men to the holding cell where they were duly locked up.

On returning to the Landrover, we were informed by the driver that we would have to spend the night in Oshakati because we were required to transport some VIP back to our camp early the next morning. This VIP, presumably some high-ranking officer, was to arrive later that night from Grootfontein. Of course we were a little annoyed that we had no sleeping bags or toiletries with us, but we were given some blankets and shown to a tent for overnight visitors.

Oshakati

Oshakati was the large military depot that acted as the nerve centre for the Ovamboland offensive. Like Grootfontein, it was a vast camp and holding pen for every aspect of military endeavour. There were thousands of tents, aerials, vehicle yards, fuel depots, magazines, offices and field kitchens.

I went for a stroll in the evening and bumped into an old friend from varsity. I noticed that he held the rank of staff-sergeant and I felt a little awkward at first, being only a corporal myself, but he wasn't concerned with rank and military hierarchy. He was beaming and glad to see me. I noticed that he wore an ornate moustache that he kept twisting into points with his fingers. This moustache was not the usual snor of the red-necked military variety. It had about it the air of the parlour, of Salvador Dali and Oscar Wilde. Chris had always been a hippie sympathiser, a magician, an admirer of the arts who had worn his hair long. This moustache was a viable substitute for a long bonnie. He took me into a dining tent. He went to the kitchen and returned with two Amstels, saying, as he sat down, that he'd laid on a good meal.

The food arrived on white plates – real crockery. Tender steak, chopped carrots and creamed spinach. Obviously he'd got some connection with the cook. The only thing that tasted of the army was the rice which had been spooned from the communal pot. Pudding followed. Tinned fruit salad and jelly. We ended with coffee, cheese and biscuits. Chris, it turned out, was the cook in charge of this particular kitchen of the SADF catering universe.

After a good chat, we bade each other farewell. I wandered off among the tents feeling strangely vulnerable and sad. Seeing Chris had awoken all kinds of memories of student days, surfing in the sun, smiling girls, civilisation, and the seeming promise of a communal future. I missed my wife. I missed my friends. I felt like a failure. Here I was, a twenty-nine-year-old corporal, a self-employed artist and musician, with my world overturned by the SADF.

There was a large screen above the tent tops and, like a drive-in, I could see the flickering images of a Bronson movie. I wandered over to the field in front of the screen. Men were sitting around in groups laughing, talking, drinking and watching the movie. I stood alone at the back sipping a bottle of ginger brandy that I had kept in my kidney pouch for some such occasion. I didn't want to be here. I couldn't get involved in the film. I hated the crass violence of American media as I watched Charles Bronson shooting the bad guys with a huge magnum pistol gripped in both of his hands. Dumph, dumph . . .

I confess that I can enjoy a Bronson movie, but on this particular occasion I could see only the lostness of western civilisation. The foolishness of screening violent American movies under the great stars of the South West African sky. Our presence in this place seemed to me to be an outrage. Our noise, machines and garbage were spread everywhere. I needed to escape.

I went back to the tent, drained the bottle of ginger brandy and, feeling slightly numb and insulated, wrote a letter to Gill. I slept well while the movie of the night raged on in the background. I had strange dreams that had to do with a drive-in scene. A small boy has climbed the ladder behind the screen. Hundreds of feet above the ground, he looks down. Far below, a tiny parent stares upwards, waving, angry and concerned.

At dawn I washed my face under a tap and took a stroll in the early morning quiet. I drifted past the walk-in movie with its screen blank and empty. Piles of discarded beer cans lay everywhere. I passed the doorway of a beer tent where a hungover soldier, unshaven and with a nasty black eye, was sweeping empty beer cans into piles for later removal.

Further on I came across some brick buildings and barracks. Around the corner I was confronted by a pile of human bodies. *Oh, jeez*. In a confusing intimacy of torsos and limbs lay six dead men. All brown-skinned ... African. Dusty olive-green uniforms – not ours. I looked at the faces. They had been killed by fire from above ... must have been taken out by choppers ... machine guns ... shot down while running to find cover. This was their last time in the sun before being taken to the cold metal fridges of the mortuary. I could see that they had been thoroughly searched ... all belts and possessions removed ... pockets turned inside out ... nothing left.

I kept going until my way was blocked by a high barbed-wire fence. It was the side of a large enclosure, about four acres in area. I could see rows of tents inside. Guards were posted in towers at each corner of the enclosure. Their LMGs were at rest, but the barrels pointed at the inmates. As I was trying to figure out what I was looking at, a bearded man emerged from one of the tents inside the enclosure and made his way to a urinal that was screened off with sheets of hessian. The man wore a greyish greatcoat I had not seen before. It hadn't been washed in a long time. He was carrying a writing pad. I could tell that he was foreign. Then I realised that I was looking at a Cuban prisoner of war, captured on South Africa's recent offensive in Angola. I watched the back of his head and shoulders as he stood urinating. He returned wearily to his tent. I imagined him writing a letter to his loved ones in Cuba.

Each day he would watch the sun rise and set. During the hottest part of the day he would seek shade under the canvas of the tent. His future? Well, it depended on the outcome of the war. He was a victim of politics and military bureaucracy.

A pawn in the game?
No, a lot less significant than a pawn.

DB – Part Two

It was late afternoon at Ruacana, almost twilight. There was a thin sickle moon above the trees on the horizon. The manne were sitting around. James asked Eddie to carry on with the story of 'ol' Johnny in DB'. The others nodded in agreement. So, after a short recap, Eddie continued:

'That first morning when Johnny woke up in the dark and he heard the slamming of steel doors, he realised that it was no dream. This was DB . . . for real. Then he heard the instructors shouting.

'When the cell doors were opened each man had to emerge fully dressed in his overall and boots, carrying his slop bucket. They had to cover the bucket with their polishing cloth so that the instructors wouldn't have to see or smell the contents. They emptied them down the toilets and each oke was issued with his own razor. After shaving, razors were handed back in. Then they started polishing the concrete floors of the cells and the long central corridor. They had to shine so that the instructors could see their reflections if they wanted to.

'On Johnny's second morning one of the instructors tuned him to lift his boots up behind him as he polished away on his hands and knees. All the weight of his lower body was now resting on his knees. They began to ache and throb, so he dropped his feet for a moment's relief, but the instructor saw this, and kicked him hard in the ribs. Two ribs on his right hand side were fractured. He swallowed the pain and lifted his boots. He had no choice. His knees would have to take it.

'Breakfast was taken standing, each oke issued with a varkpan of mealie meal, a slice of bread, a lump of white margarine, and a cup of tea. Like during basics, it contained copper sulphate to stop the okes from getting randy.

'From breakfast they were marched to the parade ground for the Lord's prayer and a formal inspection. The okes were klapped and insulted. The rest of the morning was spent drilling at double pace. The commands were shouted so quickly that it was difficult to know what the instructors were saying. A stack of the okes made the wrong moves . . . like taking a further step or two before halting. Then the instructor would stand in the squad on the spot where the oke should have been, and punch him as he tried to reclaim his position. One oke, quite a sterk, blocked a blow and stared at the instructor. That evening in the showers he was beaten up by six okes with clubs. He had to go to hospital.

'After a tea break, the drilling continued. Johnny's knees started suppurating from the early morning polishing session, but he kept going. Suddenly the drill instructor's voice changed, and he started praising them. The okes stared in disbelief. He tuned them that he couldn't believe how well they were drilling. That they did everything perfectly. The okes were amazed. Then he tuned them he was going to do something he had never done before. He was going to give them a break. So he tells them to go to the shower room and says that they can drink as much water as they like. He also lets them rest for a bit in the shade.

'The okes were a bit confused by this kindness, but they ran into the bathrooms and filled their bellies with water. It was beautiful and cool and they put their heads under the taps and drank deep to make up for the days of rationing. After a while they heard the instructor calling them. They jogged out into the sun. The instructor was smiling. Then he tuned, "Op die grond! On the ground! Lie on the ground!" They all fell to the ground. "Now, you greedy fucken pigs, roll to the fence and then roll back again!" There was nothing they could do. They had to obey. They started rolling along the ground from the one end of the parade ground to the other. All the okes became dizzy and vomited as their systems got rid of the water in their bellies. They rolled through each other's puke. The squad was released for lunch, each oke coated in puke and too nauseous to eat.

'Pole PT took place as usual with the Jehovah's Witnesses providing the background music – the *Halleluja Hit Parade*. Because Johnny was tall he suffered more than the short okes when they took the weight of the pole on their shoulders. When they did the duck walk which involved holding the pole above their heads and moving forward in a crouched position, kicking their feet out to the sides, Johnny's knees really began to hurt. He stumbled on several occasions. The instructor informed the squad that they would have to do extra pole PT because one of their number, "a bad medic, a useless medic", was "fucking around instead of doing the duck walk." Suddenly one of the okes in Johnny's squad turned around and slapped him across the face. The instructor laughed. He dug to see the okes fighting among themselves.

'Johnny reckons that that was the worst thing that happened to him in DB. He realised then and there that there was no one on his side because anyone could be turned against him. Life was like a snarling hell. All it needed was pain and people became animals. He reckons that at that moment, any patriotism that he might have felt for South Africa, died. One way.

'The next morning after shaving Johnny was ordered to polish the full thirty-three cell length of the corridor on his knees, again with his boots lifted. He was near to unconscious when he completed the task. His knees were swollen to twice their size, and they were leaking pus.

'At sick parade he tried to report for medical treatment, but he was told to get back in line. They reckoned that because he was a medic, he should be able to look after himself. If the following day hadn't been Sunday he would probably have collapsed, but because South Africa is a Christian country, Sunday was a day of rest.

'So he had some time to recover, even though his knees continued to throb and suppurate. After breakfast on Sunday the padre led the service. Then the commanding officer, a man with a ruddy, pink complexion, a moustache and beady eyes, reminded all the prisoners that DB was for their betterment as soldiers, and that they must not complain if his instructors hurt them. *Psychopaths and demons grinned.*

'On Monday morning the nightmare continued. Johnny was ordered to polish his cell and the corridor on his knees again. In great pain, he stepped forward at the sick report, but was again told to get back. His overall didn't smell too good and his knees were constantly throbbing but he was forced to carry on with the usual routine. Drill, Pole PT, Obstacle Course and work in the gardens and orchard.

'His body ached, his hands were blistered. His overall was coated in dried vomit and starched stiff below the knees with pus. Two of his ribs were fractured, and during the course of the week he collected a black eye and a cracked jaw. By Saturday, both his eyes were swollen. His mouth was swollen and it was bleeding inside where the skin had been ruptured – caught between his teeth and an instructor's fist.

'On the second Sunday he figured that he still had four days to go, when he was called in front of a captain who offered him four days remission of sentence. All he had to do was sign a form to say that he was leaving detention barracks without complaint, and in a physically fit condition. Who could refuse four days remission from this hell? Well, Johnny signed on the dotted line, despite his swollen knees and battered body. He reckons that they did this to all the okes so no one could hold them responsible for the injuries inflicted there.

'So, he returned to his unit having served ten days in DB. He reported sick and was hospitalised for two weeks. To this day he has trouble with his knees. Luckily the infection didn't reach his joints as it did with some of the other ous, like Les, who lost the use of three fingers.

'Ja. So that's DB, okes.'

Mine

While a convoy was breezing back to camp one afternoon, the right front wheel of a Unimog went over a mine. The sound of its detonation was deafening. The men on the back, seated over a layer of sandbags, were thrown up into the air like dice from a gambler's hand. The engine of the truck, which must have weighed an ugly ton, ripped through the bonnet, spinning out through the air to land fifty metres along the road, gouging a deep furrow until it came to rest. One of the men who had hand grenades attached to his belt had a deep gash in the side of his stomach. The pin had been pulled from the grenade in the impact and it had gone off. Another man had landed on the roll bar as he tumbled down in his arc of flight and broke his arm.

In the stunned hush, the memory of the explosion was still reverberating. A plume of black smoke and dust was thinning out on the air which smelt pungent and sulphurous. All surveyed the scene and moved to recover. Despite the horrific power of the detonation – it was an anti-tank mine – everybody was alive.

Besides a few bruises and a massive shot of adrenalin, only four of the men were injured. One clearly had a broken arm, another a deep wound in his side, which, though bleeding, was

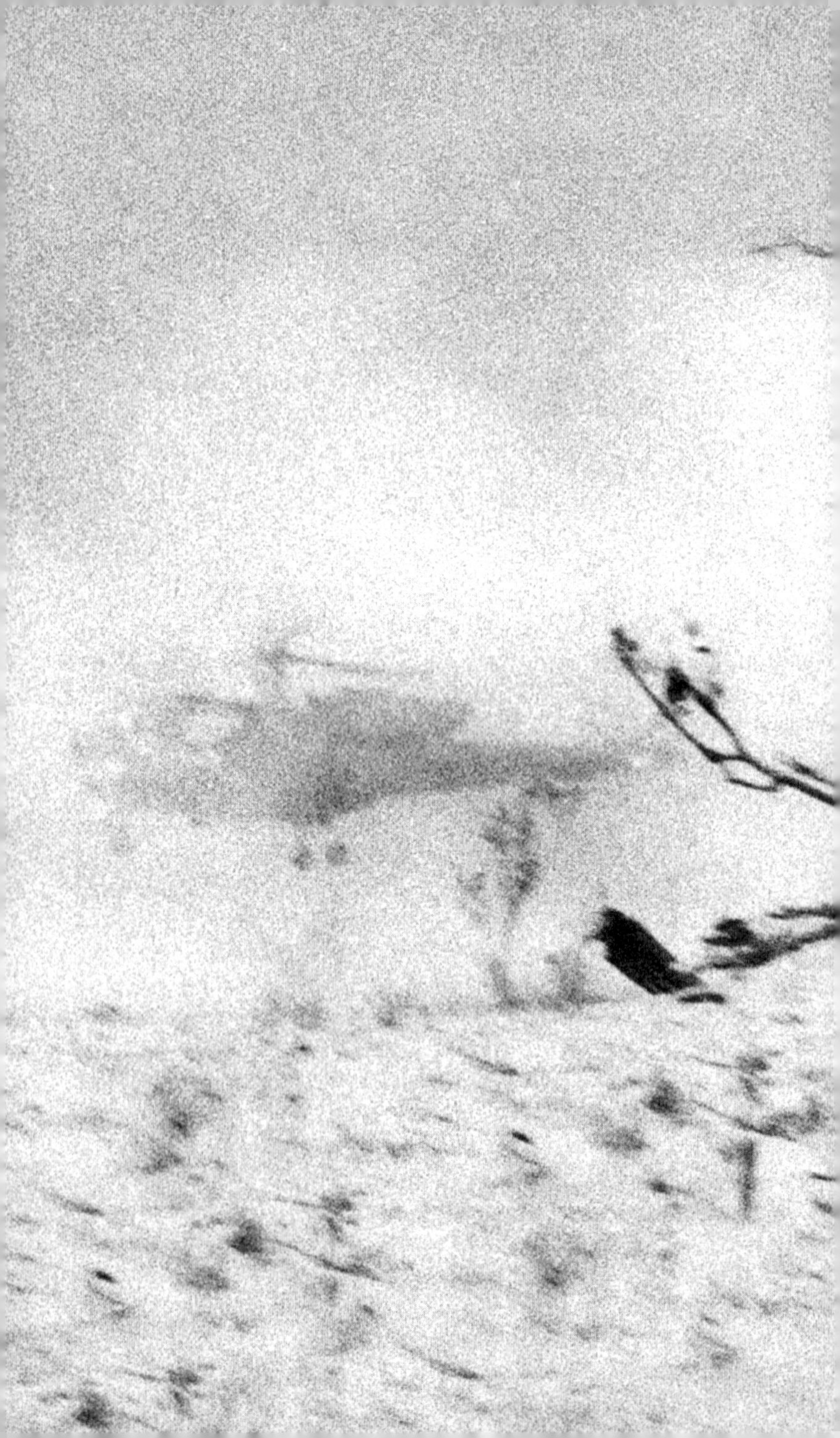

being staunched with someone's towel. There was no arterial damage. The driver and co-driver were quite badly burnt, their lower legs having been mildly roasted. Still in a state of shock, their trousers like blackened ribbons, they stared at the black socket that had been the cab. Torn metal . . . no engine. Thanks to the sandbags, both still had their legs though there was no floor left in the cab.

There was much speculation about providence, miracles and luck, as they stood in the aftermath.

The truck which had been driving ahead of this one in the convoy turned around and joined in the meditation. Their wheels had missed the mine.

No-name Brand

The manne were sitting around a small fire one evening with a good supply of cold beers, when Manie decided to tell a story.

'I had this one mate . . . in armoured cars . . . old Gav. He won a silver medal for bravery under fire . . . serious.'

Everyone got comfortable and listened.

'Ja . . . he was one of the first okes to go into Angola. He'd only done three months of basic at One Special Services Battalion before being selected for combat. Some of the major brass came in and offered the okes the opportunity to go on a special, secret mission . . . to become – as they called it at the time – an "American mercenary". All they had to do was sign some papers to say that they were volunteering for a special, secret mission, and that they'd made their decision voluntarily. Most of the okes were sick of being fucked around in camp so they grabbed at the chance for something different . . . some excitement.

'The okes who volunteered were issued with a single silver dog-tag . . . just their blood group . . . no names. Their fatigues were American . . . no badges, nothing . . . and the smokers were given no-name brand cigarettes. No way could you identify that these okes were South Africans. Even their tank suits . . . made out of like an asbestos fibre . . . were from some other country. They were no-name brand troepies.

'They rode all over Angola, even into Zaire. They got into some heavy shit all over. They fought against the Cubans and the MPLA. Full-on battles that destroyed whole towns, bridges, airports and banks. Gav and them used to lead the way in their Elands, all with ninety-mil cannons. Following behind was usually a convoy of bats, infantry, mortars and artillery.

'Anyway, on their way to Luanda they got into some really heavy shit. Old Gav was ordered to leave the main convoy and recce this one pozzie where there was a bridge, and some reports of enemy presence. Their orders were to secure and destroy the bridge. Old Gav was in the number one car with the others following. They had four Elands in front, followed by two Unimogs of infantry, and one of engineers. Some lieutie was in charge of the whole operation.

'They had just passed a little village of mud huts when there was a fucking unbelievably loud explosion somewhere close behind them. Gav could hear what sounded like bullets flying through the air, and he thought they were being ambushed. He told the driver to stop the car. He opened the hatch and looked back. He checked this huge mushrooming cloud of black smoke climbing high into the sky behind the grass roofs of the village. He's scheming . . . certainly not anti-personnel . . . must be anti-tank . . . for sure. The bullet-type noises that he heard were pieces of the wheel and steering linkage exploding out from the vehicle which triggered the mine. Old Gav was still feeling like it was an ambush, so he fired a few shots into the bush along the road. He thought he heard a single shot in return, but the okes tuned him nooit . . . no way.

'He ran back along the road, keeping carefully to the wheel tracks made by his Eland until he came to the second car. It was fucked, both front wheels blown away, but the okes were OK. He ran back to his car just in time to stop the driver from reversing into a better position. The engineers were up now and they unearthed a mine six inches behind the back wheel of Gav's car. The road was a fucking minefield!

'The engineers, the officer and a couple of other okes started probing for mines. They pulled out three from under the wheels of the armoured cars and another nine along the road to the bridge, which, as it turned out, had already been destroyed by the enemy.

'Gav could feel that something was wrong. Across the river were bush-covered hills and there were all kinds of scrapings and tracks in the sand on the road. It looked like a major force had just left the area.

'While the engineers were disappearing in the heat down towards the river valley, sweeping for mines, Gav was scanning the hills across the river. At that moment shells from a recoilless gun started flying at them from across the river. Ambush! Gav grabbed his rifle, three extra magazines, and keeping low, ran towards the river. He was thinking to himself that he must try and get the okes out . . . or their bodies or whatever.

'For some or other reason old Gav keeps calm under fire. He shits himself like anybody else, but his mind doesn't panic. He hit the deck behind a tree, the worst tree he could have picked for cover in a fire fight that lasted two and a half hours. When it was over he reckoned that this tree was just a single thin trunk, pruned clean by flying steel. As he lay taking cover, with leaves, twigs and branches falling on his head, he saw that the okes were OK. Most had got reasonable cover but they were too freaked out to return any accurate fire. He sussed out the position and started carefully and accurately firing off single rounds. This immediately drew an incredible amount of fire down onto his little tree.

'One time he checked this Cuban oke stand up just across the river – about seventy-five metres away – and fire a rocket directly at him. Old Gav schemed it was all over, so he put his fingers in his ears and nose and turned aside as this thing came towards him. It hit the river sand about thirty feet in front of him and exploded upwards . . . luckily. Gav shot the oke in the chest, and he literally flew into the sky before he dropped. The R1 is a fucken killer of a weapon. Gav's eyes were so used to the bush, that he could see the okes across the river, manning rifles and machine guns behind their cover of camouflage and bush. He took careful aim with his FN and picked out five okes on four machine gun nests. The lieutie was also firing, and each time he or Gav hit an oke he tuned, "Dead centre".

'All the firing made it possible for the okes in the Elands to start locating and shelling the okes on the ridge across the river. One by one they put out the mortar nests using their ninety-mil cannons . . . also a fucken accurate weapon. You can choose whether you want to hit the top, or the bottom, of a forty-four-gallon drum at a distance of one kilometre.

'Next thing, a heavy calibre gun downstream started firing high explosives around old Gav's tree. He could do fuck all, so he stopped firing and played dead, and then when they lifted their fire towards the armoured cars, he and the lieutie killed all five of the okes. Gav used up three magazines with selective fire. He was basically having to be a sniper . . . and an accurate sniper is fucken demoralising.

'All of a sudden five black enemy troops appeared from the bushes, their rifles at the ready. They all dobbed Gav. Everyone froze. He was surrounded. He stood up with his hands raised and made as if to offer them his rifle, and started talking to them in Italian . . . old Gav's family is Italian – his surname is Pizzoni or something. Anyway, because he had no recognisable uniform on, the okes were a bit confused and he was pointing and making all kinds of talk like he was a part of their whole setup. Maybe they thought he was Cuban. They were really nervous and a bit confused, so Gav pretended that he was getting on with things and he just turned away and ducked behind a tree. They disappeared into the bush towards the river. He fired a few rounds in their general direction but he didn't scheme that he got any of them.

'The okes in the armoured cars didn't know that the landmines had been removed, so they stayed on the ridge giving the enemy shit with their mortars and ninety-millimetres. Under cover of this fire, Gav managed to organise a withdrawal. He grabbed the lieutie and ran along a donga beside the river. They found the other engineers along the way, and they all moved along this donga in a buddy-buddy system. The sand in the donga was fucking hot – like Durban beach in December ... only hotter. Gav and the lieutie ran ahead to give covering fire while the other okes scrambled past and did the same for them. Eventually they got back to the armoured cars, and true's God ... not one oke was hurt or wounded!

'They put all twelve of the mines that had been unearthed, into the knocked out Eland. Then everyone withdrew to about two kilometres behind the knocked out car.

'Gav, with his driver and gunner, was given the task of destroying it. Just over half a K from the damaged car, they closed the turret and fired at it with their cannon. It exploded like a bomb. Each mine contained twenty-five kilograms of high explosive! Nothing was left behind for the enemy.

'The okes behind them reckon they heard the barrel of the ninety-mil gun from the wrecked car growling and humming as it passed high above them, twisting madly through the air.'

Silver Cross

'Ja, so anyway, that's what happened to Gav.

'So, six months later they're all at Rundu and a mate comes up to Gav and tunes, "Congrats, china, you're getting a medal ... for that scene at the Lumege river. Remember ... the ambush."

'Old Gav remembered OK, but, you know ... like, a lot had happened since then. He'd lost a few good mates.

'Anyway, next morning the wheels rolled again. They had to take up a defensive position on the border near Fort Doppies. From there they went out on patrols in their Eland.

'So Gav and the okes are pulling into the camp one evening, when his name is called. He goes to see the captain who tunes him to pack his kit and to smarten up because there's a chopper coming to pick him up first thing in the morning. "You're going to Pretoria, corporal. They're giving you a decoration or something."

'Old Gav reckons that everybody else seemed to know more than he did about all this. So, anyway, next morning the chopper pulls in and he's taken back to Grootfontein, and then by Hercules to his regimental headquarters in Bloem where he's royally welcomed . . . all the war hero stuff . . . toasts in the officers' mess . . . his contribution to "land en volk" and all that.

'All this time Gav's thinking that he didn't do it for "land en volk". He wasn't too sure which land and people they meant anyway. He did it because he wanted to help his mates . . . real people that he knew . . . and because he was afraid . . . and because he wanted to survive . . . and . . . he didn't know what else to do in the situation. So he schemes that since the okes are in such a generous and flattering mood, he'll ask them for some time off . . . to check his folks at home. They give him a pass and a train ticket to Durban.

'At the Bloemfontein station, the train that he's booked on starts heading for Kimberley. He doesn't realise that it will turn around beyond the station before heading east to the coast. He panics . . . he wants to get home . . . so he goois his kit through the window, and his rifle, and jumps. He rolls along the gravel beside the track. His uniform is filthy and he's scratched and bleeding, but he gets his kit together and starts hitching to Durbs.

'The first oke to stop is driving a Merc, and he offers Gav a lift to Howick. OK, it's not home, but at least it's Natal. As Gav is putting his kit on the back seat, his flash-hider rips the soft roof upholstery of the oke's car. This is a larney Merc, hey. White diesel with soft cream upholstery. He feels really shit, but the oke is cool and tunes, "No, nooit, don't worry . . . it's OK man. It's okes like you that are defending the country."

'Of course, by the time the oke heard why Gav was going home an' all, he couldn't do enough for him. He took him all the way to his front door in Zululand.

'Home . . . was home. He kipped late in a soft bed with sheets. Chatted with his old nanny from when he was a kid. Jolled with his dogs on the lawn. Lay under the old trees checking the sky . . . remembered those who would never be coming home . . . looked at his old school uniform and the books in his room . . . his pellet gun . . . and the Zulu spear given to him by Dumisani.

'He was only nineteen, but he felt like his childhood belonged to somebody else.

'He chowed bacon and eggs, and went to check his chick. She was pretty glad to see him because she knew that he had been through some shit. You see, they'd agreed before he left for Angola, that every time he was involved in a contact he'd put a cross down on the page, like a kiss. Some of his letters had many kisses and she could tell that he was in it . . . big time. The censoring officer, if the oke could remember one letter from another, would have thought, "Fuck. This corporal Pizzoni is a moody bastard . . . one week full of kisses . . . the next . . . fuck all."

'The family all drove to Pretoria together for the big day. Gav was given the Honoris Crux Silver, a decoration that was awarded to okes who were unusually brave. Gav and I used to try and understand the definition that was used. It was put in a book. I remember some of the actual words, something like . . . performing exceptional deeds of bravery while in great danger.

'Bands played. There was a huge parade and Gav only looked smart in his formal gear, all his badges shining, and his shoes. He stood to attention while the Minister of Defence, P W Botha, pinned the medal to his jacket. On the left side . . . where the heart is supposed to be.'

Carrying the Cross

'When he got back to Rundu, the okes were out in the bush, but there were a few okes still in camp. Same dust paths, same handball net, same smell of petrol. Then he checked a mate of his cleaning the swimming pool, and he felt glad to be back. He went up to the oke and tuned him howzit, but something was a bit off, like. The oke seemed distant . . . he didn't smile. Gav asked how the okes were, and the ou tuned him, "No, everyone's cool . . . we're just carrying on . . . doing our jobs. This is my job today . . . cleaning the pool . . . a good graft . . . not too strenuous."

'When the okes pulled in from patrol that evening they all chirped about the "hero" returning, but no one treated him like before. No one really spoke to him or asked him about his trip to Pretoria. It felt like a divorce. Some of the okes were tuning . . . like, "Why should one oke get singled out when everybody was in the action?" One of the gunners read Gav's story by a journalist . . . in some military mag . . . and he tuned that the story was a load of crap . . . and he used to say, "Gavin was not the only star of the fucken show."

'You check . . . all the okes had suffered through many things together. Gav even felt that they had a right to be jealous. He started to feel guilty.

'Old Gav got quite depressed, and then he got pissed off, tuning himself, "Hey, I didn't ask for this. Nobody consulted me . . ."

'So, one night, when all the okes are in camp, he goes up to the OC to ask if he can speak to all the okes, formal like.

'He got up and tuned them. At first they were pissed off for being called together by him, thinking, "Who the fuck does the ou think he is now . . . this fucken medal has gone to his head." But when he tuned them his story, the okes changed towards him. The divorce was over.

'He tuned that it was unfair that he had been singled out. He tuned them something like – "There are stacks of okes who could just as easily have been singled out. I didn't ask for this medal, so I want you all to know that I hold this medal on behalf of all of you . . . all of us, really . . . for the okes who aren't with us anymore . . . and for all the many times that we stepped in it and we helped each other get out. I hold it on behalf of all of us who volunteered to become 'American Mercenaries'" . . . and here he laughed, "The okes whose only contact with America was from thirty thousand feet when they dropped us a crate of M-16 rifles and daggers."

'Ja, they laughed because they remembered their surprise when they removed the 'chute and opened the crate. Of course they weren't allowed to take anything. But they often used to wonder where all the knives and guns had ended up. They kind of vanished.'

On Automatic

Major Rutling was not pleased to have the seven back at Ruacana, so he looked for tasks which would remove them once more from the vicinity. A Transvaal regiment was camped further south and they were in control of an airstrip. C company DLI was in fact supposed to fall under the command of this regiment while in the Ruacana area, but by keeping themselves apart, they were able to avoid dancing to a Transvaal tune.

Anyway, when the seven appeared at breakfast on Monday morning, they were called by Major Rutling and told to get their gear. They were being sent to do special duty on the runway below the Transvaal camp.

On arrival at Regiment Noord-Transvaal the seven were given a tent alongside the runway and briefed on their next assignment. They were to drive along the dirt track beside the runway as planes were taking off at night. Their vehicle was to be an old Eland armoured car, and they were to work in shifts. This old Eland, actually a Panhard 'Noddy Car', had no cannon, only an old defunct mortar, which they used for storing their cans of beer.

The idea was that in driving along the runway they would chase off any would be ambushers – those who might try to set up a rocket launcher or shoot at the planes as they took off in the night. Also, they were to drive off any animals which might have wandered onto the runway. Once again the seven were being marginalised by their special duties.

The seven discussed their task and Manie felt that it was a stupid idea, especially after they'd tried to keep up with some of the Lear jets which soared up into the night sky, leaving them batting along beside the runway in the old Noddy car which backfired with some frequency.

One night as they were driving down the runway with the searchlight on, they saw buck grazing in the scrub beside the track. Some were even crossing onto the runway. The buck were blinded by the light and stood staring into it.

It was boredom and beer which led to the idea that they should shoot a buck one night. The plan was to pull the trigger while the armoured car was backfiring so that no one would hear the shot. At the big camp, the one with generators, typewriters, movies and night lights, all that would be heard would be the old Eland backfiring.

'I'm lekker on,' said Deon. 'Let's crack it.'

They lurched onto the runway without lights, three of them in the cab and the other four riding on the outside. The old bus usually started to backfire after changing into third gear, so Neil kept it rolling gently until they were within range of the buck. They turned on the searchlight. There they were, ears alert, looking up into the glare. Neil put his boot down and the engine farted to keep up. It backfired loudly, once, then twice, and then Neil heard the loud and frenzied sound of a whole series of backfires which bore no relation to the compression of the engine.

It was a weapon firing on automatic.

Eddie killed the searchlight, shouting, 'What the fuck are you doing, Manie?' The firing stopped. Then Neil heard Eddie shout down to him, 'Drive, Neil, drive! Manie left his fucken rifle on automatic!'

All around them the night fell silent. The generators at the main camp were cut simultaneously. All lights went out. Some illumination flares arced over the runway, drifting down behind them near the distant wire. The Alouette helicopter at the main camp with the air-to-ground searchlight was starting its engine.

'Oh fuck, we're in the shit!'

The seven raced back along the runway without using their headlights. They had no sooner arrived at their tent when the lights of jeeps, Landrovers and trucks came bearing down upon them.

'What the fuck happened? Who was shooting?'

The seven had had no time to think, before they heard Manie's voice.

'I saw what I thought were terrorists advancing towards the runway. I opened fire immediately. I used automatic because they were widely spread. I would estimate there were about five of them.'

He had been raucous and fairly inebriated when they'd left for the hunt, but he seemed pretty sober and convincing now.

An intelligence officer came into the tent and they were all subjected to deep questioning. Despite the smell of beer on his breath, Manie's explanation was pretty credible and the seven needed no prompting to adopt it forthwith. After all, Manie was the boss.

Officers and men were caught up in the excitement. A lot of people began to feel justified at being there. Others felt the suffocation of fear. All this heavy equipment and days of boredom had found a focus.

The truth had to be withheld lest the seven be lynched for making a fool of the military. DB for all seven would have been on the cards. For sure.

For four days patrols moved out from the airfield. There were so many footprints and beer cans in the bush beside the dirt track along the runway that a group of flame throwers were called out to burn the scrub and bush for about thirty metres. There were thousands of buck spoor in the area. Not a single buck was found dead or wounded. Manie had missed.

Trackers were brought from Ondangwa. Choppers flew about scouring the area, but the 'terrs' had just vanished.

Three days later, the manne were sent back to Ruacana.

Bushman Trackers

The Bushmen got drawn into the war like everybody else in the vicinity. It's difficult to ignore a war. People change. The night changes. The scenery changes. Vehicles arrive with cargoes of men in uniform. Mechanical dragonflies come and go. Generals, producers and directors carry clip-boards and salute each other with manic formality. Moustaches are as varied and exotic as the parrot family.

The Bushmen – now called the San – were hunter-gatherers, and were called in to help the SADF because they had an intimate knowledge of the land. They could track a man or an animal across any terrain, reading the signs – the tiny scratchings and scrapings, decisions made in haste, the weariness and fear of the fugitive.

Bushman trackers never got lost. Their bodies were slender and well muscled, and they could run for miles at a fast pace and on a minimum of water. Our tracker stopped after leading the convoy for about fifteen kilometres in the heat. He took a drink of water from a water bottle and lit up a Texan plain. His lungs must have been powerful, because he took only about four deep and lengthy drags at the cigarette and it was smoked ... finished. Then he looked along the road – his eyes were slits in his wrinkled face – and he jogged off again.

The reason we had a Bushman tracker with our section was because of a blunder that occurred one night soon after our arrival on the border.

We had set up camp for the night. The vehicles were hidden among the trees and sentries were posted. Two men were in a listening post about three hundred metres to the north. Once the noise from the camp had died down, these two began to

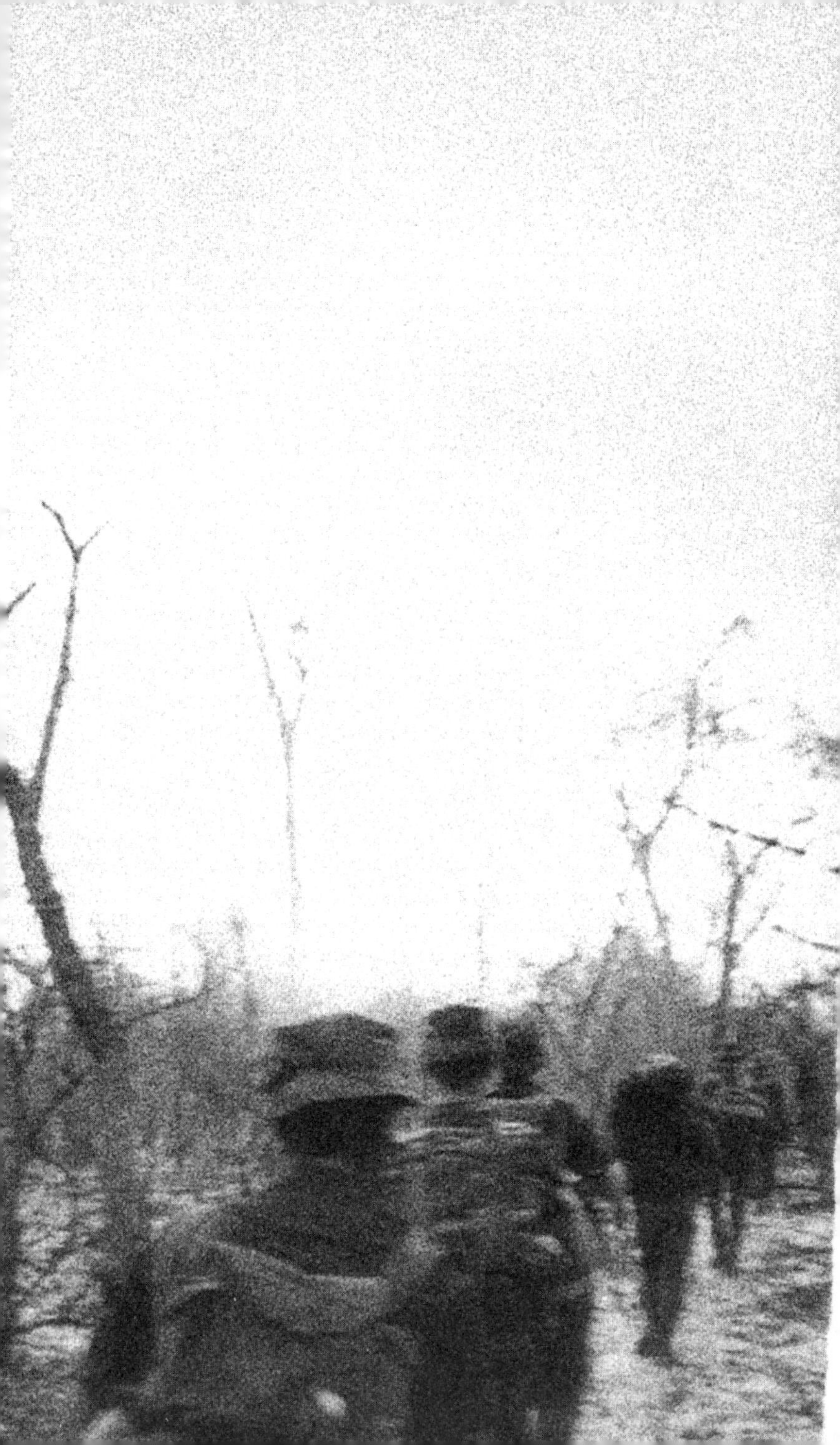

experience a change in the darkness. Bushes and trees moved and changed shape. They could hear living things breathing, slithering, or flying through the air.

Suddenly they heard a heart-stopping sound. Human movement! A heavy boot in the sand. They held their breath, and scanned the darkness from right to left, as they had been trained. They couldn't see anything. Then they heard it again. But this time they could hear someone out there leopard-crawling towards them . . . dragging equipment along the sand! Fear and panic started choking them. The more they listened, the more the horror of their situation became clear to them. They heard the enemy whispering. Something heavy was dropped out there . . . a rifle? They could hear enemy soldiers creeping forward along the ground, occasionally bumping a tree or branch in the darkness. They crept back as stealthily as their panic allowed and reported to the officer on duty. He could see their fear.

He crept forward with them, about a hundred metres or so, and listened. Yes! He confirmed their worst suspicions. They were about to be attacked. They moved silently to the camp and woke us, indicating that we were to keep silent and to take cover, pointing in the direction of the coming attack. There was a choking sense of collective fear. When everybody was ready, the officer fired a flare out in the direction of the abandoned listening post. Pop . . . we watched the hissing ball of flame swaying below its little parachute, and a ghostly white light illuminated the area. Shadows were black, and trembling. We had three minutes of illumination.

'Fire!' the officer shouted.

R1s, Uzis and LMGs, with a tracer round every four bullets, ripped the night open. Some fired on automatic, their rifles bucking madly. Others fired more selectively. We watched the graceful arcs of tracer trajectories, more magnificent than any firework could ever be. A light-show of fast flying fire. A few grenades were thrown and the explosions punctuated the chaos of noise and light. After about thirty seconds of sustained fire, the officer called out, 'Cease fire!'

Our firing died down sporadically until complete silence reigned ... an unearthly silence. Everybody's ears were ringing, and most were temporarily deaf. No fire was returned. We called out into the darkness. There was no reply. Just the maddening silence. Eventually the officer and a few men went out to investigate.

They returned, looking troubled and confused. We had killed about thirty head of cattle which were grazing in the vicinity. The officer realised that this mistake would cost us dearly in the eyes of the local people, so the next day he requested to have a Bushman tracker with our section whenever we went on patrol.

A Bushman's ears would have 'seen' the cow's hoof placed in the sand. Understood the weight and movement of the beast, the innocent muzzle chewing and pushing through the undergrowth. A Bushman's mind is still intimately entwined with creatures and creation.

The Bushman who joined us could speak a little Afrikaans, and he was glad of his posting. For him it meant work for pay – a chance to get on in the world. One night around the fire I watched him telling a story. It was firelight theatre. Enchantment. He mimed and mimicked the animals which were major role-players in his story. He became an ostrich with a long neck, eyelashes, and brisk movements. Then a chameleon, with its slow, deliberate movements, and its eyes swivelling independently. He even became the moon, and fed lizards with his fingertips.

Taking deep draws on a Texan, he showed me his SADF registration number and his bank book, crumpled and soiled on his yellow palm.

Dream On

He could smell the sea. It was fragrant. It was clean. Smooth, and coppery-pink in the cool morning light. The wind was a gentle westerly. Crisp sets of waves pushed towards the shore. Glassy tubes broke from right to left. It was a perfect day. He turned to his buddies and laughed. They were all smiling. They had the surf to themselves.

They waxed up on the cool, damp sand. The sea shells of the night lay scattered along the tide line. Small crabs scuttled across the sand and disappeared into their tiny holes. A bright blue butterfly was resting on a piece of driftwood, opening and closing its wings.

They paddled out together in the rip along the rocks.

He felt so alive as he breathed in the scented ocean. He was riding a long board, paddling on his knees. The water was cool. He leaned forward, taking deep strokes, pushing the board forward, leaving a wake in the smooth water. He raised his arms as he crested the swells which lifted the board under his knees. He got out the back without really wetting his hair.

With an almost surreal clarity, Spek could see the dark twizzler trees on the hills inland. He could see pawpaws, and the leaves of banana trees moving in the breeze. The Indians had terraced the sea-facing slopes into a patchwork of vegetable gardens, surrounded by cane fields. None of the workers were up yet to tend the fields. He could see rows of marigolds and he remembered the garland across the door of Shaku's blue corrugated iron house. He remembered the garland she made for him when they were young . . . he was fourteen, she was thirteen. Her father used to fish off the rocks on the weekends.

Shaku, short for Shakundra, with her thick, shiny black hair. Her earrings. Her neck. Her ochre skin and dark eyes. She was beautiful. The flame of the family shrine burned gently in the darkness as they loved each other. Her parents were out . . . it was against the law.

He called her Bambi because of the way she stood, and because her skin was so many different shades of caramel, copper and brown.

Suddenly someone shouted. Spek looked around to see fins churning the water. There was always that moment of doubt, *sharks*!? soon dispelled by the bobbing motion – dolphins! To be out there with them was always something else. Spek watched two of them surf glittering down the face of a wave.

Their grey-green bodies were held within the wall of water. They undulated in sheer exuberance. They leapt from the water and cut back ... out ... ahead of the closing curl. Huge, smooth mammals bearing no malice. They snorted and blew. The guys were all smiling and laughing. The dolphins were everywhere.

Spek took off on a wave and dropped down into his turn. The face was glassy and the dolphin within it kept alongside of him. He was smiling. So was the dolphin with its small good-humoured eyes. He could see the nicks and scars on its fins and body. Then he heard the tube catching up, its crashing, crunching sounds closing in fast behind him. Powerful juice started pouring onto his face and over his head. A wall of water took him under in a soupy turbulence, but the sound of the closing curl continued getting louder and louder. The wave kept churning. Something was wrong! He burst to the surface to see a brown canvas wall. The tent! But the sound was still there. In the fucken army! he remembered. But the sound of the water was still there! The wave was still closing out. It was real. He panicked. He staggered up out of his sleeping bag and stared confusedly into the sunlight. Outside, Deon was washing the major's Landrover with a thick canvas hose attached to a water hydrant.

The rest of the day in camp was difficult and depressing for Spek. He told Neil about the dream because he loved surfing too, but no one could really understand his deep sense of loss.

All Neil said was, 'Good one, Spek. Dream on.'

Fire and Water

When we first arrived on the border I used to wake early and collect firewood to heat my shaving water. In the coolness of the early morning with the sunlight palely touching the sand, I'd enjoy breaking the twigs and lighting the kindling of dried vegetation. I'd watch the fire take hold and fill the air with the fragrant incense of wood smoke. The flames blackened the outside of the firecup that I used to boil small amounts of water.

As we became familiar with the area, and daily routine was established, we found more convenient methods of heating water.

We found a four-gallon paraffin can and neatly trimmed the inner edges where the lid had been. It had been opened rather crudely, so we had to remove all the jagged bits of metal to prevent cutting our hands. We borrowed tools from the tiffies to get the job done. We lifted the tin above the fire on two metal bars that we supported on some large stones. We would collect a large pile of firewood and leave it near the tin, then each morning we'd fill the tin with water, place firewood underneath, douse the wood with petrol, stand back and apply a match. Woof. The petrol would ignite, and we'd stand around chatting while our shaving water heated. This fireplace of ours made an interesting still-life. The smoke-blackened can, with its various blacks and greys and silvery charcoal colours.

As time went by, we became more callous. We used to pour petrol into an old paint tin, place the tin under our water can, and light the petrol directly. There was no more wood smoke in the mornings, just the smell of petrol. It was easier to stroll over to the fuel depot and get a jerry can of petrol than to wander about collecting firewood. Besides, there was plenty of petrol, thanks to the generosity of the taxpayer.

I'd see our group, Phil, Butch, Eugene and Clive, standing around the petrol fire in the dusty mornings, some still wearing greatcoats from the duty of the night. Others were half dressed and half awake, talking, or sipping tea out of water bottle cups. A beat and homely atmosphere of domesticity reigned.

Recce

One evening, while we were waiting for supper, and sitting around among the mounds, trenches, bushes and tents, a Recce section called by. They dispersed immediately on arrival in the camp and as individuals entered the society as they found it. Although observing the rituals of rank, they retained the independence of assassins.

Members of the reconnaissance units were admired because of their skills in living off the land and their general hardiness, but they were also treated with reserve and caution. The story was that the first test for a recce was to be dropped one hundred and fifty kilometres behind enemy lines, preferably in lion country, with a box of matches and a hunting knife. Get back on your own ... and then, 'when you've done that, we'll see if you've got the guts to get through our training.'

Stories were told about their prowess in recon – laying ambushes, setting booby-traps and silent killing ... getting dressed for the show ... for night walking. Like actors, applying their black is beautiful face paint, and checking their props. No less superstitious than actors ... each man in ritual, checking his amulets and good luck charms ... preparing to walk with the angel of death.

In an enemy camp, on the other side of midnight, figures move silently. The fire-man stalks towards the centre of the camp, to the fireplace. He listens closely to the sounds of the night. Once he feels the moment of advantage, he moves forward. Crouching over the warm ashes of the fire, he is still listening. Then, silently, he starts to blow the flames into life.

By the time the fire gives warmth and light, every sleeping enemy soldier is dead. Sticky blood is being wiped from the blades of knives ... some smooth, some serrated. The fire-man grins and starts to heat the coffee water.

There were further tales of the taking of souvenirs. Of unshaven recce members returning from patrols with human ears dangling from their belts. A human scrotum placed over the gear knob of a truck. Rumour and imagination inflamed our minds.

Yet these are only men who have the task of reconnaissance, and, because they are first on the scene, they are often called

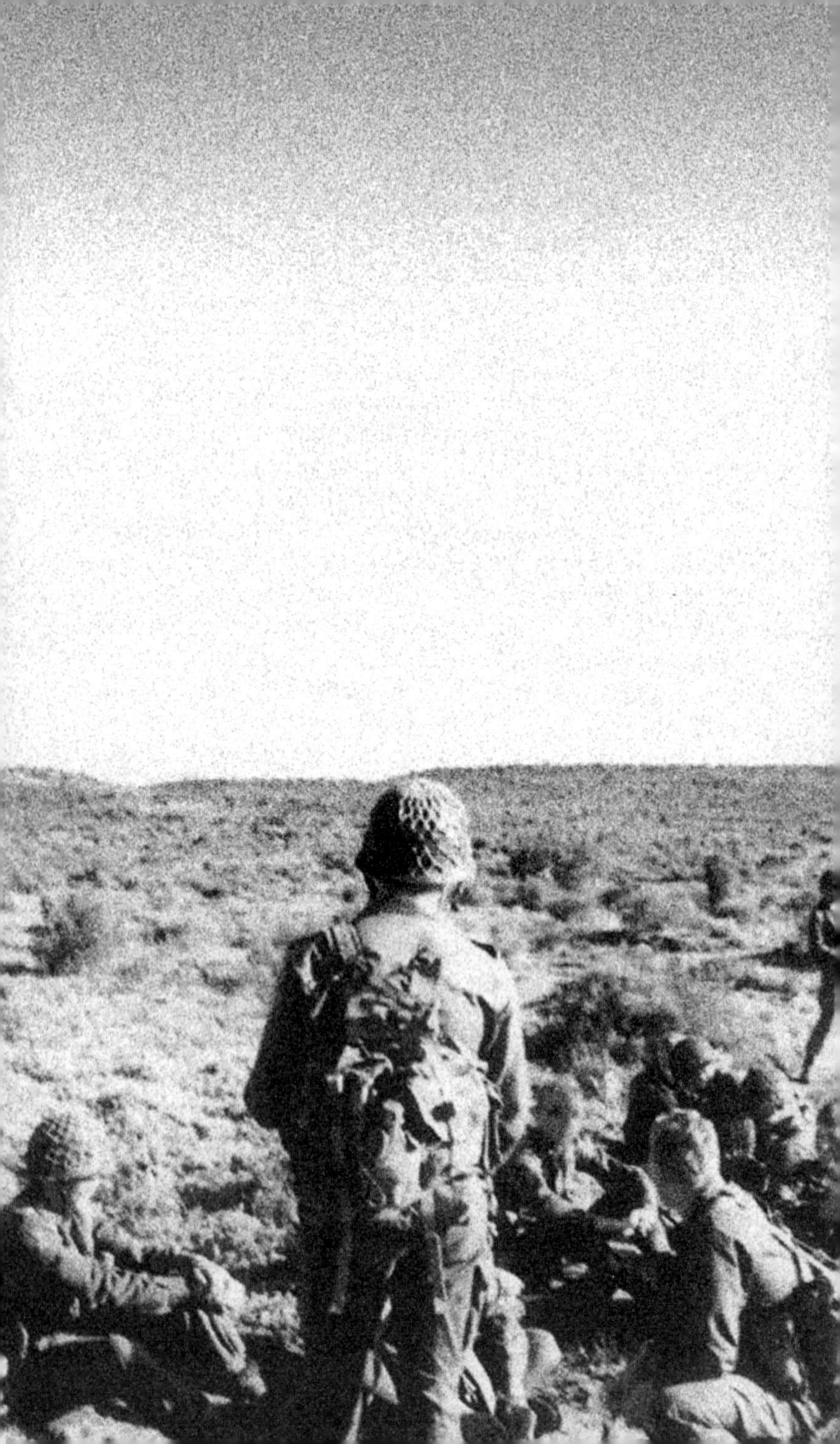

on to act with swift initiative. Do the dirty work. No one teaches them how to live with themselves, their memories, or their wives, once they return home.

The individual who came over to our section was a sergeant and he looked surprisingly neat in his uniform. He was thickset and vigorous, with red hair and a freckled skin. We noticed that his rifle was different from ours. It hung from his shoulder with the barrel pointing to the ground. The butt was made of metal and could be folded up to make the rifle smaller and more portable. We asked to see it – to hold it in our hands – and we noticed that it was lighter than our standard R1 rifles.

He disclosed little about his activities in the vicinity except to say that they were moving north soon and would be crossing over into Angola to investigate rumours of arms caches being stored in villages just above the border.

He joined us in the food queue for dinner, and I remember looking pensively at the large sheath knife he wore on his belt.

After supper he was gone.

Red Moon

Somehow the mood of the evening had been changed by the visit of the recce patrol. It had reminded us of the more horrific aspects of the war. Perhaps it was this that prompted Butch to bring me up to date with his correspondence with Keith.

Once more we were sitting in our candle-lit tent when Butch started, and once more I found myself in the twilight world of the psychiatric ward, living again in the consciousness of Keith.

That evening Keith felt calm, almost comfortable, for a while. Then he felt an agitation building up all around him as it grew dark. The patients in the ward were behaving strangely. Some went into themselves, a dark and coiled withdrawal. Some became snappy and impatient. Others, with tics or twitchings, twisted and jerked in an exaggerated way, almost caricaturing themselves. Some gibbered and moaned. Even the addicts, usually so confident and aloof, were changed, and displayed furtive expressions of fear. The atmosphere was charged.

Keith didn't know it, but it was the night of the full moon. That close, bright orb – that silent presence – that draws the tides and lifts the seaweed, loosened their frail grip on reality. Particularly affected were those who never spoke, who were in the place of twitchings and wide-eyed confusion.

An hour after dinner the psychic explosion took place.

One of the addicts was lying on his bed reading a *Surfer* magazine. He was moving his foot briskly from side to side as he tried to override the vibes. His big toe was sticking up, like the head of a hand puppet, and moving like a metronome. It was orchestrating a crescendo of emotion in the man in the opposite bed, who followed the movements of this toe with a pained fascination.

The reader of *Surfer* magazine didn't see the man crawling forward like a cat stalking a bird. He only knew the sudden horror and pain as the man grabbed his foot and bit deeply into his big toe.

A struggle followed with the patients trying to pull the attacker off, but his jaws were set like a steel trap. They pulled at his face and ears, but the attacker's eyes were bright with insane determination. The victim, in a frenzy of pain, punched at his face and kicked at his head with his other foot. The attacker didn't flinch, but blinked only momentarily with each blow. No one dared to prise open his mouth . . . they didn't want to lose their fingers.

The medics rushed in, followed by two nurses. At first they just added to the panic and confusion, but eventually they managed to sedate the attacker by means of an injection. The victim was taken through to casualty, his toe barely attached to his foot, and the attacker was taken to an isolation ward, blood dripping from his chin.

For a while, there was calm. Then some of the patients began to whine and moan. One of the addicts jumped up and began to rail against the medics and the nurses for locking him up with 'people like this'. He stirred up a group of patients who joined him in pushing the door closed. A few medics tried to prevent this, but they were beaten back with belts and fists. As the door slammed closed, the patients barricaded it with a table. They seemed to feel as though they had achieved something. Some were even smiling. Reason had fled the ward.

The military police were called. They came equipped with batons and forced the door open. A few quick, angry strikes and they were once more in charge. They put out the lights and left one of their members on duty at the door. The patients fell into a troubled silence . . . some slept . . . others pulsed with confusion.

As a nurse made a final round, looking at each patient in turn, Keith saw a tall, gangly figure in pyjamas moving towards her. The figure whispered hoarsely to the nurse, 'Sister . . . I also need a injection.' He moved closer, his mouth close to her ear. In a strange voice, cowed yet menacing, he said, 'I'm a nocturnal cat. I never sleep.' She obliged him with a shot in the rump. The nocturnal cat stalked off to bed.

The full moon shone down vertically on the corrugated iron roofs of the hospital and on the fly-screen door of the morgue, isolated in a circle of gum trees.

Morphine Sister

Being back with C company after their long absences, the seven were treated like the strangers they were. No one made any effort to include or assimilate them. It was fine by them. They had nothing to prove.

Sitting around a fire one night, Neil managed to get Manie to start talking about some of his own experiences in the operational area and in Angola. Manie's talk was terse and to the point. He didn't waste words.

'Ja, we were coming around this corner in a valley when heavy gunfire stopped the first armoured car in the convoy. The shells penetrated the armour-plating and took out two okes. We tried to reverse but someone else got hit before we could take ourselves out of sight.

'Through binoculars we checked out where the fire was coming from. It looked like someone was holed up behind a whole lot of old boxes in the trees on the other side of a dry water pan. Then we checked the weapon's barrels! Fuck me. It was a Russian twenty-three-millimetre double-barrel anti-aircraft gun! We had nothing to match the fire power of a weapon like that. The thing could comfortably shoot up to eight hundred rounds per minute per barrel and it could penetrate twenty-five millimetres of armour-plating. Some okes got on the radio and called for a ninety-millimetre Eland to come up and get rid of the gun.

'Then, and you won't believe this, we check that the gun is being manned by a chick! True's God. This black chick is handling the gun like a mamba! Holding up the whole fucken convoy.

'Well, we shot at her with rifles and rocket-propelled grenades, but she kept her head down. She was well dug in. We gooi'd the few mortars that we had. One burst near her position. I was sure that she took a hit, but she kept firing. The slightest movement and she opened up. She kept us down for nearly two hours before an Eland arrived and started shelling her position from the back of the convoy. We could more or less talk the shells onto her position. The fifth shell exploded near her gun emplacement and the firing stopped. We waited a while. Fired at her position with rifles. No return fire. I stood up in full view. Still no fire. We went to see.

'The shell had exploded in front of her position. Thousands of bits of hot shrapnel sizzling through the air. A chunk of metal hit her in the thigh and came out just below her right shoulder blade. It passed through her lung and probably through a whole lot of her organs. We found her lying on her side, still trying to breathe. Little bubbles of blood were coming out the hole in her back. Even though she was dying she checked us out with hatred. Then she lost consciousness and died. The two hot barrels of the twenty-three-millimetre were pointing up at the sky.

'We checked out her setup there. All she really had to protect herself from our fire was a whole lot of old ammo boxes and supply crates, although the gun itself had been really well dug in. We couldn't believe how many wounds she had. On her arms and neck there were deep holes where bits of her flesh had been nicked out by bullets and shrapnel. These wounds had been received during the battle, not from the last shell that got her. She had a lower leg wound that must have been about three days old. Her water was running low. All around her on the ground were ampoules and discarded syringes. She had been shooting up with morphine to get through it.

'We reckoned that she had been pretty badly wounded some days previously and that, unable to walk, she had decided to man the gun there and give her chinas a chance to get out of the area.'

'Do you know what her name was?' asked Spek.

They all turned to look at him quizzically.

'I looked at her ID document, but I can't remember what it was ... some Angolan name ... a bit like ... Portuguese to pronounce ... ag, I can't remember.'

'Well, I've got a name for her,' said Spek.

'Ja?' said Manie, looking sceptically at this surfer cum dreamer.

'Her name is Marianne ... because she was faithful!'

No one quite understood, even though they quite liked the name, and some remembered Marianne Faithfull, the singer.

'We don't get it, Spek. Why Marianne?'

'Sister Morphine?' Spek prompted.

No one knew what he was talking about, so he had to resort to prosaic explanation, once again realising that his world of music, movies and dream surfing was not the collective reality.

'A couple of years ago, Marianne Faithfull, the singer, did a number called *Sister Morphine*, so that's where the idea came from.'

'Dream on, ou Spek,' said Manie.

'Ja, I remember her,' said Neil. 'She did that Stones number *As Tears Go By*. Wasn't there also a whole scandal about her being busted with the Stones and having a Mars Bar up her twat?'

'Oh ja, I remember,' said James.

'I wonder if it was wrapped or unwrapped,' mused Eddie.

'What's a Mars Bar?' asked Manie.

'It's like a Bar One, only a bit bigger,' explained Neil.

'Jeez, I wonder why she had it stuck up there anyway?' said Spek. 'I always thought the Stones were stoned at the time and into some kind of kinky sex trip. I always used to imagine Mick Jagger's lips catching a bite at the other end. The bastards probably have to work out new things to do with all the groupies they've got.'

'Anyway, here's to sister Marianne . . . Chipinga,' said Eddie, lifting his beer can in salute, 'one of the bravest chicks I've ever heard of.'

'Was she a big chick, Manie?'

'Ja, she wasn't small. She wasn't fat. She had a dark skin, almost black, and black, black eyes. She was strong. I'll never forget her expression when she checked us out. We were the enemy and she hated us. Her eyes were fierce, man . . . woes. She never gave up. She just left her body behind . . . that's all.'

Manie's Secrets

'Another time,' continued Manie, 'we were on patrol right on the border. It was fucken hot, so we used to lie low during the worst part of the day, and move at first light and in the evening. Some officers tried to make us march at midday, but after a few okes had to be casevaced out because of heat fatigue, the tits learned the lesson. These cunts from the city think that you have to fight like a routine machine. They depend on a system. They don't know how to think with their guts.

'Anyway, we were coming to the end of an early morning march, and were about to drop our gear and relax for the day, when we were fired at. We hit the deck but rapid, and started crawling back towards some trees nearby. The bullets were mowing the grass. We returned fire, but we couldn't see the ous shooting at us. No one took any hits. We kept firing away. Eventually we stopped. No return fire. My ears were singing.

' "Fuck, what now?" I'm thinking. Then I scheme, "No, we have to track and catch these bastards." So I take three okes with me. We leave our kit and we go for it, keeping low, but moving fast in the heat. They didn't expect us. We chased them for about two hours. And we killed them.'

The manne were a little surprised at the sudden ending to the story. They wanted more excitement and detail, but Manie had finished. They noticed how his tone of voice had changed from the excitement of 'we chased them', to the quiet, almost ashamed resignation of 'and we killed them'.

But they knew not to push Manie. They could see the hauntings in his eyes. They'd all heard the other story about Manie which was usually only told when he was well out of the vicinity. Perhaps it was only rumour. Some time back, when he was still with the SADF, they'd just got back from a raid in which Manie and his manne of the time had made four kills. They were utterly exhausted and traumatised and one of them had been wounded. Instead of resting, they started drinking and ended up at a shebeen cum Cuca shop. Apparently an officer found Manie in the back, on his knees in front of some black woman. Her shirt was open to the waist and she was cradling Manie's head to her breast. They reckon he was crying. They had to pull him away from her.

Snakes' Tails

The equestrian camp was quiet in the midday sun. The horses were resting in the shade and the men lay under canvas. Suddenly a high-pitched scream cut across the drowsy silence. Jan and Tony, alias 'the Worm', jumped up and moved quickly to investigate.

In one of the police tents there was a hubbub. They went inside. A tall cop, at least six foot six, was holding a spade and pointing to the sleeping bag spread out on his bed. As they looked at it, they could see the thrilling movements of a long, strong snake inside the bag. Tony was immediately concerned as to whether the tall cop might have been bitten by the snake.

'No, I was just lying down on my sleeping bag to have a bit of a kip, when I felt this thing move under me. I shat myself. I jumped up, and then I realised it was a snake. If I kill it now, it'll fuck up my sleeping bag – maybe even poison it inside.'

Jan told the cop that Tony collected snakes, and assured him that 'Worm' would handle it.

Worm folded over the open end of the sleeping bag so that the snake couldn't escape, and shook it down to the bottom of the bag. He could tell from its weight that it was a largish snake. He carried the bag out of the tent to his snake pit, which was outside the perimeter of the camp. There he shook the snake out of the bag.

It emerged angrily into the sunlight – a boomslang about five feet long. Wriggling, glassy, grey-green, and ready to bite. Its eyes were big in its blunt head. When no one continued to interfere with it, it withdrew into the shade where Worm's prized possessions lay – a black and yellow puffadder, fat and sluggish; a vine snake with a head shaped like a screwdriver, and patterned like a Persian carpet; and two dwarf pythons.

The cop was relieved to get his sleeping bag back, but when he was told what snake it was, his eyes grew large. Although the boomslang is a back-fanged snake and doesn't always manage to get a full grip when it bites, it is deadly. The venom breaks down the blood system and causes bleeding through the skin, the eyes, mouth and ears. Unless a victim has a blood transfusion, the chances of recovery from a full bite are nil.

Worm's reputation as a snake collector grew, and all snake incidents were referred to him. His nickname had been earned at school, where his interest in snakes, crawling things and blind worms, had attracted the attention of his schoolmates.

One night, on guard duty in a bunker, the guard heard a strangely heavy shuffling noise. He switched on his torch and there, about a metre from his boots, was a cobra, drawing itself up into a defensive posture, its hood swelling . . . its eyes in trance. The guard went and woke Worm.

Using one of his snake sticks, he held it down while the guard stood by with the torch. Then he grasped it behind the head. Its body moved angrily, but he held it firm.

'Just hold the torch here,' said Worm. He scrutinised its large copper-brown scales and pink underbelly, and concluded, 'Ja, what I thought. It's a spitting cobra.'

He dropped the snake into a hessian sack and tied it at the top. He thanked the guard and returned to his tent.

In the morning he put the snake into a cardboard box and placed a sheet of glass over the top. Everyone had a chance to tap on the glass or make sudden movements which would cause the cobra to spit. When the glass was dripping with venom, Worm decided it was time to put the snake into the pit. Before he did this, however, he decided to take some photographs with his Instamatic.

He let the snake go on the sand and crouched down behind his camera. He patted the ground, and waved at the snake, which began to pull itself up into the striking position. Worm continued provoking it. He moved forward, trying to get a close-up. The viewfinder on an Instamatic makes things look very far away, so Worm was seeing a small and distant snake going through its aggressive posturings. He kept provoking it until he heard one of the guys yell at him. When he looked up from his camera, the snake was very close – too close – and it gave him a full burst in both eyes. He cried out and leaped backwards, dropping the camera.

Jan caught the snake while Worm washed out his eyes with water and then with milk. He had to remain in a darkened room for three days.

The snake joined the others in the pit. Their tails hung from a small tree in the centre.

Resting in the Ruins

The manne were discussing *Exodus* again. They had all managed to read enough of the book to form opinions about the situation in Palestine.

'I was just thinking about that Jordana chick in the book, at Gan Dafna,' said Neil. 'I think . . . when she said something like "it's good to die for your country, but it's also good to have a country to die for"? Well, I was scheming . . . I have absolutely no interest in dying for my country. I mean, what is my country? I don't dig the government. I've always felt a bit ashamed about being South African . . . you know, the privileged whitey shit.

'I was with another oke in London one time, and we were with some Jamaican okes, and this oke – the South African – wouldn't tell them where he came from. He thought they'd hate him because he was a white South African. The Jamaican okes were amazed. They thought it was quite funny, but I could see that they felt a bit sorry for him.'

'Well, I've never been afraid to say I'm South African,' said Deon confidently. He was sitting cross-legged, flexing the muscles of his tanned torso.

'Oh ja? You've never even left the country. I reckon there's a few places on this planet where you wouldn't be so keen to admit it,' chipped in Spek with his eyebrows raised.

'Look, I'm South African. I was born in South Africa. End of story,' said Deon. Manie nodded in agreement.

'Well, if everything's so cool, how come the rest of the world is blocking us and protesting about apartheid?' asked Neil.

'It's the same as Israel. We're being persecuted like the Jews.'

'Ah, come on, Deon! Get real! The next thing you'll be telling me is that you are one of God's chosen people.'

'Well, I . . . we are. Who do you think built the country up to what it is now? Started all the farms? The Afrikaner . . . that's who! Check all the churches we built. Just like the Jews, we took a desert and turned it into something. The Afs are like the Arabs, lazy and jealous. They want to pull things down to their own level, or steal the clothes off your back. And the English . . . as usual . . . are there interfering. All the time I was reading the book I was thinking how much the Afrikaners are like the Israelis.'

'How can you be serious, Deon, man?' asked Neil in amazement. 'The Afrikaners were pro-German during the Second World War. They sided with the Nazis. The Nazis hated Jews and tried to exterminate them in gas chambers. This is the reason for the whole *Exodus* story in the first place! All this racial purity shit to do with apartheid – where do you think that comes from, hey, Deon? From the fucken Nazi philosophy . . . all that Aryan master race shit . . . that's where.'

'Kak, man. We Afrikaners have had to fight our own battles like the Jews in Israel. The English tried to break us during the Boer War. They killed thousands of women and children in their prisoner of war camps. That's something you don't hear them bragging about too often, hey, Neil? Actually, you ous probably don't realise that the English were the first to invent the concentration camp . . . not the Germans. Did you know that? Did you know that, Neil? They burnt our farms, but we're still here. And where are they now? Most of them have fucken run back to England where they make lank propaganda about how we must give everything away to the blacks.'

There was a pause. Then Spek spoke.

'You have to admit that the English have been major shit causers this century. I mean, just look at the way they interfered in Palestine.'

'Ja, and now they are interfering in South Africa. They're trying to do to us just what they did to the Israelis,' said Deon.

'Bullshit. They're just trying to improve the situation so that we can live in a civilised country, and not in a fucken cage that has a *Whites Only* sign on it,' said Neil. ' "Please do not throw food to the white men." I mean, if the Afrikaner is such a big fucken Christian, how come he won't mix with black okes? Either God's the Creator or he isn't. If he is, then he created everyone, including the Kaffirs, the Charous, the Chinks, the Yids, the Rockspiders, the Goffels, and the Pommies ... and cunts like us.'

Deon was unmoved by this appeal. He'd heard it all before.

'Ja ... that's your usual liberal bullshit. But there *are* people God has chosen. Some are going to heaven and some aren't. I read my Bible. I don't have to answer to any man ... only to God.'

'Well, I reckon I'd rather go to hell than to heaven,' retorted Eddie. 'I'd hate to spend eternity with some of the religious cunts I've met. Everyone else is going to hell except them. They can tell you which seats are booked for them up there. None of them are going to be too far from the stage ... they're gonna be right up front there with God and the band.'

Eddie laughed.

Neil ignored him and continued talking directly to Deon.

'So, what you are saying, Deon, is that your idea of heaven is some kind of a whites only trip. Apartheid with harps and haloes. Are you fucken mad or what?'

'No ... ye ... no ... of course heaven isn't for whites only. Look, man, all this integration shit is OK in theory but it doesn't work in reality. I don't want to live with kaffirs –' and here he paused and looked pointedly at Neil. 'And *you* know what I mean by a kaffir! ... And why should I?'

He was leaning forward in his intensity. He continued.

'OK, Neil, if you're such a big liberal, how would you feel if you went to hospital and the surgeon turns out to be a black oke?'

'So what? No problem. The oke's had to pass the same tests as any white oke to be a doctor.'

'Ja, but be honest, you'd prefer a white doctor. You just don't want to admit it. Or, howsabout you sit down in a Boeing and the pilot's voice comes over the intercom and you can tell he's black and he tunes "Eh, hullo, this is your pilot, captain James Makabulu. We will be taking off in two hours . . . but we have a small problem . . ."' His attempt to imitate an African accent trailed off. 'I mean, why do you think there are no black pilots? Because the okes can't fucken cut it . . . that's why. Just look at this recent raid on Entebbe airport. A couple of Israelis fly in, take over, and get back all the hostages. Idi and his boys didn't even see them coming.'

'Ah, Deon . . . you know . . . IQ is not determined by race. Just because you haven't seen black pilots and doctors, doesn't mean they don't exist. The rest of the world is not like South Africa, bro.'

'A good thing too. I mean check all the pornography and shit the people pump out in England. They even let their kids see it. They've got no moral backbone. They're lily-livered, man – decadent fucken wankers. I mean, look at America. The place is riddled with crime. But you look at South Africa . . . there's hardly any crime.'

'Ah, come on, Deon. Are you mad? Don't you realise that internationally South Africa's race laws are seen as a crime against the rights of humanity? Why do you think the churches are protesting?'

'That's easy. Look at which churches are stirring – the Anglican church mainly. Cunts like Trevor Huddleston and Alan Paton . . . they've brought politics into religion. Why? Because they're English liberals and they like to play the saint . . . you know, be the good oke to all the Afs. They've always got their English passports if the shit hits the fan. Their cocks are nearly pickled from dangling in the ocean for so long. And the blacks? The only language they understand is strength . . . power. That's all they respect . . . that's all they know!'

Before Deon could get as angry as he was becoming, Greg interrupted, holding up his large, bony hands.

'Look, you okes, we're getting off track here. Israel is not South Africa. The question was, "Do we have a country to die for?" '

'I suppose we do in some ways,' said Spek. 'Durban's my country . . . Natal. The rest you can keep. I dunno if I'd be prepared to die for it though. I mean, does Durban need me to die for it?' His raised eyebrows emphasised the absurdity of the question.

'I suppose we must believe something if we're here in the army,' replied James cynically.

'Balls,' said Greg. 'I'm only here because I was forced to be here. Get real. Do you think I'd be here voluntarily? Sitting here eating the shit they give us? Living in my underpants and these fucken boots? Fighting this so-called war for a fucken crooked government? I mean, would you like to have B J Vorster for a buddy? The oke's a cunt! Why do you think those riots took place in Soweto? Because cunts like him tried to force the black kids to learn in Afrikaans, that's why. You better hope that the blacks don't force you to talk Zulu if they get into power.'

'Fucken dream on. That'll be the fucken day. We've got the strongest army in Africa. We can bomb the townships . . .' said Deon dismissively.

'Well, cool, Deon, if you believe all that shit, but I'm telling you that I'll only feel like I have a country to die for when there's a fair and just kind of law in South Africa,' said Neil.

'It's to die for, doll!' squealed Eddie, in the fruitiest voice he could muster. No one laughed, but Eddie continued. 'Have you heard the joke about old Vorster and the little coloured oke at the gate?'

He felt compelled to lessen the tension and anger growing among the manne, so he didn't wait.

'Well, old Balthasar and some of his VIP chinas and ja-boeties are motoring along a dirt road to one of their grape farms in the Cape. They're all dressed up in suits and ties. Old BJ is wearing sunglasses, and one of his black hats . . . Nat hats . . . a cross between a diaken's top hat and a Viennese pork pie. Anyway, the Mercedes pulls up at a farm gate, and there's this little coloured oke sitting there in the grass. So one of the okes in the car tunes him to open the gate. "Maak oop die hek!"

'There's no "please" or "thank you" . . . you know, the usual "ek is baas" attitude. So the little oke just checks them out. He's not impressed. He's seen hoods before. These are just white ones. He's got an uncle in Cape Town who also has a fancy car, wears hats, and does crime. His mother and aunties warned him about these kind of okes. So he tunes them "Fok jou!"

'Ay, the okes in the car freak. This is heart attack stuff this. They can't believe that this little coloured kid, this fucken little klonkie, has just said "Fuck you" to the prime minister of South Africa. One of the okes in the back of the car is scheming that he'll have to kill this little cunt, so he starts opening his shoulder holster. The other oke in the front stops him. He's a bit liberal like . . . so he takes off his sunglasses and leans out of the window.

' "Hey, boytjie, do you realise that you are speaking to the prime minister of South Africa?"

'The little oke looks again at the oke in the back with the hat and the heavy jowls. Then he says, "Sorry, meneer, I didn't know who he was. If I had known that, I would have said Fok U!" '

They all looked at Eddie and laughed. Spek, whose Afrikaans wasn't good, didn't get the joke, so Eddie had to explain the punchline to him. It depended on knowing that Afrikaans has a respectful form of 'you', 'U', so in effect the kid had really said, 'fuck you, your highness'.

A pause was needed. Manie had grown ominously quiet, and Neil and Deon were still a little ratty.

Suddenly Manie spoke.

'The part I liked best in the book was when Kitty and Ari went up Mount Tabor with all those teenagers from the kibbutz and they all kipped up there on the ruins from all the previous civilisations. And they sang and all. And some of them went off alone. That's it, man. We're all just resting in the ruins of the past. I look after myself and I do my duty. What's mine is mine. What's yours is yours. End of story.'

RSM Gutridge

It was growing dark when Butch lit the candle in the tent. We were talking about how some guys are so completely fanatical about rank and military things. Then the name of RSM Gutridge came up. I had met a sergeant of the same name during basics in the '60s. He was one of our instructors. All I could remember of him was his snarling mouth and the pride with which he wore the bat's wings on his beret.

In Butch's latest letter from Keith there was an interesting tale about a man of the same name, though he now held the rank of regimental sergeant-major. As Butch began to talk in the candle-lit darkness, we joined Keith once more in the restrictive atmosphere of the psychiatric ward.

Keith had heard many stories about sergeant-major Gutridge, the RSM of One Military Hospital. It was rumoured that he was mad. The story was that RSM Gutridge had been a member of a recce unit, one of the first to reconnoitre Angola back in about '73. He spent a year in the bush. Some of the medics had seen his photo album, and they reckoned that he used to be big – a huge oke – but that after that year in Angola he was thin as a rake – skraal. He was divorced and often lonely, so occasionally he would invite some of the medics to his quarters for a drink or two. This usually ended up with him showing an eight millimetre film that he had in his possession – a kind of conspiracy movie – all about the communist plot to overthrow the western powers. The American voice-over was urgent and convincing. The camera panned over the dark, grainy images of mutilated bodies, surreal cities, crowds in the streets, flags, the hammer and sickle, and long ranks of marching soldiers. The announcer's voice made a last desperate call for the west to rally, before the film boiled with light bubbles and flickered to an end. They reckon that before TV came in the sergeant-major used to watch it every night in his room ... the soundtrack booming along the corridors.

The word was that he had cracked during his time with the Recce. The oldest medic there had some years previously spent an evening with the RSM who, well under the influence of alcohol, had confessed to his breakdown. Apparently what triggered it was not the night walking or the throat cutting, but that he had entered a dwelling in an enemy camp where he had come upon his comrades stomping their boots on the ground ... popping the heads of the babies whose mothers had been taken out in the fighting. It was the popping sound of those soft heads, their skulls not fully joined at the fontanelle, that had made him flip.

He never really recovered. Most times he seemed balanced, but if anything provoked his anger he became dangerously irrational.

The following morning Keith had occasion to meet the RSM. Early, before breakfast, he heard a loud, snarling, cutting voice ordering all the medics to assemble on the parade ground with their rifles. The patients watched through the windows. The parade of medics looked like a gathering of clowns who were intent on ridiculing the military. They had done so little parade ground work, that when RSM Gutridge started ordering them about the results were farcical.

He had a disparate bunch to deal with. Some of the medics were strong and manly. One was about six foot seven. Some were obviously gay, and some were the overweight and protected progeny of wealthy families. None of them was interested in drilling. Their antics as they tried to keep pace, stand to attention or about turn, made the RSM even more angry.

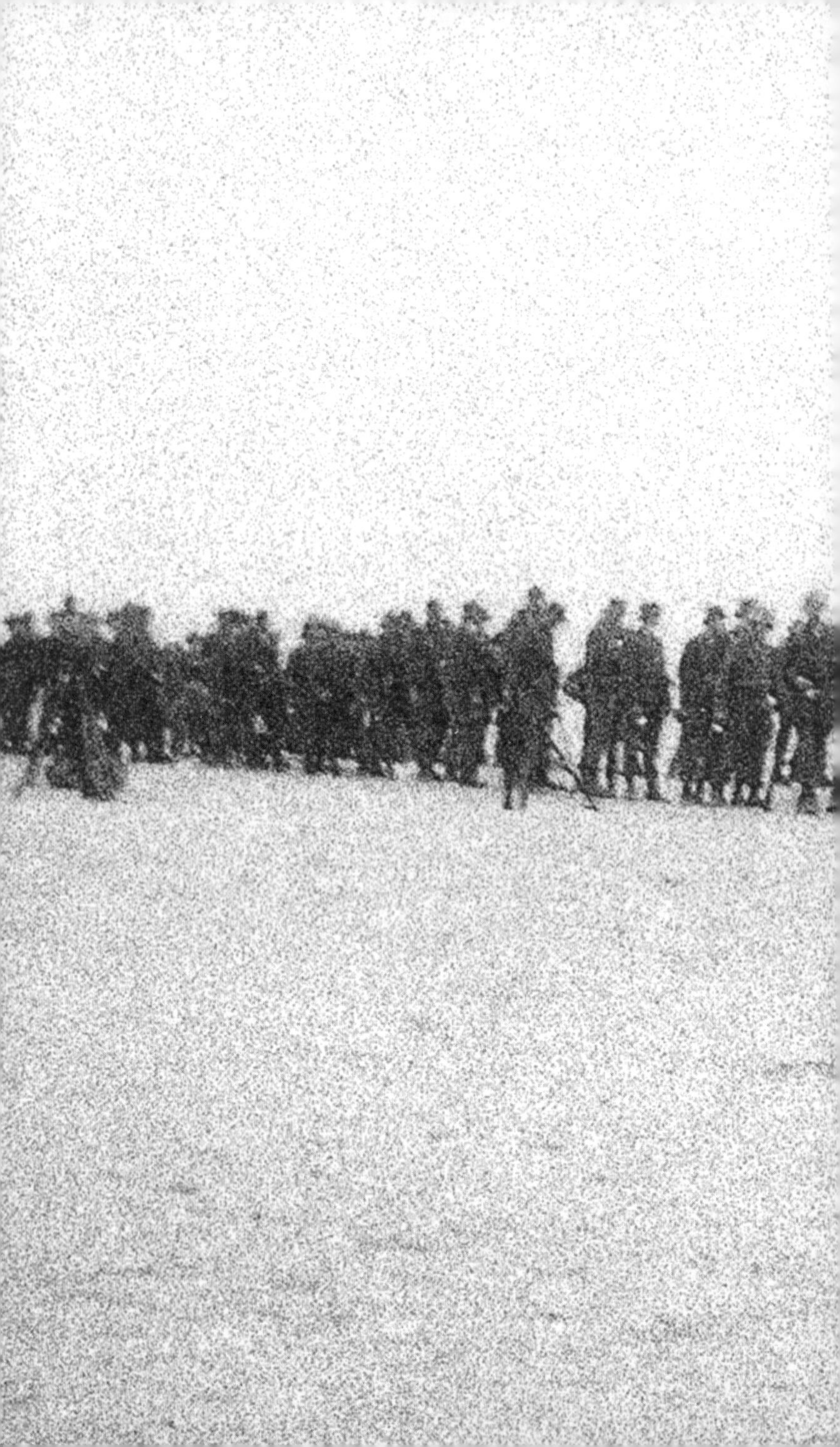

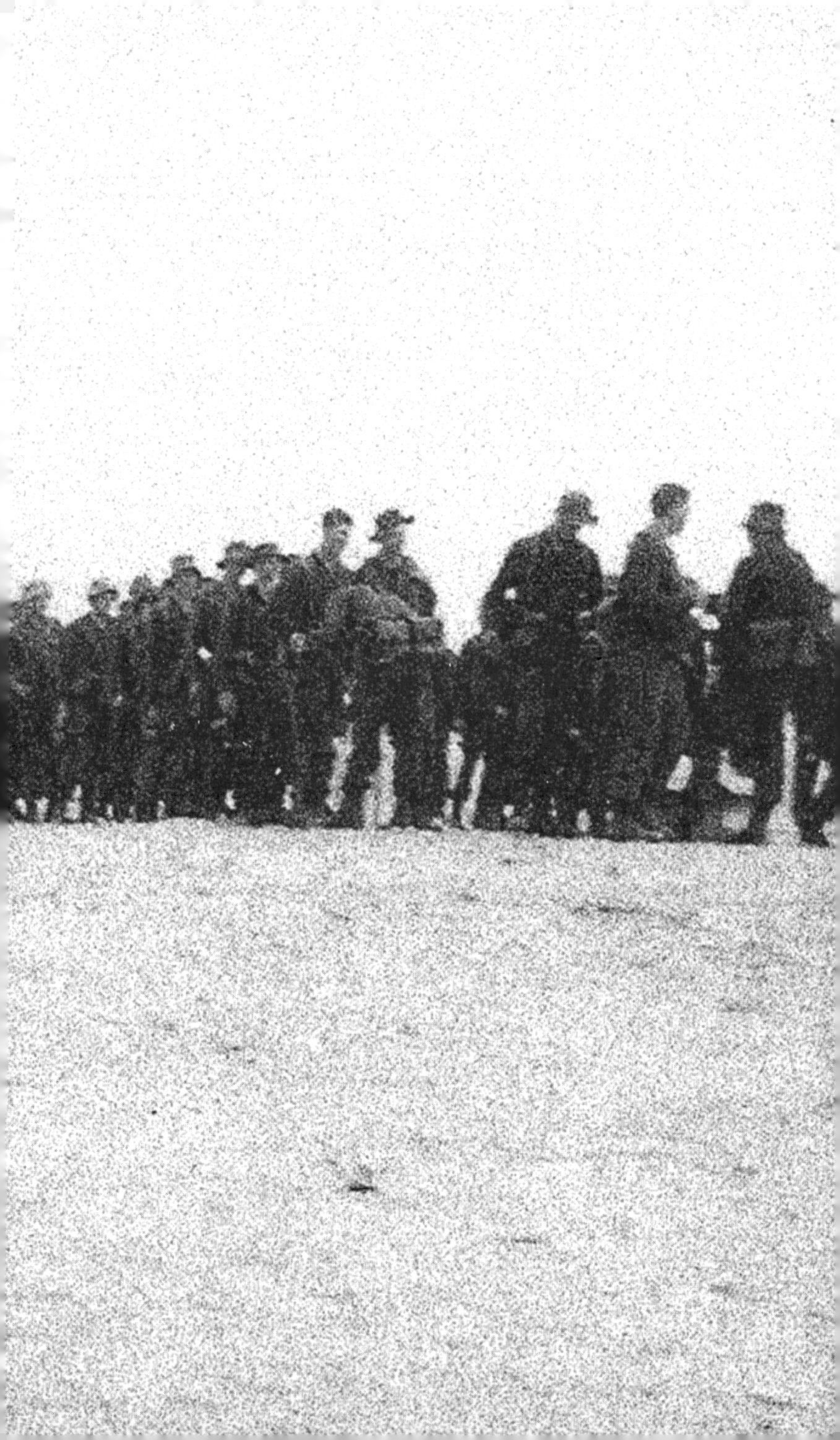

With his eyes half closed and his nostrils flaring, he announced:

'Last night there was trouble in ward 28. My septic medics were too bloody useless to handle the situation. The military police had to take control . . . again! You bloody useless bastards! But no . . . as if that wasn't enough . . . one of my men was seen gafooffling with a nurse in the intensive care ward!'

One of the medics (the envy of many) had been caught in the very act with a nurse on one of the empty beds in the moonlit gloom of the intensive care ward.

'Now, you useless bunch . . . I'd like to take you out of your little rat's holes here . . . out! . . . into the real war that is being fought by real men, while you just lie about smoking and doing women's work.

'Come with me and I'll take you into some real action . . . I'll lay booby-traps for you . . . I'll plant landmines . . . I'll set up ambushes for you . . . so you can wake up . . . and feel what it is to be a soldier.'

Needless to say, not one of the medics had any intention of accepting the RSM's raving invitation. It was a good bit of theatre, full of sound and fury, but it signified nothing.

Eventually the medics were dismissed for duty, and Keith could hear them clattering back to the wards, chatting and laughing.

At that exact moment an unearthly scream rang out at the end of the ward. A patient was taking a fit and was thrashing around in a mad trance. The medics and some of the patients started to clutch at his arms and legs to slow down his movements . . . to get him to lie on his side . . . to calm him . . . to restrict his oxygen intake by getting him to breathe into a brown paper bag.

While this routine struggle was going on the RSM burst into the ward. He was out of his mind with fury.

'What's going on?' he demanded.

They all turned to look at him.

'And you!' he said to the patient who was having the fit, 'Stand up! Stand to attention! That is a lawful command!'

The medics stood back. The patient seemed bewildered. His eyes rolled in his head as he tried to focus on this source of aggressive power, but he couldn't manage it. He got to his feet and stood there swaying, unable to gather his wits. The RSM charged him formally.

'I am charging you with malingery! Attempting to fake a fit! Arrest him immediately!'

With expressions of numb disbelief, the medics held him fast and 'marched' him from the ward. The RSM looked around at the patients on the beds with his nostrils flaring.

'Your time will come too . . . you fucking shirkers!'

The Boet's Second Letter

Neil received the second letter from Peter in early September, about a week before the regiment was due to strike camp and start the journey home. The letter had English stamps on it and it had been opened, but nothing had been scratched out or changed.

53 Solent Road,
West Hampstead,
London NW6
10th August 1976

Dear Neil,
Howzit, boet. As you can see we've made the move. England is a hard reality. The climate's depressing and the place is class ridden, but there is a broad spectrum of information available on the South African situation that would blow your mind. The things I've heard and seen only confirm that my decision to leave was the right one.
It's taking a long time for me to get residence here, but we're working at it. Julie is happier in some ways, but we're shitting-off in a single-roomed bedsit with the baby.

I have joined the Namibia support committee and I've picked up a few underpaid freelance jobs, putting together leaflets for SWAPO. It's been difficult earning money so far, but I'm making some connections.

Well, boet, we're on different sides now. No hard feelings, but wake up to the facts and get your arse out of there.

*Love and best wishes,
    from
        Peter, Julie & Paula*

On the Road

As their time on the border drew to a close, the manne became increasingly careful and superstitious. As much as they tried to avoid it, their minds were haunted by all the last days stories – horror stories, absurd stories – of tragedy that had ambushed soldiers in the last few days of border duty: a rock crushing a sleeping man's head as his buddy pulled away the ground sheet that they'd been using as a shade cover ... he'd forgotten about the heavy rock they'd used to hold the cover in place; last minute cuts, blindings and vehicle accidents, not to mention landmines and accidental shootings.

It was in the last days that Neil and Eddie found themselves on a mine-sweeping operation north west of the camp. The engineers were moving slowly along the road with their mine-detectors, covering every inch of the pale ochre sand, and listening through their earphones.

Neil and Eddie had the task of walking in the bush alongside the road, about one hundred yards ahead of the mine sweepers. They had to look for any signs or tracks through the bush which might indicate that the enemy had approached the road to lay a mine. Neil chose the left side, and Eddie the right.

The day was hot, and the bush was thick with thorns. Neil

looked back along the road. It was the colour of beach sand, and it shimmered in the sun. A few white butterflies fumbled and sailed in the dusty air. The engineers were a long way behind. The heat was oppressive and he had large sweat patches under his arms. He looked down at his hands holding the rifle. They were thorn-torn and dust-covered. He felt tired and thirsty. He decided to move closer to the road.

He walked along the edge of the road for a while and then sat down. He took a drink from his water bottle and shouted across to Eddie to let him know what he was doing. Eddie told him to get off the road, but Neil told him that he was just resting, and proceeded to draw pictures in the dust with a stick.

Eddie came up on the opposite side of the road and with an uncharacteristic urgency, shouted at his friend, 'Get off the road, Neil!'

'Why, Eddie? It's such a drag walking through this thorn bush.' He held up his hands to show his bleeding scratches. 'No oke is going to put a mine down on the edge of the road. Let's rather walk closer in.'

'Don't fuck around, Neil. Get the fuck off the road!'

Neil accepted Eddie's sense of danger and they both continued struggling through the bush on either side of the road.

Half an hour later they heard the men behind them shouting.

'What now?' Eddie muttered to himself.

'Come and see! Come and see!' shouted the engineers.

When they got to the mine detection party they saw the circular shape of a cheese mine in the dust on the edge of the road. Anti-tank. Twenty-five kilograms of high explosives.

Just three inches to the side of the mine were Neil's boot prints and drawings.

This story swiftly reached us at HQ in Oshikango, bringing last days horror stories that much closer to home.

Butch was deeply affected because he started talking about Keith again . . . and about how he had managed to get himself out of ward 28.

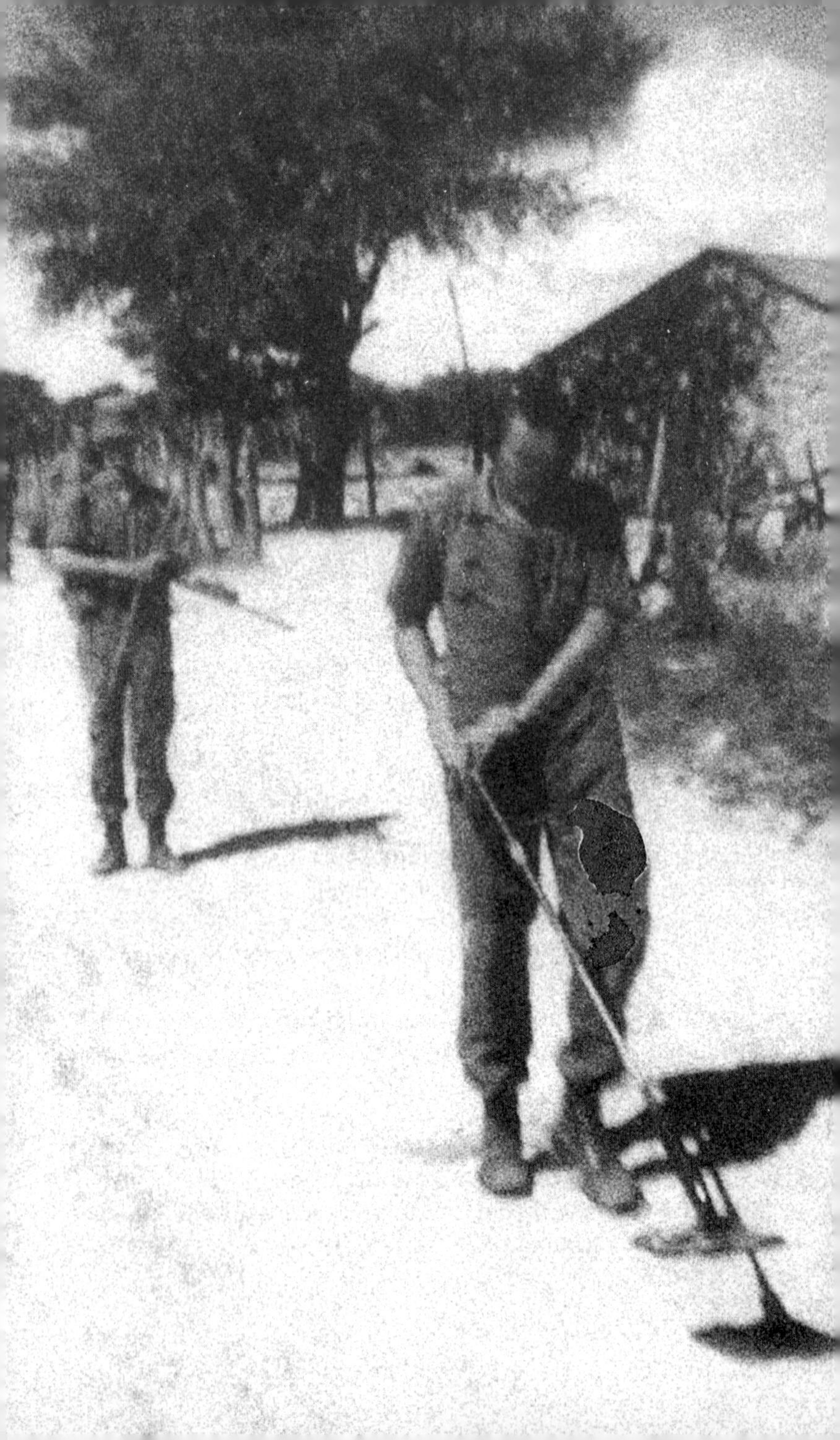

Under Observation

Keith had begun to find the psychiatric ward a very disturbing place, more disturbing than the normal military madness outside. His regiment was somewhere on the border and well into their time. He decided then that he would make every effort to get out and return to his unit. Only, this time, if he lost it again . . . he'd escape. He'd go AWOL and get the hell out of South Africa. No more ward 28. No more army. No more lies. No compromise.

He was kept under observation for a further two weeks before being considered fit to return to his unit. He realised that it was so much easier to get into ward 28 than it was to get out of it. Until you had discharge papers, you were in there for ever.

One of Keith's last and most humorous memories of ward 28 was of Papie, the night before he left.

The milk supply for each ward was collected from a depot at the head of the central corridor. A medic dispensed the milk in five-litre containers. Keith had been wandering about, visiting some of the casualties in the orthopaedic ward, when he came upon Papie standing in the milk queue. He looked like a buccaneer. His pyjama pants had been rolled up neatly to three quarter length, and on his feet he wore sandals. He was wearing his airforce coat, a blue, formal, three-quarter length garment. It had collars and straps, a belt and brass buttons. He had a bandage wrapped tightly around his head, and neatly placed on top of the bandages, was his beret . . . perched at a rakish angle.

At first Keith was concerned. He thought that Papie might have been given shock therapy or something.

'Jeez, Papie, what happened to you, man?'

He looked at Keith, and smilingly showed him his discharge papers.

'I've had a brain transplant, my china. They've taken out my army brain and given me back a civvy brain.'

Two weeks later, at Oshakati, a tired and dusty Keith climbed off the back of a Magirus with all of his kit and, reporting to the Ops tent, began the task of getting to where he was supposed to be. It was at that moment that he bumped into his old school buddy, Butch, who was delivering private Hollard's body for transportation to the states.

It was a coincidence of some note.

Casevac

Lying under trees in the heat, we heard the shaking, popping, heartening sound of a chopper. We all started to focus on it because it was coming nearer and nearer by its sound. The sound becomes ... loud ... the sound ... and the sight ... as the cab swings into view, chubbering above the tree tops, sun reflecting on the glass. Then the hovering above ... and then the landing. It's a magic scene. Takes over the head like rock and roll.

This time the engine was kept running after the chopper had landed. As we figured, it was a casualty evacuation. Someone had collapsed with heat fatigue while on patrol in the sun.

We checked out the loading of the stretcher ... into the chopper ... and the powering off into the sky.

Two sections from the equestrian regiment were following up on a spoor late one afternoon. As the first section crossed the road the lead horse stood on an anti-personnel mine. In the reverberating aftershock, with dust and smoke eclipsing the late afternoon sun, the section moved to recover. The horse was dead. Its front had been ripped away – both legs and chest gone. The rider was lying close to the remains of his horse in a sulphurous haze. The blast had mangled his lower leg and the weight of the falling horse had snapped his femur. They radioed for immediate casevac, but at that moment it began to pour with rain. They had to wait three quarters of an hour for it to clear, before the chopper could land. It was getting dark as they finally took off with the wounded man.

As they watched the chopper dip and power away over the treetops, they knew he had lost his leg. Reports from One Military Hospital confirmed this. His leg was amputated just below the pelvic girdle, leaving an inflamed stump of some six inches.

Three months later they heard that he had died at home. Of gangrene. Maybe some of the contents of the horse's bowel had infected the bone marrow? Maybe it was the delay caused by the rain?

Does it matter?

The Colonel Reads the Map

Selected by agencies beyond our volition, I and two others were chosen to be the colonel's bodyguards. Our task was to accompany the colonel in his jeep, and to move quickly from the vehicle at any place it stopped, and to cover him with our loaded automatic rifles.

The vehicles of the convoy were standing stationary along the road. The area had many tall trees and we moved along in dappled shade. Some two hundred metres distant we could see three African men, Ovambos, sitting on chairs in the shade of a large tree. A bicycle leaned against another tree. Some butterflies wandered and flickered in the sunlight. The men were talking and drinking beer. They were, of course, very aware of our presence, but did their best to pretend to continue their conversation in a natural way.

'I'll never understand these people,' said the colonel as he indicated towards the Africans under the tree. 'This country could be a paradise. It looks like a desert, but there's an endless supply of water under the ground. Some of the pools are so deep that divers can't find the bottom. All that's needed is to pump the water up into a system of pipelines and the whole bloody place could be irrigated. This area could be economically prosperous, with farms providing food . . . but no, these people just can't . . . just don't . . . just won't . . .'

The officer to whom he was speaking was an Afrikaner and he spoke English with rich and rounded r's. I could tell that he'd heard this kind of notion before, but after many generations of living in Africa, farming the land, working the mines, and finally joining the permanent force, he was not as confident that paradise could be established by another grand, technological scheme. He merely said, 'Ja, there is water here, but the people have their ways.'

As we were about to climb into the back of the jeep, the colonel requested that we find our position on the map. The map had been with us in the back so I produced the clipboard that held it. The colonel took it from me and gave it to the sergeant standing next to me.

'Can you pinpoint our position, sergeant?'

Not wanting to disappoint, the sergeant looked at all the lines and contours and dots indicating roads and boundaries, and pointed with his index finger at a point on the map. He sounded sure and confident. 'We're right here, sir.' The colonel craned his head forward and looked briskly at the position indicated by the sergeant's dirty finger.

'Jolly good,' he said. 'Carry on.'

Once under way again and bumping along in the jeep, the sergeant confided to me that he really had no idea of our position on the map. 'I just hacked it,' he said, smiling. We both pored over the map and eventually felt that we had found our position in relation to what markers or beacons we had seen. It was a hell of a long way from where the sergeant had indicated. *Oh well.*

The day dragged on with various stops at tribal offices, villages and Cuca shops, which were nothing more than corrugated iron rooms with padlocked doors. We listened to the colonel's ideas on how to establish paradise in South West Africa more than once because he shared it with several different officers, some of whom believed that the local people were just downright useless or degenerate, while others were more circumspect.

We must have driven for about three hours, a hundred kilometres maybe, when the colonel requested another finding of our position on the map. We had been taking note a lot more carefully and, ironically, this time we were pretty well at the spot which the sergeant had indicated previously. His dirty finger print was still visible. I wondered what he was going to do. He put his finger on exactly the same spot, and said, in a confident voice, 'We're right here, sir.'

Again the colonel craned his head forward and looked authoritatively at the map.

'Jolly good, sergeant. Carry on.'

The sergeant winked at me and flashed the 'min dae' sign.

Getting Out

We'd been on the border for just under three months when I began to take a serious look at my predicament. I had a wife and child at home, no job to return to, and I began to feel the pressures mounting. I responded by biting my nails, smoking heavily and thinking hard. I watched the flickering white wings of the butterflies gathered at the water-trailer. I wondered whether they were even aware of us at all. *Could they even see us?*

I figured that the best plan of action was to explain my situation to the adjutant, and see if he would let me leave camp about ten days before the regiment so that I could start looking for work at the beginning of September. In other words, as soon as possible. I wrote a motivation to Captain Browne and he supported my request.

So it was that I found myself, loaded with all of my kit, on a truck heading for Grootfontein. The journey took most of the day and we passed through the Ovambo gate in the afternoon. From that point on, we were no longer on danger pay. There were two others with me who were also on their way back home, and we all smiled at one another as we watched the gate receding in the dust. We were getting out.

Grootfontein, a vast, sprawling military depot, was the main artery for the whole SWA campaign. The driver asked us where we wanted to go, but we didn't know, so we drove about between the rows of tents and the vehicle parks until, by chance, we came upon our regimental paymaster's office. There we were directed to a group of tents which housed those who were waiting return passage to the states. We reported to the staff-sergeant on duty there, and he gave the official stamp to our release forms. He smiled when he saw the dates set for our return.

'I don't want to discourage you okes, but it's not so easy to get out of here. It's very difficult for me to find space on the planes or trains leaving here. Most have been organised for regiments, officers or special groups. Non-commissioned individuals don't get preference, unless of course your mother is dying.'

It was sobering news, but we were still in a jubilant frame of mind and weren't too upset by it. However, when we entered the tent where we were to bed down, all the men who were there said that they had been waiting for days to get out. Some said they'd been there for weeks. This was bad news and I could feel my heartbeat increase and my palms beginning to sweat. I had to get out of there. I couldn't, no, I *wouldn't*, allow the momentum of my journey to be broken.

I had made friends with one of the guys who had been on the truck from Oshakati. His name was Rob and, like me, he wasn't inclined to passively accept this delay in Grootfontein. We drew together, turned our backs on all the negative stories of the others, and made a commitment to each other. We'd work together relentlessly, day and night, to get the hell out of there. Our options were limited. Hitch-hiking from the gate was not allowed; besides, there were few vehicles, whether civilian or military, that travelled by road from there to the bigger centres. If you were lucky you might get to Windhoek. And then? No, it was a train or a plane that we had to take.

Not So Definitely Flying

The following morning we were packed and ready for anything. An open jeep, piled high with luggage, pulled up, and an officer shouted out for those who were on the flight to Pretoria. No one responded to the call, so I said to Rob, 'Come on, let's go.' We slung our gear onto the loaded jeep and climbed aboard. The officer who was driving turned around and asked, 'Are you the guys who are booked on the flight to Pretoria?'

'Yes', I said, 'we have to be in Pretoria as soon as possible.' It was only half a lie.

Without another word we drove to the air field.

At the airfield there were two queues standing in the sun before the Hercules that was being fuelled for flight. One of the queues, the long one, contained various military personnel in step-out dress, a voluptuous blonde woman – an officer's wife, I assumed – and a few civilians. This was the queue of definites. They were booked and they were flying . . . no question.

The other queue, the shorter one, was for the others . . . like us. The not-so-definitely flying. Rob and I looked at each other and went to work. First we went to the sergeant at the head of the queue who had a list of names on a clipboard. Half of them were hand-written. We gave him our names as if we expected him to have them on the list.

'What? We must be there! The captain (one didn't want to mention that this captain was many miles away in a tent somewhere) assured us that we were booked on this flight.'

The sergeant assured us that we weren't – our names were not there. We stood around for a moment or two, pretending

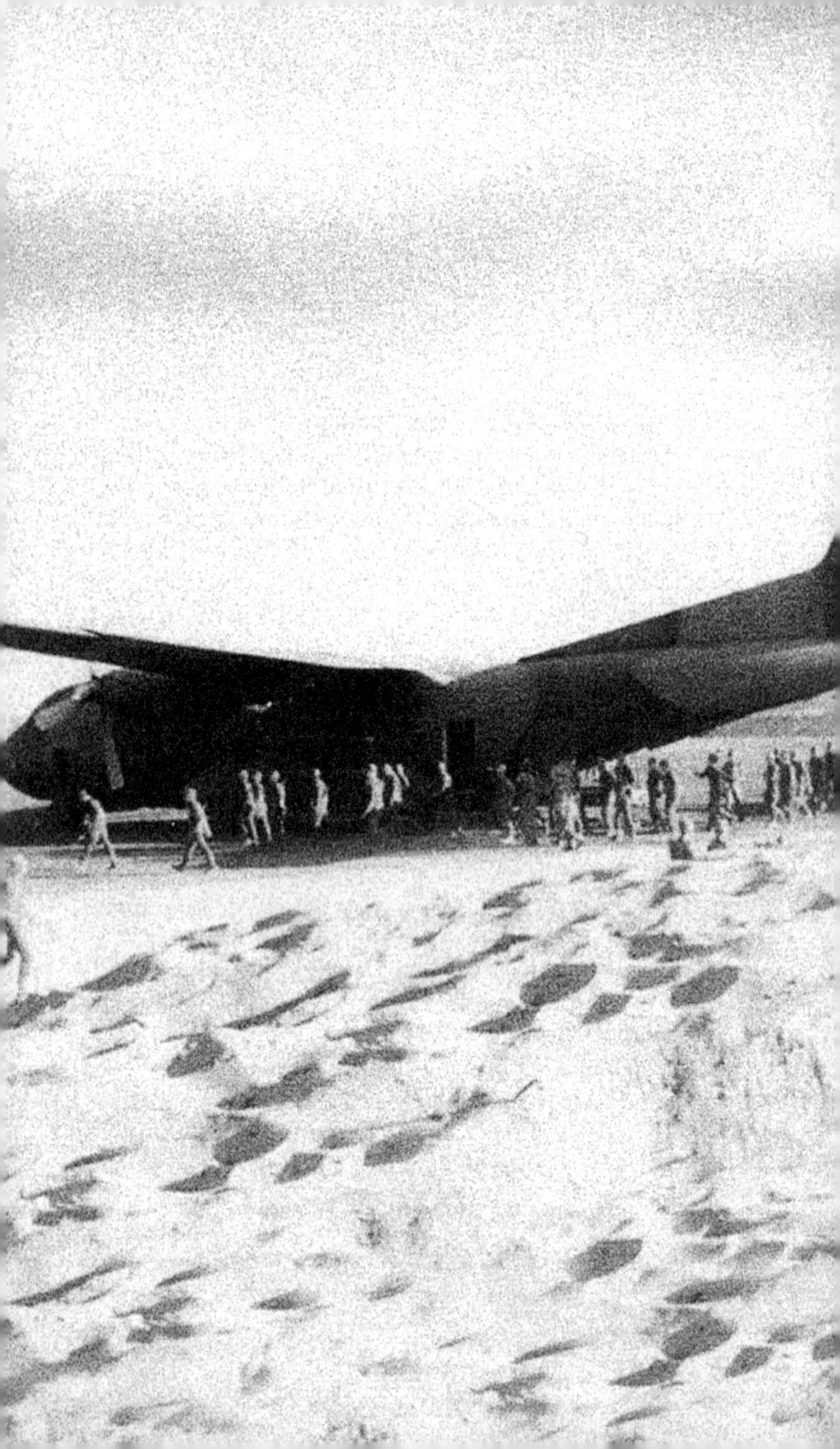

exasperation and indignation. Then I suggested that the sergeant at least write our names down in case there were any vacancies. Besides, we assured him, someone would be bringing our names forward at any moment. Ours was an urgent case. He looked a little sceptical but wrote them down anyway. We thanked him warmly.

Step one . . . our names were on the list, and we were there . . . standing in the queue, but anything could happen between now and take-off. The guys who were booked for Pretoria, and whose places we were attempting to usurp, could arrive at any minute. While we were standing there watching luggage and kit bags being loaded on to a pallet, Rob said to me in a voice of quiet determination, 'Let's get our luggage on to that pallet over there.' We walked over briskly and placed our kit with the rest of the luggage that was there. Another sergeant came over and asked who had told us to put our kit there. We indicated vaguely towards the sergeant with the list and said, 'We're listed for the flight, and we're obeying captain's orders.' He looked at us searchingly, but he was used to this kind of loose organisation on the runway. After all, there was a certain measure of elasticity in the situation, with a standby list changing by the minute. He shrugged his shoulders and ambled off. We smiled at each other and returned to the queue. Now we really had a chance!

We watched the people coming and going and then we saw the pallet being picked up by a forklift truck and driven up the ramp at the back of the plane. Our luggage was aboard! We continued waiting. Suddenly the queue of definites moved across the runway and started boarding the plane. The sergeant at the head of our queue called the typewritten names on his list and told them to board the plane. He was about to leave the remainder to try another time, when Rob and I asked him about us. He didn't seem particularly interested, but when we told him that our kit was already on the plane he waved us forward, and we jogged gleefully onto the Hercules.

I couldn't believe that we had escaped until the aeroplane was airborne and, leaning into its climb, revealed the dusty camp below us and the endless tree-covered landscape. What Rob and I hadn't realised was that the plane wasn't flying directly to Pretoria. It headed straight back to Oshakati.

The Hercules flew along with its engines rumbling. We were strapped into our seats along the centre. The seats ran the length of the fuselage, and we sat opposite the passengers seated below the portholes along the left hand side. As we prepared for landing, the plane descended in a series of braking movements and creaking noises. Eventually we were stationary on the runway in Oshakati, the place I had left one and a half days before.

The doors were opened, and military personnel boarded. It appeared that some high-ranking staff needed seats on the plane, so an angry-looking major walked down the aisle to see if he could persuade someone to give up his seat, and to wait for another flight. He looked at me and asked, 'Why are you here, corporal?' I told him that I had leave of compassion and that it was an emergency. I had to be in Pretoria as soon as possible. He couldn't find anyone prepared to give up his seat, so he left the plane.

Rob and I sat there in deep stress, expecting him to come back with a list of names and find us out. Nothing happened. We waited grimly, but relaxed when the navigator closed the doors and we taxied down the runway. The next stop was Rundu. From there the plane turned south and headed back to South Africa.

The States

It was late afternoon when we landed at Waterkloof airbase in Pretoria. We worked our way through the bureaucratic requirements and then, standing beside the road into town, we started hitching. It was growing dark and streams of headlights were flowing by. We were still a long way from home, but at least we were in the states . . . homeward bound.

A car stopped for us, and we were reminded once more of civilian life by the driver, who was wearing a tie, and who transferred his briefcase and jacket to the back seat to make space in the car.

We got a ride to the station where we presented ourselves and our papers to the station master. Rob was so eager to hasten the process that he saluted the station master. The old SAR lifer, with his black cap, leathery face, and thirty-Lexingtons-a-day breath, smiled. He consulted his schedules. From his black waistcoat dangled a chain, a whistle, and a ticket clipper.

As military personnel, returned from active service, we were entitled to utilise public transport. If a train was fully booked, we were allowed to stand in the corridor. Rob was going to Jo'burg, and I was on my way to Natal. He'd be home before midnight, while I'd have to wait until some time after lunch the following day. I phoned Gill and told her to expect me.

Needless to say I hardly slept that night. I didn't care about anything except the fact that I was moving in the direction of home. I'd have stood all night in the corridor if I'd had to, but the conductor found me an empty bunk near his compartment.

The following day I sat watching the countryside rolling by. I could see my reflection in the corridor window. My head was shaved and I was tanned.

Pmb

The fragrance of pine trees filled the air as the train descended into Pietermaritzburg along the sweeping curves and hills. I could see the diesel locomotives pulling us along. The shadows of the coaches were doing a rapid dance with the bushes and trees along the track.

Ka tick ka tick . . . roar . . . ka tick ka tack.

I dreamed my dreams of Maritzburg. The spaces between the orange brick buildings. Corrugated iron roofs, sash windows, fireplaces and chimneys, and the distant tree-covered hills. And behind them, more hills ... to Edendale ... to Bulwer ... to Underberg ... and then the mountains. The cold clean rivers and peaks of the Drakensberg.

Herders from the cold heights of Lesotho walked into town from the station. Their stepping out gear was a clean pair of powder-blue overalls, with the top unbuttoned to reveal the T-shirt beneath, usually white or pale yellow. Their leather belts were decorated with silvery metal shapes, rivets and old copper coins. They wore gumboots, and stylish felt hats from trading stores. And blankets ... always blankets. Dark and medieval, the Bantu Eating House nestled in the armpit of the station. Salesmen stood at the doors of furniture shops. Backyard dreamers dreamed under washing lines. Secret gardens hid behind backyard walls. Housewives dandled babies. In windows of mystery, curtains moved on a breeze scented with the fragrance of frangipani.

Maritzburg was my first symbolic town. My town of deep dreaming ... of stoned mooching. It was an early source of sustenance ... of live music ... and friends – my dear, beat, voiceless friends.

Suddenly I was walking along the station platform in Maritzburg and there was Gill with our child on her hip. We embraced. I was home.

Adjusting

Gill and I had nights in Eden, but slowly the pressures of the world forced us to venture out of the garden in search of employment and society. I was still wearing my army jacket with its familiar pockets.

We stood before my father-in-law, a major, and his first words to me were, 'Oh, so you're back, are you?' A decidedly rhetorical question. The relationship between my father-in-law and me was not one of easy familiarity. He had been witness to my youthful arrogance and idealism, but he tolerated me because his daughter loved me.

He offered us the use of a cottage on his estate. He had made money providing weapons for the military, and could afford to be generous, as suited his nature. I was confused and tired and could not afford to stand on principle. Having a place to stay, rent free, took some of the pressure off us. We moved in gratefully.

I suffered the perennial anger of the returned soldier. The sense of betrayal, easily triggered by unfriendly shopkeepers or people whose culture was the cash register. I would happily have turned my guns on some of my so-called 'fellow countrymen'.

A café owner in Mooi River got angry because I asked him what his chips were like. He looked at me coldly and said, 'They're chips.'

'Yes,' I answered, 'but there are chips, and chips. Some are fresh and crisply fried. Some are old, greasy and carcinogenic.'

He continued to stare at me. Then I asked the African staff behind the counter whether they ate the chips they were selling. They were too afraid to answer me, but I could see that they knew as well as I did that the boss's chips were up to shit.

He made a move towards me and I was just longing to smack his ugly face. I think he saw that I was 'disturbed' and backed off. My wife took me back to the car. 'He probably had a gun under the counter,' she said.

This is my country? This petty, limping place? For this I spent three months in purgatory?

Wherever I went, I felt like a distant observer. I kept thinking of strategies to defend my family against an enemy. I was concerned that our cottage was made out of wood and wasn't bullet-proof. I sat on the rocky hillsides at Shongweni staring down at the railway line in the valley below. I directed imaginary battles, placed LMGs and mortars ... cut up the spaces into grids based on distances and trajectories.

I went for long walks on Sunday afternoons, watching the Zionists at worship in their brightly coloured vestments. Blue and white and red robes against the sky . . . and the beating of drums . . . arms lifted to Zion.

Visits to Durban or Pinetown overwhelmed me. I was stunned by the amount of stuff that surrounded us, the goods that fill the plate-glass windows of shops, air-conditioners, newspaper headlines, lurid colour photographs, paving stones, porcelain toilet bowls, flickering screens, little ceramic dogs, street lamps, parking garages, cardboard boxes, steak houses, plastic drinking straws, traffic – the vast, throbbing urban infrastructure, with its dumps of smouldering garbage.

This sudden contrast to the open spaces of South West Africa, and the simple lives we had lived as soldiers, made it difficult to adjust. We'd walked under the moon and the stars where there were no streets and no plumbing. We'd slept on the earth in the great glittering womb of the night . . . seeing stars fall . . . watching satellites winking.

The Regiment Returns

On the 15th of September, two weeks after my return, the regiment was due to arrive in Durban at ten am. I dressed myself in my new blue velvet jacket, grey trousers, leather shoes and a white shirt – an outfit my wife had encouraged me to buy for my resurrection into civilian life – and drove to Durban station. There I waited for the regiment to return.

The train came powering into the station with a wild load of men spilling out of the windows, waving and shouting and singing. I saw sergeant Cameron jump off before the train had come to a standstill. Everybody was smiling as their eyes searched the platform for family and loved ones.

When the officers began to form the men up for the final

march through the streets back to headquarters, I turned and headed home.

Past Returning

Once back in Durban, we dispersed along the streets and paths of civilian life. Few border friends remained friends as we re-entered our lives.

Butch and I had dinner together with our partners, but they weren't particularly compatible so the friendship ended there. Besides, I don't think Butch and I would have had that much in common anyway, once the pressures of the military were removed.

I looked up Butch's name in the Durban telephone directory when I started writing this memoir, but it was not to be found. Perhaps he, too, had left the country like so many others.

Anyway, cheers, Butch, wherever you are.

In 1984, on a train trip to Cape Town, I had another encounter with the SADF. It was completely unforeseen.

As the train passed through Bloemfontein in the early morning I was visited by memories. I recognised the station in the early morning light and saw once again my civilian clothes scattered across the platform. A white cotton shirt, a pair of jeans, shoes and socks.

In my haste to get back to camp before 06h00, I had swung my kitbag around so fiercely that it had disgorged my civvy clobs, the ones we were not supposed to have, the ones I had rather hurriedly stuffed into the top of my kitbag. Basic training . . . '65. *Ja . . . a long time ago.* Then I remembered the deep sense of relief I felt as I handed in my kit at the DLI headquarters when I was finally discharged in 1978. *Over and out.*

The train moved on towards Kimberley and I settled back against the green leather of the seat. I had the compartment to myself. My sketch book was at hand, and I sat cross-legged, watching the dry lands and fences passing by.

As the train pulled into Kimberley station – a covered station – a whole battalion of soldiers was standing in formation along the platform. My reaction was one of immediate anguish. I was reminded – at a time when I thought I had escaped it – of my captivity in South Africa's social, political and military grip. I didn't want to see the soldiers. I was flooded with anger, disgust and hatred for the spirit which surrounded and animated our times. My heart was beating fast and my palms started to sweat. Why was I so completely thrown by this situation?

The train was stationary for quite a long time. I wanted it to get going so that I would no longer have to see (and deal with) all the guns, loud talk, uniforms and bush hats.

Then, and I don't really know how to describe my anger and consternation, I saw the whole battalion climbing aboard the train. My train . . . my privacy! I locked the compartment door and waited.

Sure enough, the conductor opened the door and, seeing me sitting alone, asked if I would please accommodate some of the soldiers who, by force of some problem or other, would be travelling with us as far as De Aar. I couldn't refuse and so, reluctantly, I packed away all my possessions, but kept my place at the window. Five soldiers moved in with all their kit and rifles. I had to override my feelings and did my best to be friendly. My visitors seemed like nice enough guys, and it wasn't long before they went off to the dining car to get some beers . . . 'for everyone'.

I was sitting alone in the compartment with army jackets swaying from the hooks, kitbags and rifles stashed on bunks and under seats, when the door was opened by a plumpish, thickset soldier . . . with a cause. He rattled a Coke can at me just as beggars or collectors for charity do in the streets of the city.

I ignored the rattling can and waited for him to speak. He told me that he was collecting for the conductor of the train who had been so very generous in accommodating his regiment. He was all ready to sing, 'For he's a jolly good fellow' to the conductor, while I would have preferred to sing 'Why d'ja have to do it?' So I shook my head and said, 'No, I don't feel like it.'

He looked at me with contempt.

'Ah, come aahn! Any donation. Anything. Even if it's just two cents, man!'

I took out some money, and carefully sorted through the coins until I found a two cent piece. This I dropped into the can. He took it as an insult, which it was, and looked at me aggressively.

'You haven't seen the last of us, ballie. The okes will be interested to hear about you.'

We stared hard at each other before he shut the door and moved on.

I was in a state of extreme stress. My hatred of the military and everything that was wrong with South Africa was projected at this individual who had shoved a collection can under my nose. All kinds of possible retributions against me began to run through my mind. Most of them were violent and ugly. The whole situation seemed unjust and infuriating. I felt victimised, outnumbered. I was so hostile and paranoid that I decided to prepare a weapon ... just in case.

I took my knife from the pocket of my satchel and went into the toilet, bolted the door, and stood staring at myself in the mirror as the train clattered and swayed. I looked at the knife. Ironically, it was the knife issued to me by the army in 1965. Made of silver stainless steel, it had a mark stamped into the handle – an M inside a U.

The main blade was sharp and strong but it didn't lock, and it had no means of keeping the hand from sliding down onto the blade. I'd have to wrap it with a hankie to use it. There'd be no time in an emergency to do that. It was no good for my purposes.

Then I opened the wedge-shaped tool that emerged from the centre of the handle at the back of the knife. A short three-sided spike that came to a sharp point. If I gripped the handle tightly, not only was my fist hardened and reinforced by the handle, but the spike emerged from between my first and second fingers ... a sharp and lacerating weapon ... medieval ... sneaky, mean and ugly. Just the way I was feeling. I closed the knife and kept it accessible in my righthand trouser pocket. I decided to go to the dining car to try and cool down. I had my weapon.

A while later, returning to the compartment in some trepidation, I found three soldiers in there, one of whom was playing a guitar. These three were friendly and generous in sharing their beer, and it wasn't too long before the guitar was in my hands. I had a lot of material that I could share – songs, and stories about the border. The audience grew and soon the compartment was a smoky hive of music and laughter with the door open to the corridor.

When my enemy returned for revenge, he was confronted with this scene. He stood just near the doorway, watching, sizing up the situation. Then he tried to talk to some of the soldiers ... looking and pointing at me, but no one was really interested. I looked at him hard while I was playing the guitar ... just to let him know how the situation had changed. I was safe ... thanks to music. And then I relented, and gave him a let's-just-jag-it-in smile, but he was too angry to let it go, and wandered off along the corridor.

When the guys got off at De Aar I felt quite lonely in my compartment. Beer cans and cigarette butts were lying about. I cleaned up and turned my mind once more to my own journey.

Epilogue

I was driving out of Pinetown the other day when I saw a guy hitching on the M13 to Durban. His stance seemed unusual. He was facing the crash barrier and looking over his shoulder, while hitching with his left hand. I pulled up, and as he opened the passenger door, I saw that he had no right hand.

He was wearing a short-sleeved shirt, so the stump of his right arm was visible to all. I could see that he was a nice enough guy and, being curious by nature, I asked him what had happened.

He looked at me.

'It was in the SADF . . . back in 1988.'

I nodded. And to reassure him, added that I too had experience of the SADF. At once we understood each other. We knew about the army and its madness.

He continued.

'It happened on the 14th of July, 1988. I was nineteen at the time. We were in Zeerust . . . actually at Rooisloot, the shooting range . . . when this one lieutie comes there and tunes, "You, you and you, come with me." So we go with him and he shows us a pile of spades and rakes and tells us to start cleaning up the range.

'While the other okes were raking up the cartridge cases, I was picking up the duds and unexploded mortars left by the previous regiment. I picked up an M-26 practice grenade . . . it's got a blue casing, with like holes in it . . . but as I picked it up, the detonator went off.

'It blew up in my hand.

'I just stood checking what was left of my hand . . . it was gone . . . buried in the sky.

'From there it's a long story. They amputated my wrist and I spent five months rehab at One Military Hospital. I finished my time at Natal Command and klaared out in 1990.'

'So how do you feel about all this now?' I asked him.

'Well, I get a military pension, but I can't say I've recovered . . . for true. I always try to be optimistic about life . . . but deep down inside . . . I can't explain it like . . . there's a depression. I get angry . . . at the loss of a hand. I have to fight the feeling. I have to be strong . . . it's a conscious battle.'

As we pulled up in Durban, I told him about this book.

'Ay, I wish my story could be there too,' he said.

Acknowledgements and special thanks to:

James Phillips (alias Bernoldus Niemand) for his contribution to the spirit of rock and roll in South Africa. His songs and laughter punctured that bloated Zeppelin of fascism that used to police the skies and overshadow our lives.

Breyten Breytenbach for his book *The True Confessions of An Albino Terrorist*. Germinated in solitary confinement, it's an inspired confession of humanity in the hard and dark '80s.

Charlie Berea, Pierre Venter, Tyrone Toombs, Ekkie Eckhart, Leighton Alcock, Mike Kantey, Gert Swart, Hylton Alcock, Kevin Piccione, David Fletcher, A J Brindley, Barry Downard and Adam West for their stories and memories.

Pierre Venter, the present Adjutant of the DLI, who has been a generous and willing help with technical and historical details about the border war and the history of the regiment.

Willem Steenkamp, whose book *South Africa's Border War 1966–1989* (Ashanti Publishing, 1989), has been a useful source of reference.

I would like to thank Shirley Bell, Chris Chapman, Rika Thomson, Doug Macdonald, Piers Carey, Jim Phelps, Peter Strauss, Chris Mann, and Alison Lowry for their editorial contributions.

Country Joe McDonald and the Fish for *I-Feel-Like-I'm-Fixin'-To-Die Rag*. Graham Nash for *Military Madness*. Richie Havens for *Freedom*, and Leonard Cohen for *Suzanne*.

Extra special thanks to Bob Dylan for providing us with a rich and portable culture of poetry and music which, besides being fun to play, fed our souls during some trying times.

Leighton Alcock and Pierre Venter for the photographs. Pierre Venter for the map.

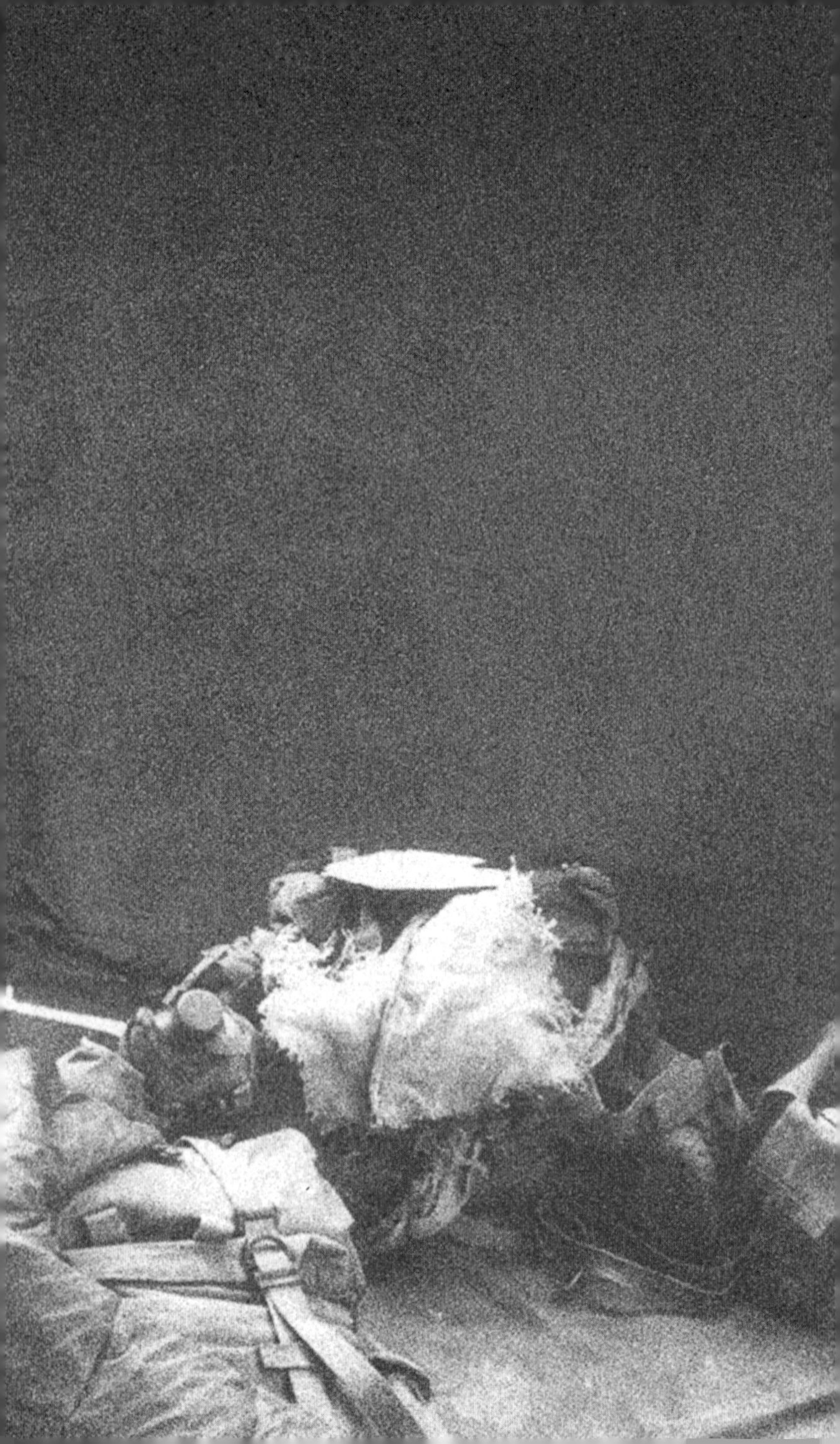

Glossary

appy	apprentice
AWOL	absent without leave
ballie	old man (slang, Afrikaans) A term used to describe an older man who has lost his vigour or stands on the other side of the generation gap. If used face to face, and especially if there is not a great age difference between the two protagonists, it is a provocation and an insult
balsak	ball bag (Afrikaans) Literally means ball bag, but in the army is used to describe a large black standard issue kitbag
Bedford	a three-ton truck used for the transport of soldiers and equipment
boet	a fond term for brother (Afrikaans)
bonnie	a long or luxurious head of hair on a man
bossies	a term used to describe the psychologically disturbed state of soldiers who had been in the bush on military duty for a long time and were not easily able to cope with normal civilian life (Afrikaans)
boude	limbs or haunches (Afrikaans) In this context refers very specifically to the female anatomy, namely, backside and thighs
breker	literally a 'breaker' (slang, Afrikaans) Used to describe a hoodlum or street fighter
casevac	casualty evacuation
check	to look or see
china	friend
civvy	civilian
clobs	short for clobber or clothing. Pronounced 'clawbs'
Cuca	the Ovambo name for a shop – usually a corrugated

iron shack – which sells Cuca beer in bottles

DB	detention barracks
DLI	Durban Light Infantry
dob	to look or see
dog biscuits	large square biscuits with the colour and consistency of dog biscuits, issued as rations
dog tag	silver metal tags with names and numbers worn by soldiers for identification in case of death or casualty
donker	dark (Afrikaans)
dood	dead (Afrikaans)
dop	a drink – used as both a noun and a verb (slang, Afrikaans)
Eland	originally an imported Panhard armoured vehicle with a sixty-one millimetre mortar and two machine guns. It was developed to become South Africa's primary attack weapon in the open spaces and long distances – fitted with a ninety-millimetre cannon
Esbit	compact white substance (solid paraffin) in the form of a large tablet used for heating food or water
ETA	estimated time of arrival
gat	a gun (slang), pronounced with a soft g as in gamble
gil	yell (Afrikaans)
goed	goods or stuff (Afrikaans)
gooi	throw (Afrikaans)
grensvegter	a border fighter (Afrikaans)
Hercules	a four-engined aeroplane used for transporting vehicles or heavy loads. Also used to drop paratroopers
Hippo	large, armed, anti-mine vehicle constructed on a Bedford chassis and used to transport troops
hoor	hear (Afrikaans)
HQ	headquarters

Hyena	enclosed anti-mine vehicle used mainly by police on the border to transport troops for swift pursuit
induna	an elder, chief or headman (Zulu)
jol	a party, or 'to play' (slang, Afrikaans)
joller	a party-goer and 'wild cat'
jou	you (singular) (Afrikaans)
julle	you (plural) (Afrikaans)
Jusses	Jeez (slang, Afrikaans)
kak	shit (Afrikaans) Pronounced cuck as in cuckold
khaya	home or house (Zulu)
klaared out	clear out of the army. To be demobilised (Afrikaans)
klapped	slapped (Afrikaans) The word suggests a heavy cuffing by a male hand
klim	climb (Afrikaans)
kop-toe	over-conscientious in holding to military rules (slang, Afrikaans)
lank	a superlative. Anything which is extreme, whether 'nice' or unpleasant. From Afrikaans, but pronounced in English like plank
lappie	a small cloth – used in this context to cover the mouth end of a dagga pipe and to filter the inhalant (Afrikaans)
larney	posh, or fancy, having pretensions. A word coined and used frequently by the Indian population of Natal
lekker	nice (Afrikaans, pronounced like lacquer)
LMG	light machine gun
Magirus	large Deutz truck with six-wheel drive and air-cooled engine used to transport troops or supplies
mahangu	corn similar to millet (Ovambo)
manne	men (Afrikaans) Usually used in the sense of a team, a group or a gang

meisies	girls (Afrikaans)
mense	people (Afrikaans)
min dae	literally 'few days' (Afrikaans) A term used by troops as their time of duty was coming to an end. The term was often accompanied by a hand sign ... the index and little finger raised high
moffie	a homosexual (slang, Afrikaans)
môre	morning (Afrikaans)
mosdop	the plastic inner belonging to the steel helmet. It was worn separately for purposes of training (Afrikaans)
MPLA	Popular Movement for the Liberation of Angola (acronym from the Portuguese)
naam	name (Afrikaans)
nooit	never (Afrikaans)
OC	officer commanding
oke	guy or man (pronounced 'oak')
ongeluk	accident (Afrikaans)
ongelukkig	unhappy/unlucky (Afrikaans)
oom	uncle (Afrikaans) Used in Afrikaans society to show respect for any male adult whether related by familial ties or not
OP	observation post
Ops tent	operations tent. Centre of communications and administration
optel	pick up (Afrikaans)
ou	guy or man (pronounced 'oh')
PA	public address system
PF	permanent force
phutu	thick, dry porridge made of mealie meal (Zulu)
Pmb	the abbreviation for Pietermaritzburg
poephol	arsehole (Afrikaans)
poes	crude word to describe the vagina (Afrikaans). Similar to the English 'pussy'

pozzie	place or position
praating	an anglicised form of the Afrikaans ... means 'speaking'
PT	physical training
Puma	a troop-carrying helicopter used primarily by paratroopers for swift attack or follow-up
R1	standard issue 7,62 automatic rifle manufactured in South Africa, based on the model of the FN (Fabrique Nationale) of Belgium
reg	right (Afrikaans)
rookparade	a smoke break in which all the smokers stand in a straight line as if on parade (Afrikaans)
RSM	regimental sergeant-major
ry	drive or ride (Afrikaans)
SA	South Africa
SADF	South African Defence Force
scheme	think
Scope	a popular magazine with a centre-spread of pin-up girls – more discreet than contemporary magazines like *Hustler*
skaam	shy (Afrikaans)
skate	an anglicisation of the Afrikaans word 'skyt', which means a ducktail, rebel or rough person
skraal	thin (Afrikaans)
skrik	fright (Afrikaans)
skyf	a smoke, or a cigarette (Afrikaans)
sluk	swallow (Afrikaans)
snor	moustache (Afrikaans)
stadig	slow (Afrikaans)
states, the	the term used to refer to South Africa by soldiers on military service outside its borders
sterk	strong (Afrikaans) but used in English slang as a noun to describe anyone of powerful physical strength
SWA	South West Africa

SWAPO	South West African People's Organisation
taal	language (Afrikaans) In this context the word refers specifically to the Afrikaans language
tannie	aunt (Afrikaans)
tiffie	army terminology for a mechanic or technical engineer
trommel	standard issue metal trunk for a soldier (Afrikaans)
tune	to tell or speak to
U	you, or 'your honour' (Afrikaans) Respectful and formal version of the more familiar 'jou'. Similar in meaning to 'your highness'
uitstap uniform	stepping out uniform (Afrikaans) The formal wear of a soldier on special occasions
ungypo'd	army term to describe anything that has not been tampered with. Rookies were forced to keep their caps ungypo'd ie as they were issued, with flat postman-like tops. The more experienced soldiers gypo'd their caps by bending them down at the sides to give them a more menacing and 'experienced' look. The term originated with ex-servicemen on their return from Egypt during the Second World War where the 'Gypos' or Egyptians tried to sell all kinds of goods which had been tampered with. For example bottles of whisky purchased by soldiers were found to contain urine. Such a purchase would be said to have been 'gypo'd'
Unimog	all-terrain four-wheel drive vehicle used on patrols for swift pursuit. Initially the floor of the vehicle was covered with sandbags as protection in case of landmines, but it was later converted to the Buffel anti-mine troop carrier
UNITA	National Union for the Total Independence of Angola (acronym from the Portuguese)
Uzi	a 9mm hand-carbine of Israeli design
varkpan	literally a 'pig pan' (Afrikaans) Refers to the metal

	alloy trays on which soldiers collected their food, and used as plates
vinnig	fast (Afrikaans)
wag	wait (Afrikaans) The w is pronounced as a strong v, and the g is guttural
weerman	rifleman (Afrikaans)
weet	know (Afrikaans)
woes	angry, irate (Afrikaans) The w is pronounced as a strong v
zoll	a finger of marijuana wrapped in brown paper